DIANA

A Strange Autobiography

The Cutting Edge:
Lesbian Life and Literature
Series Editor: Karla Jay

Changing Our Minds:
Lesbian Feminism and Psychology
BY CELIA KITZINGER AND RACHEL PERKINS

Sophia Parnok: The Life and Work
of Russia's Sappho
BY DIANA LEWIS BURGIN

Elizabeth Bowen: A Reputation in Writing
BY RENÉE HOOGLAND

The Angel and the Perverts
BY LUCIE DELARUE-MARDRUS
TRANSLATED BY ANNA LIVIA

The Cook and the Carpenter:
A Novel by the Carpenter
BY JUNE ARNOLD
WITH AN INTRODUCTION BY BONNIE ZIMMERMAN

Lesbian Erotics
EDITED BY KARLA JAY

The Marginal Woman:
The Challenge of Bisexuality
to Lesbian Politics
BY PAULA RUST

Diana: A Strange Autobiography
BY DIANA FREDERICS
WITH AN INTRODUCTION BY JULIE ABRAHAM

Heterosexual Plots and Lesbian Narratives
MARILYN R. FARWELL

The Cutting Edge:
Lesbian Life and Literature
Series Editor: Karla Jay
Professor of English and Women's Studies
Pace University

EDITORIAL BOARD

DIANA

A Strange Autobiography

DIANA FREDERICS

INTRODUCTION BY JULIE ABRAHAM

NEW YORK UNIVERSITY PRESS
New York and London

NEW YORK UNIVERSITY PRESS
New York and London

Foreword © 1995 by Karla Jay
Introduction © 1995 by Julie Abraham

Library of Congress Cataloging-in-Publication Data
Frederics, Diana
Diana : a strange autobiography / Diana Frederics.
p.   cm. — (The Cutting Edge)
Originally published: New York : Dial Press, 1939.
Includes bibliographical references (p.).
ISBN 0-8147-2632-1 (cloth : acid-free paper).
ISBN 0-8147-2635-6 (pbk. : acid-free paper).
1. Lesbians—Fiction. I. Title. II. Series.
PS3511.R4145D53   1995
813'.52—dc20   94-42094
                              CIP

New York University Press books are printed on acid-free paper, and
their binding materials are chosen for strength and durability.

Manufactured in the United States of America

10   9   8   7   6   5   4   3   2   1

Contents

[ix]

CONTENTS

Part IV: LESLIE

Foreword

DESPITE THE EFFORTS of lesbian and feminist publishing houses and a few university presses, the bulk of the most important lesbian works has traditionally been available only from rare-book dealers, in a few university libraries, or in gay and lesbian archives. This series intends, in the first place, to make representative examples of this neglected and insufficiently known literature available to a broader audience by reissuing selected classics and by putting into print for the first time lesbian novels, diaries, letters, and memoirs that are of special interest and significance, but which have moldered in libraries and private collections for decades or even for centuries, known only to the few scholars who had the courage and financial wherewithal to track them down.

Their names have been known for a long time—Sappho, the Amazons of North Africa, the Beguines, Aphra Behn, Queen Christina, Emily Dickinson, the Ladies of Llangollen, Radclyffe Hall, Natalie Clifford Barney, H.D., and so many others from every nation, race, and era. But government and religious officials burned their writings, historians and literary scholars denied they were lesbians, powerful men kept their books out of print, and influential archivists locked up their ideas far from sympathetic eyes. Yet some dedicated scholars and readers still knew who they were, made pilgrimages to the cities and villages where they had lived and to the graveyards where they rested. They passed around tattered volumes of letters, diaries, and biographies, in which they had underlined what seemed to be telltale hints of a secret or different kind of life. Where no hard facts existed, legends were invented. The few precious and often available pre-Stonewall lesbian classics, such as *The Well of Loneliness* by Radclyffe Hall, *The Price of Salt* by Claire Morgan [Patricia Highsmith], and *Desert of the Heart* by Jane Rule, were cherished. Lesbian pulp was devoured. One of the primary goals of this series is to give the more neglected works, which constitute the vast majority of lesbian writing, the attention they deserve.

A second but no less important aim of this series is to present the "cutting edge" of contemporary lesbian scholarship and theory across a wide range of disciplines. Practitioners of lesbian studies have not adopted a uniform approach to literary theory, history, sociology, or any other discipline, nor should they. This series intends to present an array of voices that truly reflect the diversity of the lesbian community. To help me in this task, I am lucky enough to be assisted by a distinguished editorial board that reflects various professional, class, racial, ethnic, and religious backgrounds as well as a spectrum of interests and sexual preferences.

At present the field of lesbian studies occupies a small, precarious, and somewhat contested pied-à-terre between gay studies and women's studies. The former is still in its infancy, especially if one compares it to other disciplines that have been part of the core curriculum of every child and adolescent for several decades or even centuries. However, although it is one of the newest disciplines, gay studies may also be the fastest-growing one—at least in North America. Lesbian, gay, and bisexual studies conferences are doubling and tripling their attendance. Although only a handful of degree-granting programs currently exist, that number is also apt to multiply quickly during the next decade.

FOREWORD

In comparison, women's studies is a well-established and burgeoning discipline with hundreds of minors, majors, and graduate programs throughout the United States. Lesbian studies occupies a peripheral place in the discourse in such programs, characteristically restricted to one lesbian-centered course, usually literary or historical in nature. In the many women's studies series that are now offered by university presses, generally only one or two books on a lesbian subject or issue are included, and lesbian voices are restricted to writing on those topics considered of special interest to gay people. We are not called upon to offer opinions on motherhood, war, education, or on the lives of women not publicly identified as lesbians. As a result, lesbian experience is too often marginalized and restricted.

In contrast, this series will prioritize, centralize, and celebrate lesbian visions of literature, art, philosophy, love, religion, ethics, history, and a myriad of other topics. In "The Cutting Edge," readers can find authoritative versions of important lesbian texts that have been carefully prepared and introduced by scholars. Readers can also find the work of academics and independent scholars who write about other aspects of life from a distinctly lesbian viewpoint. These visions are not only various but intentionally contradictory, for lesbians speak from differing class, racial, ethnic, and religious perspectives. Each author also speaks from and about a certain moment of time, and few would argue that being a lesbian today is the same as it was for Sappho or Anne Lister. Thus no attempt has been made to homogenize that diversity, and no agenda exists to attempt to carve out a "politically correct" lesbian studies perspective at this juncture in history or to pinpoint the "real" lesbians in history. It seems more important for all the voices to be heard before those with the blessings of hindsight lay the mantle of authenticity on any one vision of the world, or on any particular set of women.

What each work in this series does share, however, is a common realization that gay women are the "Other" and that one's perception of culture and literature is filtered by sexual behaviors and preferences. Those perceptions are not the same as those of gay men or of nongay women, whether the writers speak of gay or feminist issues or whether the writers choose to look at nongay figures from a lesbian perspective. The role of this series is to create space and give a voice to those interested in lesbian studies. This series speaks to any person who is interested in gender studies, literary criticism, biography, or important literary works, whether she or he is a student, professor, or serious reader, for the series is neither for lesbians only nor even by lesbians only. Instead, "The Cutting Edge" attempts to share some of the best of lesbian literature and lesbian studies with anyone willing to look at the world through lesbians' eyes. The series is proactive in that it will help to formulate and foreground the very discipline on which it focuses. Finally, this series has answered the call to make lesbian theory, lesbian experience, lesbian lives, lesbian literature, and lesbian visions the heart and nucleus, the weighty planet around which for once other viewpoints will swirl as moons to our earth. We invite readers of all persuasions to join us by venturing into this and other books in the series.

We are pleased to include *Diana: A Strange Autobiography* by Diana Frederics in our series of reprints. This 1939 work fits into a unique historical gap between the medical texts of the early part of the twentieth century and rare novels like Radclyffe Hall's *The Well of Loneliness* on one hand and the lesbian pulp fiction of the 1940s and 1950s on the other hand. Since scholars have been unable to uncover any information about its author, it is impossible to verify whether Frederics is honestly recounting events from her own life, creating a composite of several women she knew, or writing a work of fiction disguised as autobiography. In a new introduction, Julie Abraham places this work into the last category and reads it against the background of similar fictional works. But whether fictional or not, readers will be intrigued by the story of a woman who tried to find love and a meaningful relationship at a time when the obstacles seemed overwhelming.

KARLA JAY

Introduction to the New Edition

DIANA FREDERICS' *Diana: A Strange Autobiography,* first published in the United States in 1939, belongs to the period between the emergence of recognizably modern lesbian and gay identities in the late nineteenth century and the revolution in lesbian and gay consciousness and culture produced by the gay and women's liberation movements of the late 1960s.[1]

Despite a few frequently noted exceptions—Marlene Dietrich in drag in *Morocco* (1930), or Lillian Hellman's *The Children's Hour* (1934)—representations of lesbianism before Stonewall were largely confined to the written word.[2] Public perceptions of lesbianism were shaped by scientific texts, newspapers and magazines, and especially by novels about women in love. Highly publicized attempts to ban what would become the best-known "lesbian novel," Radclyffe Hall's *The Well of Loneliness,* when it first appeared in Britain and the United States in 1928, created the impression that such novels were likely to be censored. In practice things were not so simple. If the narrative was satirical, like Compton Mackenzie's *Extraordinary Women* (1928), or sensational, like G. Sheila Donisthorpe's "story of a wife who was spoiled for marriage," *Loveliest of Friends!* (1931), there were no difficulties.[3] In the United States after World War II, paperback publishers saw a market opportunity and went looking for writers to produce melodramas about the women of "the twilight world."[4]

But lesbian writers did not usually write "lesbian novels."

INTRODUCTION TO THE NEW EDITION

Some feared public identification as lesbian; others rejected the lesbian novel's focus on women in love, or the novel as a form. Sometimes they wrote "women in love" into experimental narratives that were not read as lesbian. If they wrote a novel likely to be read as lesbian, they did not publish it. Or they wrote and published one lesbian novel before going on to a career devoted to another genre of fiction.[5]

Moreover lesbianism is not "the subject" of most of the autobiographies written by lesbians in the first half of the twentieth century. In Margaret Anderson's *My Thirty Years' War* (1930), Mercedes de Acosta's *Here Lies the Heart* (1960), and Bryher's *The Heart to Artemis* (1962), for example, the writer discusses her life, including her female partners, without specifying that her relationships with these women were sexual, without discussing "lesbianism" as an experience or source of identity.

Diana was presented as an autobiography, "the confession of one . . . destined by Nature to gather forbidden fruit in the gardens of deviation" (xxxi). But, like many lesbian novels from the 1930s through the 1960s, it was published under a pseudonym; we know nothing about "Diana Frederics" aside from the contents of this book. *Diana* begins with its heroine's childhood, as the unexceptional daughter of an unexceptional "plutocratic" family. She is unusually close to her father before his sudden death at the beginning of her adolescence. During adolescence she finds herself drawn with mysterious intensity to a girl friend. Stumbling across a book about sex in her father's library, she is horrified to discover the possibility of her own perversion. This discovery prompts her to abandon a promising musical career; she cannot bring herself to perform before an audience who would scorn her if they "knew." The narrative then follows Diana's progress through college, including sorority life; through the trial marriage that proves she is incapable of heterosexuality; through further intellectual and sexual education in Berlin and Paris; through the promise and failure of her first lesbian relationship, with the ultimately faithless Jane; through the trials of a closeted social and professional life as a "ladylike" French professor; through her development of a new identity as a writer and a second relationship, with the younger and more pliant Leslie; and through her final tormented triangular struggle with Jane and Leslie for the individual salvation to be found in a happy couple. Diana is told that her short stories have enough plots for two novels. This autobiography has enough plot for half-a-dozen novels. And unfortunately for Diana's claim to the authority of true confession, *Diana*'s plot echoes many more than half-a-dozen novels.

What was to be gained by presenting *Diana* as an autobiography? Autobiography has offered lesbian writers more freedom than the conventions of the lesbian novel allow. These freedoms were demonstrated before Stonewall by modernist writers such as Virginia Woolf and Gertrude Stein, who challenged the conventions of autobiography in order to expand the possibilities for representations of lesbianism.[6] Since Stonewall, the coming out story has developed as a central genre of lesbian writing; lesbian autobiographical writing is surpassing the lesbian novel in quality and scope.[7] Claiming autobiography allowed the author of *Diana* to string enough material for half-a-dozen novels along the narrative line offered by the story of one life.

Lesbianism as a subject has a tendency to strain readers' assumptions about the distinction between autobiography and fiction. Although the full-length narratives touted as "about lesbianism" in the decades before Stonewall were usually novels, *Diana* by "Diana" shares its autobiographical claims with a significant subset of these texts, such as Elisabeth Craigin's

[xix]

Either Is Love (1937), and *Olivia* by "Olivia" (1949), which are equally difficult to distinguish from fiction.[8] Many other lesbian novels were discussed as if they were autobiographies, even when they were explicitly presented as fictions. *The Well of Loneliness* was treated as its author's story from the moment it was published, and the most recent edition still claims *The Well* is "the thinly disguised story of Radclyffe Hall's own life."[9] The combination of "lesbian autobiographies" that are difficult to distinguish from fiction and a general desire to read lesbian novels as autobiographies together reflect a cultural premium on identifying texts about lesbianism as autobiographical.

The conventions of "autobiography" promise a true and individual but exemplary story. *Diana* is presented as the true story of one woman's deviant development, which is nevertheless representative of the sad fates of not a few modern women. In a social context in which any representation of lesbianism might be condemned as obscene and feared as corrupting it was, of course, useful to lay claim to the autobiographical. At once true and representative, *Diana* could be presented, as such texts routinely were, as a contribution to the general store of grim but necessary knowledge about a regrettable social phenomenon. The autobiographical claims made by and about such narratives about lesbianism made them easier to justify. But the claim that *Diana* is autobiography positions the text, and the reader in relation to the text, within the frame of dominant assumptions about lesbian novels as well. On their covers, in their introductions, and in their texts, lesbian novels presume that nothing accurate is known about lesbianism and assert that theirs is the definitive account. "Truth" lends them authority while the claim to definitiveness supports the view that "the lesbian" is a strictly limited and easily explicable social type.

[xx]

INTRODUCTION TO THE NEW EDITION

The truth claims of lesbian novels imply their grounding in "real life," but if they are read as a group, it becomes apparent that "real life" has extraordinary consistency: the same settings, the same protagonists, the same crises and the same resolutions appear again and again. In view of this consistency, one is forced to conclude either that all lesbians led identical lives, in Paris or later in Greenwich Village, or that these novels more than most were shaped by ideological imperatives.

The lesbian novels and the pseudonymous "lesbian autobiographies" of the first half of the twentieth century are formula fictions. Their structure is based on preexisting conventions for the representation of women. The lesbian's narrative is no different from that of the heterosexual woman: the paradigmatic lesbian story, like that of her straight sister, remains a story of romance. Like a generic heterosexual romance, or lesbian novel, *Diana* follows its heroine through the course of her emotional development, ending with the resolution of a climactic relationship. But the lesbian novel added its own conventions to this basic structure. Lesbian novels focus on middle- and upper-class white women. Lesbian novels characteristically present certain external features, such as a medical introduction; they pursue specific narrative subjects, such as the heroine's discovery of her lesbianism; they are governed by particular ideological necessities, such as an explanation of the heroine's lesbianism, and proof of her inability to be heterosexual; and they employ standard tropes, such as the heroine as writer. Lesbian novels are often explicitly didactic.

Given *Diana*'s historical moment, it is hard to tell which conventions of narratives about lesbianism are initiated here and which are already in circulation. The proliferation of conventions and the contradictions in the text would seem to

[xxi]

reflect *Diana*'s position in the ongoing evolution of the lesbian
novel, not yet in 1939 a stable form. On the cover, in the
introduction, and in the text, *Diana* tells you that what it is
telling you is true. Chapter titles like " 'Am I a Lesbian?' "
and " 'I Am a Lesbian!' " telegraph the purpose of this and
every other lesbian narrative: to tell the reader who "the
lesbian" is. Under the banner of autobiography, *Diana* hits all
of the high and low points of the lesbian novel. The chaos of
conventions is impressive. Diana goes through the process of
"becoming a lesbian" over and over: in adolescence; after her
trial marriage; the night of her first lesbian sexual experience;
with her first lover, Jane; as she establishes a new life with
Leslie. She seems to be unable to decide on the relationship
between lesbianism and gender transgression: as a child she
was a tomboy, but she does not grow up to be a man; she
insists on her feminine appearance while casually referring to
her "masculine qualities"; she is hostile to mannish women
while declaring that the "emotional range" of the lesbian is
"masculine as well as feminine" (121). She offers a series of
labels for her interesting condition: she is a member of the
third sex and an invert (although hers is an "emotional inversion," presumably the kind that does not show). She is em-
phatically "not a normal woman." She is initially horrified at
the idea of being "another 'case' on file in a psychological
laboratory. I was, then, a 'pervert,' 'uranian,' 'homosexual' —
no matter, all added up to the same thing. *I* was subject to
arrest! *I* was grotesque, alienated, unclean!" (18). Nevertheless she presents her story as a case study. Her narrative is
about a lesbian discovering she's a lesbian, demonstrating that
she's a lesbian, examining the meaning of lesbianism. But in
the tradition of American individualism, Diana denies her
connection to any larger community of lesbians.

True to form, Diana establishes herself in the first pages of

[xxii]

her narrative as an upper-class woman of northern European descent whose family has been in America since the "earliest settlers" (3). Her race and class are presented as a neutral background from which her sexual deviation is dramatic. Although there were women of color in lesbian and gay novels from this period, such as Sybil in Blair Niles' *Strange Brother* (1931) or Tris in Ann Bannon's *Women in the Shadows* (1959), these were marginal characters.[10] The narrow focus on white women in pre-Stonewall lesbian novels was exacerbated by the convention that "real" lesbians were wealthy women to be found in Europe, particularly in Paris, like those in *The Well of Loneliness*.[11] Diana's family owns a bank, and has for generations. Even though the bank fails in the course of her narrative, which coincides with the Depression, she pursues her education and travels comparatively unaffected by her family's declining fortunes. She expects to support herself, but she declares her disinterest in work, and chooses her profession because it is "ladylike." And predictably, she goes on to have her first lesbian sexual experience in Berlin and to begin her first lesbian relationship in Paris.

Diana is introduced by a medical preface. Victor Robinson, M.D., "welcome[s] any book which adds to the understanding of the lesbians in our midst" (xxxvii). (In the paperback reprints this comment even appears on the cover.) The doctor buttresses his own authority with references to Havelock Ellis and Edward Carpenter. In a typical pattern, his authority is buttressed within Diana's narrative by references to other medical texts, and these in turn are reinforced by the doctors in the text. When she discovers that she might be a lesbian, the young Diana races off to a "reputable physician" for an examination, so that he can pronounce her normal. When she subsequently confesses her fears to her medical student brother, he responds both by assuring her that she is not a lesbian and by reading aloud to her from volumes by Freud and Havelock Ellis, which reassure her that homosexuals "might find a worth-while place in society" (24).

The medical references in *Diana* reflect the emphasis on self-consciously learning about homosexuality that is common to lesbian novels, as well as their assumption that written sources will provide the necessary information. Diana insists on a "piecemeal" approach to the authorities, and on the existence of contradictory literatures. When she reads for herself "Hirschfeld, Freud, Jung, Westermarck, Krafft-Ebing, Gide and Ellis," she claims, "I accepted, piecemeal, what was compatible with my own observations" (70). If on the one side there are the "good" authorities—Ellis, Freud, Hirschfeld, and Gide, the medical and the literary—on the other side there is the unidentified "book on sex" she finds in her father's library, which discusses homosexuality in terms of such "phrases as 'pervert,' 'nature will have her little joke,' . . . 'uranians,' 'crime against nature,' " and offers "a gruesome picture captioned 'Homosexuals burned at the stake in Germany, 1494" (18). Diana complains about "the occasional pulp magazine article on homosexuality. Such piffle—written, I gathered, by washroom savants—was not only uninformed but vicious, for it amounted to half-truths either glorified or grotesque or sentimentalized" (71). These overtly hostile texts can be rejected outright. At the same time, the configuration of competing literatures she constructs allows her to establish the validity of her own work, authorized by its definite if skeptical relation to recognized external authorities and explicitly distanced from all "uninformed but vicious" reports.

The references to scientific and literary sources imply not only that Diana must learn about homosexuality, and that written texts are the necessary sources of information, but that lesbianism requires explanation. As in the lesbian novel generally, these explanations begin with childhood, but *Diana* offers contradictory variations. At different moments she declares that predominantly male and predominantly female environments produce lesbianism. She was too close to her father as a child, she suggests, or alternatively, her father died when she was too young. Maybe she became a lesbian because of an excess of male company as she was growing up: she spent too much time with her brothers, their friends and male boarders, and so became inured to masculine charms. But later she proclaims women's colleges "the Elysian fields of the lesbian" (72) because of the absence of men. The introduction, where the doctor opts for "Nature," endocrines, and "hormonic tides," likewise contradicts Diana's emphasis on environment. One lesson of *Diana* seems to be that it is easy to produce lesbians. Diana explains her first lover Jane's homosexuality as "largely the result of her height which, during adolescence, had made her timid and awkward with boys and, no doubt to compensate for this deficiency, aggressive with girls" (115). But she goes on to suggest that it took Jane's adoration of her father as well as a stint at a girls' boarding school to seal her fate. The family is always a potential culprit. Leslie, Diana's second lover, was burdened by a father who wanted a son, and raised his daughter as "Junior."

After the necessity of explanation comes the necessity of proof. A lesbian novel does not have to prove that its heroine is a lesbian, but it does have to demonstrate that she is incapable of heterosexuality. Otherwise her lesbianism would be inexcusable. Unlike the protagonists of many lesbian novels, Diana is not seized with uncontrollable revulsion at the touch of a man. Instead the question of Diana's sexuality is dealt with by introducing the possibility of a distinction between sexual performance and sexual pleasure, and even between sexual experience and social decisions. She has a sexual relationship with Carl, in the course of which she performs so well that he is oblivious to the fact that she, necessarily, feels nothing: "Not once . . . had physical intimacy meant anything to me but the giving of pleasure to Carl" (55). Given the success of her deception, however, and the devotion she inspires in him, Diana could live as a heterosexual. Instead she commits herself to sexual pleasure— " 'desire,' 'passion,' 'ecstasy' "—as well as honesty, when she tells him she cannot marry him (55). Turning to women, Diana is not interested in a Boston marriage, as she makes clear at the beginning of her relationship with the initially conflicted Jane: "My conclusions on sex had been a matter of compromise from first to last, for every moral and intellectual principle I knew had led me to feel shame—and yet I was enamoured with all the richness and sweetness of physical life" (115). But again there are contradictions: *Diana* first endorses, then rejects sexual pleasure. By the end of the narrative Diana sees aggressive sexuality on Leslie's part as both a problem and unfeminine. The narrator's representation of female sexuality is complicated by the question of power within relationships, a question she is unable to separate from the sexual. Diana retreats to a conventional hostility to female sexuality rather than acknowledge that she is unhappy at any challenge to her control of the situation.

The sexual is important not only to Diana but to the structure of the narrative. Diana presents herself as a rational, educated, loving—and therefore socially acceptable—lesbian. But by convincing another woman to accept sexual pleasure she produces an evil predatory lesbian. In lesbian novels the central female couple is routinely divided into a predatory "real lesbian" and her innocent victim. The victim can claim the sympathy of heterosexual readers both because she is a victim and because she is not "really" a lesbian; narrative tension is provided by the question of whether she will be rescued at the last minute or succumb completely. Diana plays with these conventions. She divides the lesbians she observes into "active" and "passive": not surprisingly, the active lesbians are described as masculine and committed to lesbianism, while their passive counterparts are feminine and their involvement in lesbian relationships is situational. But Diana needs to keep the reader's sympathy for herself while taking an active role in her own narrative. She achieves this by offering good and evil versions of the active lesbian. After Diana has overcome Jane's resistance to lesbianism, Jane goes on to develop predatory skills that she will exercise against the wives of America. She even attacks Diana herself, by trying to disrupt her subsequent relationship with Leslie. This splitting of the active lesbian allows Diana to ally herself with the heterosexual majority. She can sympathize with the husband whose wife Jane seduces, for she has herself become a potential victim of the predatory lesbian. Moreover Diana can represent herself as oppressed by lesbians as much as by heterosexual society. "The odds against happiness in the lesbian relationship were double what I had first imagined them," she declares. "No longer was it a single question of enormous social pressure from without; but even more insidious, of slipshod mores from within" (169).

Insofar as pre-Stonewall lesbian novels focus on the heroine's becoming a lesbian or resisting lesbianism, that pattern ensures that attention continues to be paid to the heterosexual world. Diana is obsessed with her place in "society": "Society, as Gide had said, eternally predestined one sex for the other—indeed it urged thoughts of love with monotonous stimulation, one sex for the other, in literature, the movies, the radio, the newspaper, the example of elders, the example of

[xxvii]

social gatherings, the very scene of the streets. None made any recognition of the homosexual" (173–74). Normal—that is, heterosexual—social life is impossible for Diana as a closeted and so apparently heterosexual, apparently single woman. She claims that lesbians have a special capacity for friendship with straight men, but that straight men are unable to resist making sexual advances to any apparently available woman. Life within a mixed male and female gay community is likewise unimaginable; *Diana*'s representations of gay men assume their hostility to women. So the individual lesbian couple committed to "normal" life is completely isolated as well as always under attack: "we wanted: the opportunity to live together without question of criticism, without interested opinion. . . . a normal domestic life. . . . But. . . . we were social outlaws. Our relationship must be clandestine: there could be no joy in sharing the knowledge with family or friends, no hint of anything more than ordinary affection. We must get used to hypocrisy and camouflage that degraded and humiliated. We must have courage to steel ourselves against coarse remarks made by unsuspecting acquaintances who tarnished homosexuality with their light contempt" (95). At one point Diana loses her job because she is known to be living with another woman. But it is necessary to note, as Diana does not, that her only heterosexual relationship also involves the deception of her family, who are not told she is living with a man, and the deception of "society," when she and Carl present themselves as married. These deceptions suggest the extent to which female sexuality of all kinds was subject to interpretive if not practical constraints in the 1930s.

Moreover, Diana's insistence on the isolation of lesbians is undermined by her reaction to her peers. In *Diana* as in many of the lesbian and gay novels of the period, a gay bar scene provides a focus for questions of self-identification, which are presented as inseparable from questions of identification with other lesbians.[12] When Diana and Jane accidentally wander into a lesbian bar in Paris, Jane immediately distances herself from the women there—" 'These people are depraved. They're homosexuals!' " Diana protests, " 'What in the name of God do you make of you and me?' " She is shocked, insisting that " 'I did not want [Jane's] love until I could be proud' " (117). Yet she claims that she returns to the bar to "discover . . . points of common likeness . . . only to avoid them" (118). While she decides that lesbians are "individually vivid and intelligent looking," with "exceptional qualities of courage," these qualities are all produced, unfortunately, by their "abnormality" (119). For Diana the real taboo remains group identification; her task is to articulate her individual identity apart from the whole.

Diana emphasizes that the difficulties lesbians experience are created partly by the world's hostility: "Society, I learned over and over again, is omnipotent." But her conclusion is that "It was smarter to indulge [society's] ruthlessness—if only for the sake of comfort" (73). She is actively hostile to lesbians who do not share her own commitment to the closet: "I disliked them for mocking society and themselves at the same time from behind an awkward guise which not only offended society but gave themselves dead away. They were the ones who were ostentatious in mannish gesture, who walked with brusque gracelessness, who smoked and drank with self-conscious bravado, who indulged in transvestitism and wore shirts and ties instead of blouses, and slacks instead of skirts. Male attire on a woman always struck me as a puerile gesture intended to appease one's self while thumbing one's nose at society, and ended only in smart-aleck unconventionality" (72–73). Not only should lesbians refrain from "offend[ing] society," but she implies that lesbians are the ones in control of whether or not they do "offend." The stigmatized, as always, are responsible for managing their stigma. Diana laments that she is cut off from what she romanticizes as "the normal individual's sense of kinship to the world about him" {sic} (97), but she is oblivious to the connection between her own hostility to other lesbians and her "sense of isolation in the third sex." That the other lesbians in the book are less tormented than she by a sense of isolation from the world's grand scheme only confirms her sense of her own finer sensibilities.

Diana's "sensibilities" are not incidental to her story. As in so many lesbian narratives, our heroine has artistic tendencies. After rejecting a musical career, Diana ends up a writer, the vocation of nine out of ten lesbian protagonists. "Writing" is the means by which "Diana" balances her commitments to individualism and to lesbianism, her need for and disdain of the group. Without the group as a subject, as she acknowledges in her preface, her "autobiography" would not be justified at all. Her observations are given value by her claim to group membership. But as the narrator "her" observation of herself and others allows her to maintain her detachment from "the lesbian" in herself and from lesbians as a group.

Writing, unlike musical performance, is presented here as unrevealing. Diana's writing is described as based in her lesbian experience and so important as to determine the direction of her life: Diana's most successful story is derived from her relationship with Jane; she ultimately chooses Leslie as her life partner, on the grounds that Leslie will support her writing. Nevertheless, in order to represent Jane's character in her best story she writes about a heterosexual relationship. There is not even any discussion of this translation of the lesbian into a heterosexual narrative.

Yet the questions of gender at the center of Diana's contradictory presentation of herself as a lesbian are clarified by her position as a writer. Diana is surrounded by writers. Carl, who offers her his fortune as well as his hand, likewise offers a literary standard toward which she can only aspire. His friend Claudia, a hack writer of "magazine serials . . . lightweight, sentimental stories of popular appeal" (49), once wrote a well-received "arty novel" — "the only decent thing" she ever produced — but took three years to produce it and earned only $630. She explains to Diana that she moved on to serials that take a couple of months to write and pay $20,000 each, because " 'I've got four poor relations dependent on me' " (49). Diana ends up both a serious writer and a hack, producing trash for the money while retaining her literary goals. The trash is heterosexual romance: " 'the formula: "Sin, Suffer and Repent," call your hero Mike and your heroine Cynthia, and throw in twice every bromide you can think of' " (205). But Diana needs the money that the trash provides because she is a lesbian. Having chosen lesbianism instead of Carl and his fortune, she ends up supporting Leslie as well as herself, when the younger woman, in the middle of her education, is cast off by her family for being a lesbian. Real men produce real literature, real women produce trash, and Diana because she is a lesbian produces both, which leaves her neither a real man, nor a real woman, but again a member of the third sex.

To read *Diana* in the 1990s is to read not just an "autobiography" from the late 1930s, but a tangle of narrative and editorial statements about lesbianism that circulated for many of the intervening decades. That circulation is one of the best reasons for our continuing attention to this text. Like its contents, *Diana*'s publication history is typical. Like many other such books from the 1920s and 1930s, Diana's "story of a strange love" was repeatedly reprinted after its original publication by a respectable press in 1939; it appeared in the 1940s in hardcover and in the 1950s and 1960s as a pulp paperback. Some of these works—Gale Wilhelm's novels from the 1930s and Patricia Highsmith, Ann Bannon and Valerie Taylor's novels from the 1950s and 1960s—were republished in the 1970s and 1980s in gay and lesbian series or by gay and lesbian publishers and are still in print. *Diana* last appeared as one of the Arno reproductions of lesbian and gay texts in 1975. These narratives have had such extended circulations because they were labeled "lesbian." And through their recycling they have only gained in authority and cultural impact as sources of information about lesbianism.

Diana lacks the commitment to the group with which Radclyffe Hall concludes *The Well of Loneliness*. However ambivalent, melodramatic, and self-aggrandizing that commitment was, it clarifies the progressive impulses of Hall's more widely known work. Diana's narrative ends not surprisingly, although again novelistically, with a much tidier commitment to the couple. We are faced again with the contradictions of her work. This final emphasis on the couple, achieved against lesbian as well as heterosexual opposition, underscores the conservatism of Diana's narrative. At the same time, *Diana* offers a defense of lesbian relationships that was unprecedented in 1939 and radical for decades afterwards. Questions remain: about the role of her race and class position in Diana's commitment to individualism; about what aspects of *Diana*, if any, are "authentic," and/or whether that matters; about the effects of such a conglomeration of conventions and contradictions on the claim that any one lesbian story or text could be representative; about the meanings of this narrative to the successive generations of readers to which it has been successfully served.

INTRODUCTION TO THE NEW EDITION

Thirty years after the fact, Audre Lorde could still recall "the gay-girl books" she and her downtown gay-girl friends "read so avidly" in the 1950s, "Beebo Brinker . . . Olga, of *The Scorpion*. Our much-fingered copies of Ann Bannon's *Women in the Shadows* and *Odd Girl Out*" (213).[13] That Lorde and her friends read avidly did not mean that they read uncritically: "we knew there was a world of our experience as gay-girls that they left out, but that meant we had to write it ourselves, learn by living it out" (213). Linking writing and living, Lorde underlines the resonance of these texts, and not just to the gay girls who would grow up to be writers. Patricia Highsmith evokes the "very proper atmosphere" of private gay clubs in the New York of "the 'forties and early 'fifties," where "The gays talked about the latest homosexual novel, and maybe chuckled over the ending."[14] But Highsmith also describes the "letters that poured in after the paperback edition [of her own *The Price of Salt*] in 1953 . . . twelve a day sometimes and for weeks at a stretch. . . . from Eagle Pass, Texas, from somewhere in Canada, from towns I never heard of in North Dakota, from New York, even Australia," thanking her "for writing about two people of the same sex in love, who actually came out alive at the end with a fair amount of hope for a happy future" (277). Whatever its limitations, this affirmation is what *Diana* still offers.

JULIE ABRAHAM

Notes

1. The standard history of the period is currently Lillian Faderman's *Odd Girls and Twilight Lovers: A History of Lesbian Life in Twentieth Century America* (New York: Columbia University Press, 1991).

2. For an account of lesbians in film see Andrea Weiss, *Vampires and Violets:*

Lesbians in Film (New York: Penguin, 1993). The lesbian and gay presence on Broadway is described in Kaier Curtin's *"We Can Always Call Them Bulgarians": The Emergence of Lesbians and Gay Men on the Broadway Stage* (Boston: Alyson, 1987).

3. Mackenzie's *Extraordinary Women* was published in Britain without any difficulty the same year that Hall's *The Well of Loneliness* was banned. G. Sheila Donisthorpe's masterpiece *Loveliest of Friends!* (New York: Arco Publishing Co., 1952), published originally in Britain in 1931 to cash in on the scandal surrounding *The Well*, was reprinted repeatedly in the United States from 1952 until at least 1962.

4. Discussions of lesbian pulp paperbacks include Kate Adams, "Making the World Safe for the Missionary Position: Images of the Lesbian in Post World War II America," in *Lesbian Texts and Contexts: Radical Revisions,* ed. Karla Jay and Joanne Glasgow (New York: New York University Press, 1990): 255–74; and Angela Weir and Elizabeth Wilson, "The Greyhound Bus Station in the Evolution of Lesbian Popular Culture," in *New Lesbian Criticism: Literary and Cultural Readings,* ed. Sally Munt (New York: Columbia University Press, 1992): 95–114. For an account of post-Stonewall lesbian novels, see Bonnie Zimmerman, *The Safe Sea of Women: Lesbian Fiction, 1969–1979* (Boston: Beacon, 1990).

5. Virginia Woolf's *Mrs Dalloway* (1924) has not been read as a lesbian text until the past decade. Gertrude Stein's *Q.E.D.* (1903) and H.D.'s *Hermione* (1927) were not published until after their deaths. Mary Renault wrote *The Friendly Young Ladies* (1945) before establishing her reputation as a writer of historical fiction. Patricia Highsmith published *The Price of Salt* (1952) under a pseudonym (Claire Morgan), before she went on to a career as a writer of psychological thrillers.

6. See for example Woolf's *Orlando* (1929) and Stein's *The Autobiography of Alice B. Toklas* (1932) and *Wars I Have Seen* (1945).

7. For an analysis of coming out stories see Biddy Martin, "Lesbian Identity and Autobiographical Difference[s]," in *The Lesbian and Gay Studies Reader,* ed. Henry Abelove, Michele Aina Barale, David M. Halperin (New York: Routledge, 1993): 274–93.

8. While we know that "Olivia" was Dorothy Strachey Bussy, and that her memoir of girl's school life was based on a school she attended, her account echoes the many other girls school stories with lesbian overtones, and ends dramatically with the suicide that so often concluded lesbian novels.

9. Cover blurb for Radclyffe Hall, *The Well of Loneliness* (New York: Anchor, 1990). For contrary information see Michael Baker, *Our Three Selves: The Life of Radclyffe Hall* (New York: Morrow, 1985).

10. For a survey of black lesbian material up to 1981, see J. R. Roberts, *Black Lesbians: An Annotated Bibliography* (Tallahassee, Fla.: Naiad, 1981).

11. While the characters in the novels written for the 1950s and 1960s pulp

market, such as Ann Bannon's Beebo Brinker series, stay in New York and end up working as elevator boys, as secretaries, and in shops, their fathers were professional men and they went to college. The heroines of pre-Stonewall lesbian novels are not born into the working class.

12. For an account of the role of bars in lesbian culture in the 1950s and 1960s see Elizabeth Kennedy and Madeleine Davis, *Boots of Leather, Slippers of Gold: The History of a Lesbian Community* (New York: Routledge, 1993).

13. Audre Lorde, *Zami: A New Spelling of My Name* (Watertown, Mass.: Persephone Press, 1982), 213.

14. Patricia Highsmith, "Afterword," *The Price of Salt* (Tallahassee, Fla.: Naiad Press, 1984), 280.

Introduction

THE mythographer Appollodorus, in his description of the birth of the gods, refers to Thamyris, the first homosexual. Sapphism, or lesbianism, was ancient in the days of Sappho of Lesbos. Yet such is our immunity to information, that when Havelock Ellis collected his various studies on *Sexual Inversion* (1897), he stated that before his first cases were published, not a single British case, unconnected with the asylum or the prison, had ever been recorded; worse still, he knew medical men of long experience in practice who had never, to their knowledge, come across a single case. In that year, Edward Carpenter issued a pamphlet on *An Unknown People*—found among all primitive tribes, and in every race on earth. They are still the unknowables, for though the existence of a third sex is now widely recognized, general knowledge on the etiology and prognosis of homosexuality is inaccurate and confused.

I welcome any book which adds to the understanding of the lesbians in our midst. Among these books I definitely place the present autobiography. It is delicate, yet enlightening; tense, but never lewd; passionate, without a word offensive to chastity. It is the confession of one who was destined by Nature to gather forbidden fruit in the gardens of deviation, and who saved her life from frustration by knowing herself. That charming women should be lesbians is not a crime, it is simply a pity. It is not a question of ethics, but of endocrines.

The authoress lights a little lamp on the hidden altar of les-

[xxxvii]

bianism. There is no danger that the woman biologically craving the male, will seek that strange light. Only the sisterhood enters to remain, and those who are borne here on the hormonic tides of inversion, cannot by laws or maxims or ostracism, be kept from that dark temple.

VICTOR ROBINSON, M.D.

Author's Foreword

I MUST WRITE this book as if I were a person of importance. And, indeed, I can do that if I think of myself as a type rather than as an individual. As an individual I am without importance except to myself; as a type I am quite important, for I belong to the third sex.

The history of my emotional development had only these two marks of distinction: first, my lesbianism is, I believe, the result of long environment peculiarly fitted to foster whatever inclination to homosexuality I had as a child; second, my obstinate refusal to admit the truth of my own nature to myself.

The characters and events in this book are real. But the reader will understand that because of the abnormal nature of the theme, the author has made whatever changes were necessary to protect her characters' identities. If there are characters, names or circumstances that suggest identification with living persons, that fact is regrettably coincidental.

DIANA FREDERICS

To M. AND H.

PART I
First Fears

Skeletons in My Family Closet

OTHER THAN a dipsomaniac grandfather who managed to be a fair poet, and an uncle who made a fortune in mules, my family background is almost entirely without color. While my distant ancestors were among the earliest settlers in America, my immediate family did little else than earn money, establish homes and settle into comfortable living that was occasionally even plutocratic.

The skeletons in our family closet are quite ordinary skeletons, neither better nor worse than those of many another average family. A great-grandfather who was a preacher exhausted three wives; and a musician cousin was killed in a Munich duel under circumstances that focused on an outraged husband. But these suggestions of color are neutralized on the family tree alongside general blamelessness so normal as to be almost dull. Indeed, I almost resent such a respectable ancestral front; it would be a comfort to be able to explain my own shortcomings by no more than a glance at the family album.

For generations our home has been in a good-sized town in northern Kentucky, that part of Kentucky which the South calls midwestern and the Midwest calls south. In spite of my fondness for northern Kentucky, it has always annoyed me a little that it had to be located in such an equivocal latitude. Since I must question which sex I belong to, it would be satisfying to be able to think of myself as positively *something,* as positively midwestern or southern. But I straddle the question of geography even as I do that of gender.

[3]

DIANA

My father was of German descent, a handsome man of great personal charm and fine intelligence, a tragic misfit in the banking world where he somehow succeeded in becoming a financial success, in spite of an artistic rather than a practical turn of mind. I have always suspected that his guiding hand was my mother, who is practical where my father was not. My father died when I was nine, but I recall with tenderness his whimsical wit, his love for music, his exasperating habit of expensive and short-lived hobbies, his quiet agnosticism, and his devotion to Mother and the children.

My mother, sentimental Irish and practical Scotch to her finger tips, is a sensible woman, formidably regal in her good looks, and has a sly sense of humor calculated to bewilder those who have not caught the spirited glint in her eyes. Nothing, ever, is allowed to take precedence over her maternal affection and responsibilities. And her four children are devoted to her.

From my father I inherited a German sentiment that frequently gets in the way of clear thinking, an impractical nature, and some control over the quick temper I got from my mother. My father gave me, too, his black hair and oval face. From my mother I inherited little besides blue eyes, the capacity for profound sympathy, and a stubborn will.

My childhood was that of a happy, carefree moppet who had everything—a lovely home, affectionate parents, and three brothers who were fun. Gerald was the oldest, then Billy, two years older than I, then John, three years younger.

I was proud of my home, even as a child. It was at the edge of town, a great grey stone house set at the top of a slowly rising hill and surrounded by scores of maple and elm trees. In spite of its monastic color and the formal landscaping, its appearance was comfortable rather than imposing.

As soon as I was old enough, my father allowed me to go along with him when he took Gerald and Billy on week-end trips

[4]

to his hunting lodge, a log cabin set deep in what seemed at the time a huge forest. Ready for anything, and realistic, I always dressed in my bright red and yellow Indian suit, complete even to beaded moccasins, and justified my father's pet nickname of "Feathers." I always felt sorry for my brothers: they had to go off by themselves to hunt small game, while my father allowed me to stay with him to act as lookout for bears. He gave me the stock from an old gun wired on a wooden barrel, and let me stalk among the trees until I was ready to drop, my scalp tingling with direst fears if I so much as stepped on a dry branch. My hope must have been as perpetual as milk to the miraculous pitcher; I never saw a bear. I was a long time learning that the tracks my father occasionally pointed out to encourage me were made by errant cows.

There was one thing I loved above all others as a child—my music. At the age of five, I began to interrupt Billy's practice hour at the piano by begging to be allowed to play, and at six, when my mother let me take lessons, I startled both my family and my teacher by my precociousness. Yet my facile ear for music got me into trouble—it was more fun to imitate Billy's harder pieces than it was to practice my own. And though Billy became furious and mother forbade my imitations, the impulse often got the better of me. I still believe I was the reason for Billy's switching to the trumpet, though he maintains that the Boy Scout band needed a trumpeter. In any event, he used fore-thought in keeping his instrument locked in a trunk.

When I was nine Father persuaded his friend, Dr. Roehm, the head of the music department of the men's college near town, to take me on as a private pupil. It was unfortunate that Dr. Roehm's ferocity could not stand up under close acquaintance. The longer I knew him the less fearfully I regarded him. His moustache seemed less and less militant; even his voice changed from a sharp snort to a paternal grunt, and I somehow sensed, in spite of his awkwardness with little girls, that he meant to stop short of paralyzing me. At any rate, within the first few months he was calling me *"Kind,"* and buying me stick candy in the college refectory.

A paradisiacal family life was cruelly blasted by my father's sudden death. John and I were young enough to be spared the sharp grief of full realization; Mother's silence terrified us and we wondered if she were going to die too: we were without understanding. What I needed was someone to tell me what to do, or how to stand the silence and mystery without crying. Though my body shook from holding back my tears, I could not let myself give way; Father would not have liked it.

Several hours before the funeral Gerald took John and me for a walk in the hills behind our home, slowing down now and then for a minute as if to speak, then going on without saying anything. Finally, he took us to our maid's mother, who was to keep us in her house until the next day. What he finally said as he left us is a memory of such tenderness it has become a part of my very love for Gerald: "I'm glad you two are old enough to be able to remember him."

I had always played with boys instead of girls, and growing older made no difference; I still did. Girls frankly bored me. I scorned dolls and played instead with the noisy trains my brothers prized. I scorned Elsie Dinsmore for Tom Swift, and, instead of my own *St. Nicholas,* I read my brothers' *American Boy.* I scorned my girl playmates and their games of jacks to become marble champion of the fifth grade.

Our large front lawn, beautiful with trees, shrubs and flowers, made an ideal gridiron for the neighborhood football team. Floral vandalism was no concern of ours. I often wonder now why I, the only girl permitted on the team, was not maimed beyond

[6]

recognition. Perhaps the boys were being more considerate of their feminine tackle than I thought at the time.

I was scarcely conscious of being a girl. The boys accepted me as one of them as tacitly as I assumed that position. My skill both as a swimmer and as a trapeze artist, where at the risk of my neck I would outdo the boys or perish in the attempt, unquestionably added to my privileges of equality with the male.

My mother and father had always taken my antics as they came, hopeful that time and age would season my tomboyish nature. Of course, they were indulgent with me; I was their only girl. I was a healthy young animal, full of energy and deviltry, and tomboys were common enough. They matured into just as feminine young women as did the little girls who preferred dolls to BB guns.

Years afterwards, during my adolescence, when my preference for knickers to lace panties persisted, it was too late for my mother's growing concern to matter. My acquired tastes were set; the ladylike pastimes she urged seemed sissy and tiresome.

I recall how hurt she would become by my wilful refusal to conform to her expectations. It must, indeed, have seemed peculiar to her that I preferred baseball bats to sewing sets in my room. No amount of persuasion could induce me to give up such tastes. Once she prepared a surprise for me during my absence at summer camp; when I came home my room was decorated in a girlish mode, from dainty wallpaper to lace counterpane. A new bottle of *eau de cologne* stood on my dressing table where our pony's saddle soap had always been, and a new amber manicuring set was spread out to one side.

It was a dismal failure. With the brutal tactlessness of adolescence I wept that my beautiful collection of bats and marbles had been taken away. I couldn't for the life of me pretend to like those frilly blue pillows.

DIANA

Though the threadbare theme of the misunderstood daughter is difficult to make convincing, I can understand now why my mother used to say she never knew real disappointment until I began to grow up. Naturally partial to girls rather than boys, she must have found the discouragement of trying to mold me into a more moderate feminine cast all the more disheartening since I was her only daughter.

2

Gil: A Normal Boy

IN THE LIGHT of my early hoydenish beginning, it was unfortunate that my adolescent years were also passed in proximity with boys. By this time I had started attending classes with them too, for Dr. Roehm had persuaded me to enroll as a special student in his regular theory and appreciation courses. Mother, hesitant because of the unusualness of the situation, agreed when Dr. Roehm insisted that reasons of sex and age were superficial. Besides, she was proud of his invitation.

Any thrill I might have felt by being considered ready for classes with college boys was frozen clear out by fright. The studio had never looked so big, and Dr. Roehm, transformed into a lecturer now, seemed compelled to use words of forbidding length, which he bit off with pedantic zest. For weeks I was too chilled by individual words to try to follow the context. Then quickly, I was in the second term and these classes became far more exciting than anything at school; now we could compose.

Dr. Roehm, of course, wanted us to stick to the simplest exercises in harmony. But fancy captured me heart and soul, and my imagination ran far beyond anything expected or, for that matter, wanted. I must have driven Mother, Dr. Roehm, and the class half mad with my creations which—the one thing to be said in their favor—were at least reverently executed.

The year I started going to high school three college students came to live in our house. The men's college had an overflow enrollment and since we lived close to the campus, Mother was persuaded to rent two rooms. Our house was large, and though my father had left Mother financially secure, she was glad to receive help with the household expenses. Consequently, from the age of twelve to sixteen, when I went away to college, my home life was a veritable parade of boys. Counting my brothers, there were frequently as many as six at a time in our home. This sort of ménage resulted in boys becoming my daily companions. Small wonder that constant daily association with boys over a period of years left no secret mystery or charm enshrouding the male sex! My impressionable years were flooded with male habits, male viewpoints, male ideals, male psychology.

Except for one occasion these various boys were pleasant companions, some of them delightful friends. This one exception was a shocking experience for a hopelessly naïve child of thirteen. One boy, a newcomer to our home, called me into his room one rainy Sunday afternoon to admire some snapshots. I hesitated a moment, since I never entered the guest rooms, but, reluctant to appear rude, I went. Ignorant as I was, his intentions were too abrupt to be misunderstood. I recall only my fury; in spite of my years, it was enough to upset a blundering collegian. Like many people who manage to keep their heads in a tight predicament, I suffered repercussions. For weeks afterward I felt the full impact of sordidness. Despite the sudden exit of the collegian from our home, with no more explanation to my mother on my part than on his, the scene remained indelible.

It is almost incredible to me now to recall the extent of the effects of this assault on my innocence. I was made too abruptly aware that life amounted to something more than front yard games and school and camp. My would-be seducer had said something to me which made me think more than I had ever honestly thought in my young life. I even got out my dictionary to find out what it was he'd meant by saying I was "seductive-looking." What a disturbing thought to one who until that very moment was completely unconscious of body, despite a maturing physique.

I spent days brooding over the fact that I had been born a girl. I didn't want to grow up. I didn't want to be "seductive-looking." I hated the expression, I hated the vague meaning. Oh, the horror of becoming an adult!

Shocked into the realization that I was growing up in spite of myself, I turned suddenly into an anti-social, introspective, melancholy bookworm. Life took on the proportions of a pitiless hoax. In the diary I kept at this time is entered, in the handwriting of a fourteen-year-old, such a penetrating observation as this: "It is cruel of parents to read fairy tales to children. The transition from the delicate fantasy of the fairy tale to real life is painful. Life bumps into children as they grow up. I'm glad I've found out about the falsehood that 'virtue is rewarded.'" Then, as if I'd been stilted as long as I could stand it: "That's boloney."

I didn't want to play any more games. I hated the boys for no reason except that they were growing up too. And some of them wrote notes to me in school that seemed silly and embarrassed me. My only pleasures were lonely ones—reading and suffering and practicing at the piano, and making the highest grades in school.

Mother, concerned that I was becoming aloof from friends for lonely excesses of reading and practicing, very wisely insisted that I go with her on a long summer vacation between my junior and senior years. She took me to a gay lake resort where life was active and people were not interested in soul probing, or in any music but a jazz band. I couldn't withstand the thrill of the water, and, without trying to resist, I joined the boys and girls of my own age in a whirl of exciting adventures. My mother no longer urged me to be sociable; doubtless to her surprise, she didn't have to. But her real triumph came the third day when I asked for my first evening dress to go to the country club dance.

Gil, an attractive, moon-faced sixteen-year-old who swam with me, had asked me, and I made no attempt to conceal my excitement.

On the evening of the dance I put on my blue formal and my new silver slippers. Mother fluttered nervously about, helping me dress, as excited as I. When, at length, I looked into the mirror for final approval, I was startled into realizing an exciting fact. I was almost pretty.

I felt a little backward to have to admit that I'd never stopped to consider my appearance before. Mother had given me powder and lip rouge, and I'd used them because it seemed the proper thing to do; clothes bored me and I'd always managed to shift the problem to her. But now, I thought, things were going to be different.

I needed about three more inches in height before I could think of myself as grown up, though my body was filled out. My mouth was too large and too happy-looking for me to be considered the wistful type. But my dark hair was nice, if just curly enough to be impertinent; my nose was nondescript and unobtrusive (as noses should be); and I instinctively knew my eyes were my best feature. There was really nothing about my looks to get excited about, but at least I wasn't plain-looking like some of the girls at school. Feminine vanity, which never had a chance to develop around three teasing brothers, had at last caught up with me. Suddenly I was glad to be fifteen and alive and waiting for Gil to take me to my first big dance.

I did love to dance, and Gil was expert in all the refinements of the camel walk and its variations of the season. It was a beautiful evening, and in the moonlight between dances Gil asked me to be his girl for the summer. When I shyly said I would, he gave me a compact—the first I had ever owned. I often wonder what Gil would have done with the compact if I had said no.

But I said yes. And Gil continued to be an attentive escort.

He was a daring swimmer, as well as an exciting dancer, and he had a roadster. What did it matter if Gil was a little slow-witted? Being his girl for six weeks was fun. He was popular with the younger set who had their summer homes on the lakeside, and his friends invited me with him to their house parties and camping trips.

On our last evening together we went to a dance and then sat in meaningful silence by the lake shore in front of our cottage. After a while Gil drew nearer. I was strangely affected. This scene was familiar; I had read about it somewhere, many times. Everywhere was loveliness. Gil edged closer and closer, and finally put his arm around me. When he kissed me I wondered why it seemed so very sweet and natural, and why Gil seemed so self-conscious.

Next day Gil drove mother and me to the station and, to my surprise, Mother invited him to visit us in the fall. I was glad. I could think of seeing Gil again.

I started my senior year happily and actively after long stubborn months. I was surprised and excited when my friends welcomed me back by electing me president of our class.

More meaningful than any success in school, however, was my progress in music. When, that same fall, Dr. Roehm talked of presenting me in a spring recital, I began to work with a zeal that punished my strength. Nothing had ever seemed so heart-warming as his simple statement, "You've learned well, Diana. But you have a natural something I could never have given you, a clean touch. It's clear-cut." And then, his summing up which I've thought of many times since, "It's masculine!"

Gil drove down twice in the fall and winter to see me. I was flattered, and my friends were much impressed that I had an out-of-town boy visiting me. But, I had to admit, I was slightly bored. Swimming with Gil and dancing with him were quite different from trying to entertain him in my home. And, of course, my brothers teased me unmercifully. Worse, Gil could not understand that I had kissed him as part of the mood of a lovely night; he assumed the right to be jealous of my other friends.

But I was still simply a companion with my friends at home; I had never kissed any other boy. Though I never lacked for dates for dances and parties, I was not interested in boys just because they were boys. Explaining to Gil that I didn't want to be his girl any more only made me the more conscious, in the face of his objections, that I was somehow not in harmony with the general pattern of girls of sixteen.

I never had crushes on boys and I couldn't understand girls who had. I was not in the least intolerant; rather, I felt helpless and at a disadvantage. I wished that I, too, might enjoy sitting in a drugstore just because the boy who worked at the fountain would grin back into the booths every so often. It was mystifying. What excitement could there be in that? And though I went along with my friends, and even pretended thrills to match theirs, the effort to feel comfortable became more and more forced. It seemed to me that I must be lacking somewhere. I liked boys; I believed that I honestly liked them better than my friends did, but coquetry went against my instincts. It was discouraging to try to adapt myself. Flirting got in the way of what natural poise I did have, tangling my impulses into a feeling of inadequacy I could not understand. I envied my friends their gift of banter that fed on innuendoes, or their arch expressions that meant so much —and nothing. But I could never join them without painful consciousness of my own limitations.

3

Most Exquisite Pain

MY CAMARADERIE with the boys was not nearly so exciting as my friendship with Ruth, a new girl who entered school in my senior year. On the first day of school Ruth had sat opposite me at a great wide table in the study hall. She was too thin and her mouth was too large, but she had lovely titian hair, worn in braids around her head, solemn blue eyes, and such a sweet smile that I wondered if anyone could possibly be as angelic as she seemed. What had drawn me as much as her expression was the dainty silver crucifix she wore at her throat; like all children brought up as Protestants, I was always fascinated by any symbol of the mother church.

When I made efforts to be friendly, Ruth's response delighted me. A little shy at first, she turned out to be so charming and so much fun that I began to envy her innocent expression as an accomplishment. I invited her to several parties, and from then on Ruth's popularity took care of itself. Her father was a visiting professor in the men's college, and she had a pretty Italian mother —quite enough for all of us to be impressed.

Ruth had been trained in dancing. Quick and imaginative, she loved to improvise steps as I played, and together we let ourselves go, in interpretations that would have strained more literal minds.

Soon we became inseparable. I began to neglect my other friends or ignore them altogether to be with Ruth. Mother scolded me for such tactlessness, but Ruth was satisfying and exciting, and no one else mattered. We gave our teachers excuses

[15]

of any kind to get to sit next to each other in the few classes we attended together. We wrote notes to give each other as we passed hurriedly through the halls; I could scarcely wait for her replies. Before I knew it I had become the addict of fantastic reveries in which she always had the central rôle.

When Ruth and I were invited with several other girls to a Christmas holiday house party, I knew I would contrive in every way possible to share a room with her. For a week I wondered what excuse I could use that would be tactful and plausible, and then when our hostess assigned us a room together, as I might have known she would, my happiness knew no bounds. I remember that Ruth laughed at my obvious relief.

That night when we went to bed alone, tired and happy with the day, Ruth's thoughtless intimacy and good-night embrace almost took my breath away. I had been surprised to feel curious sensations of longing the few times I had ever touched her, but I could never have imagined the exquisite thrill of feeling her body close to mine. Now I was amazed. Then, before I knew it, I realized I wanted to caress her. Then I became terrified by a nameless something that froze my impulse. The pain of resisting was torture, but the touch of her hand holding mine against her side was so infinitely sweet that I lay tense for fear my slightest movement would make her turn away from me. Long hours I lay awake after she had gone to sleep, scarcely daring to breathe for fear she might move, not daring to hope that I might kiss her lips without startling her.

That night is set apart in my memory, supreme and forever. My longing for Ruth was the most exquisite pain I had ever known.

It made a very great difference in my affection. Where I had been gay with Ruth, I now felt shy, self-conscious, too fond. Where I had been willing to share her with friends, I became jealous and morose, though I made every effort not to show my feelings. I began to brood about my growing desire to touch her, and the fear I felt at my impulse. At night when I'd go to my desk to study I would eventually push my books aside to write interminable letters I never dared send her.

My grades in every subject but music dropped from A's to B's and C's, and in one subject to D. I had never made below B in my school life before. But it didn't matter. Nothing seemed to matter except Ruth. Several of my teachers called me in for conferences, inquisitive about my new indifference. No doubt my inability to explain my own confusion only made them more curious.

I never spoke to Ruth of my feelings. Fear restrained me. I had enough sense of proportion to realize that what I felt was extraordinary. I was afraid she would not understand my affection. I did not understand myself.

4

Am I a Lesbian?

THEN, AT SIXTEEN, came the well-timed dénouement to my mental gropings, accidental though it was. Browsing in my father's library one night, I came upon a book on sex. I had seen it many times, I had read parts of it, but now I saw a section I had never noticed before. One detailed chapter was on homosexuality. I read and reread, eager, fearful, and finally sick in the pit of my stomach.

Such new phrases as "pervert," "nature will have her little joke," "queer mental twists," "Case A," "uranians," "crime against nature," jumbled on top of each other in my mind. I looked long minutes at a gruesome picture captioned "Homosexuals burned at the stake in Germany, 1494." It seemed to me that I could almost smell the burning flesh. I could reproduce that picture now from memory. There were two pairs of them: two women together, sitting, their backs against a log, faggots in their laps; and two men, standing together, faggots at their feet, their hands clasped. The executioners were jeering as flames licked at the victims.

I took the book and went upstairs to my room; it seemed miles away. I believe that nothing could ever happen to me again which would match the despair of that hour. It stands etched in my memory as a nightmare of unspeakable terror.

I felt like another "case" on file in a psychological laboratory. I was, then, a "pervert," "uranian," "homosexual"—no matter, all added up to the same thing. I was subject to arrest! I was grotesque, alienated, unclean!

AM I A LESBIAN?

Suddenly I even doubted if my body were normal. With a nausea of apprehension I examined my body carefully for any indication of abnormality. There was none that I knew of, but perhaps I couldn't tell. My mind was white with fear. I could scarcely wait for morning to come and with it the opportunity to go down to a doctor's office for a complete physical examination. I would go to a doctor who didn't know me, and give a fictitious name. I would pay him out of my allowance.

I couldn't sleep when I went to bed. The night seemed never-ending. I got up and turned on my night-lamp and read again until Mother saw my light and came to see if I were ill.

The next morning I hurried downtown to a reputable physician who, I was sure, did not know me. It was too early for his office to be open; I had to wait an hour. Finally he came, a small grey man with a wrinkled face and a large nose. I have wondered many times since what he must have thought of the child who tried to hide her trembling as she asked for "a thorough examination for any possible abnormalities." My memories of his kind smile are still vivid. His calm quieted my terror, and when I told him I was in a dreadful hurry he seemed to understand.

I was embarrassed when the nurse took me into a big room and told me to lie down with only a sheet to cover me. My mind had been too full of dread possibilities to wonder how I would be examined. Grimly I undressed and lay down, and the doctor came in. I shut my eyes against my mounting panic, telling myself that only his verdict was important.

After a stretch of time the doctor looked at me. He smiled and told me I was "perfectly normal and healthy." This knowledge, not doubted twenty-four hours before, was such a relief I was actually happy for a little while. Horrified at the thought of all kinds of impressions the book had given me, at least I now knew that my body was normal.

If only my mental turmoil could have been as easily calmed!

[19]

DIANA

My first step toward psychological treatment was compelling and involuntary. I did not even recognize it as such. Not yet in control of my emotions, I depended on instinct—and my instinct was to hide. I began to avoid all my friends, especially Ruth. I resigned my presidency of the senior class without the knowledge of my family. I refused a music award, knowing that I should have to acknowledge it on graduation night with a short speech and a piano solo. School was, with everything else, hateful to me now. My one desire was to graduate as inconspicuously as possible and go away to a college where no one would know me.

Though my piano recital was only six weeks off, I knew I could never go through with it. I kept practicing only to avoid questions, but I hated it, every note, and I lay awake nights inventing excuses to tell Dr. Roehm and Mother. No ordinary story would do; I had taken part in too many student recitals to make stage-fright appear plausible. Besides, this was in a sense my graduating recital, for Dr. Roehm was preparing me for a conservatory after I had finished high school.

It is hard for me now to convince myself that what I did was real, that my new knowledge could assert itself with so much cruelty. Yet it would be impossible to give any picture of my feelings without owning up to the desperation that demoralized my thinking.

A month before the recital I broke my left forefinger in a basketball game in gym class. To say I did it deliberately must be a qualified statement; I had played recklessly, game after game, hoping that the ball would have force enough to sprain my wrist if I held my hands stiff. Now, though my accident was more than I'd bargained for, I could not complain. I walked to the studio that same afternoon and showed Dr. Roehm my splinted finger, thankful that it explained itself and that I didn't have to say much. It came to me, after I left, that Dr. Roehm had apologized for an oath; I had been too relieved to notice what he had said.

The most difficult feature of my new mode of life was the avoidance of Ruth whom—I now admitted it to myself—I loved. Feeling guilty, fearing that if anyone found out I might even be put in jail, it was maddening but imperative to stay away from her. I could not look at her in class; I avoided our rendezvous by the fountain in the hall; I ate my lunches in the cafeteria alone, hiding behind a book in such pointed isolation that not even Ruth dared break in.

No one would ever know. I tried to be confident of that. I even tried to stop thinking, holding myself in a state of suspension that seemed more bearable than thought. But it was natural enough that Ruth should demand an explanation of my behavior.

Not clever enough to hide my misery, feeling crushed and a little defiant, I could not persuade her that my many excuses were valid. I even tried to tell her I was fickle, independent. She would not believe me. Without my knowledge she talked to Gerald, whom she knew I adored as if he were my father.

Gerald came into my room one evening when I was reading and, without warning, asked me why I had resigned my class presidency. Then, without waiting for an answer, he asked, too, why I had refused the music award. He knew I had worked hard on my music in spite of my indifference to other studies. He didn't know how hard it had been to refuse. And of course no impromptu explanation would satisfy him; a broken finger had nothing to do with recognition of past work. I was surprised and ashamed that he had found out these things. Finally he told me that Ruth had talked with him. I was heartsick. But no, of course I would not tell him. Even if I could I would not. He would hate me. He urged, kindly, even speaking of the recent moroseness which I hadn't thought was apparent. I was wilful—under no circumstances would I tell him. He could think anything he liked. Anything would, I thought, be kinder than the truth. At length, after an excruciating silence, Gerald, now anxious, asked me point-blank if I had done anything I was ashamed of. That, like a flash, was my inspiration. Nothing, I knew, could be so awful as the truth. I had an idea, and I might as well tell him. Yes, I said finally, with weary relief, I had taken some money from one of the teacher's desks. I didn't know what had made me do it. I just saw it late one afternoon when I was alone in her room and I took it. And I'd felt so wretched about it I couldn't stand any honors. I couldn't stand to be with my friends. I was going to pay it back as soon as I could save five dollars. Nothing he could say would make me feel more ashamed than I already felt. Now would he go away and leave me alone?

For a few minutes Gerald said nothing. I was afraid to look at his face. I buried my head in my pillow and I heard him walking around the room, back and forth, by my bed. Then I heard him open the door and start to go out. But he turned to say, rapidly,

"I'm glad our father can't know of this."

The words lashed me like a whip. He shut the door abruptly and was gone, without making any gesture to comfort me.

"I'm glad our father can't know of this."

Slowly I realized the horror of what I had done. I was getting to my feet to go after Gerald when he opened my door for a second to throw something on the bed. It fell short. I picked it up and saw it was a five-dollar bill. My blood froze. Without thinking I called Gerald's name wildly, two or three times, and finally he came back. I clung to him; I'd been afraid he wouldn't come. I told him I had lied, impulsively, but somehow I hadn't thought it would sound so terrible. I hadn't thought how awful it would be to be a thief, what it would be like to have our father ashamed.

Gerald, not knowing whether to be relieved or more worried, finally heard me say I'd tell him the truth. I remember he led me to the bed and sat patting my hand, and I was sure he would be kind. I did not know how to begin. Very suddenly came the thought that he would be embarrassed by what I was going to say. But I had cut myself off from any retreat. I have no idea now how I did begin. Bit by bit, without being prepared or having the truth softened, Gerald heard the miserable acknowledgment of my homosexuality. I did not tell him of my physical examination, but I omitted nothing else. I made him understand, without daring to use the word "love," that I loved Ruth. I even told him why I had wanted to hurt my hand, that I couldn't stand making a show of myself before people who would scorn me if they knew. I wanted to be out of sight and mind. I hadn't worked out what I would do with my life, but I could get adjusted somehow if only I were let alone.

Then it was over, much sooner than I had thought it would be. I could not look at Gerald but I felt him staring at the wall above my desk.

When he spoke his voice was so low I had difficulty hearing him. I recall his words as if I had made a conscious effort to memorize them. He spoke carefully but very firmly. He denied outright that I was a homosexual. He explained that I was the victim of a school-girl crush, that crushes were common at my age, that I was hypersensitive, that the accidental discovery of homosexuality had made me accept a quick conclusion. He told me of other crushes he had heard of, and he admitted that he could understand my feeling: Ruth was very attractive. But there was nothing abnormal about it. I would outgrow it. Gerald sounded reasonable. Furthermore, he was studying to be a doctor, and to my mind doctors somehow knew the innermost secrets of all human behavior.

He was naturally upset that the book in question had treated homosexuality as a vicious social disease and criminal offense. I remember how he suddenly jumped up and, calling to John, asked him to go to the library, six blocks away. I wondered why. Half an hour later John handed Gerald a volume of Havelock Ellis and a volume of Freud, the first I had ever seen. Gerald read to me a long time, first from one book then from the other, stopping here and there to explain. I was astounded. I hadn't known that homosexuals had ever been treated with reverence; I only knew that they had been burned at the stake. I hadn't known they might find a worth-while place in society; I thought they were ostracized when they were discovered. I listened intently to every syllable Gerald read. And I hadn't known that the large majority of homosexuals are intellectually sound; I had thought they frequently had disordered minds, sometimes inclined to sexual insanity.

Before Gerald left me that night he looked at me and smiled, chiding me gently for having lied so wretchedly in the first place. He added, as if to counteract what he had said before, "And even if you were what you thought you were, I think your dad would understand all right."

5

Grace

THE REVELATION had been a godsend. I was not entirely convinced that I was not a homosexual; the core of my existence had been too abruptly displaced and the memory of Ruth had burned too deeply. But I was overjoyed to learn that even if I were, my nature would not doom me to the fate of witches nor to the insane asylum. It was wonderful to know that homosexuals were not a monstrous jest on nature's part, but a fairly common group of men and women for whom the normal was, incongruously, abnormal to so-called "normal" people. Intelligent people who understood were neither horrified nor shocked by them.

My saving grace was a feeling of rebellion. It was this same rebellion which caused a radical reactionary gesture that lasted through the next five years. With Gerald's enlightenment, at least I could reject the idea that my lesbianism was developed to a point beyond redemption I recalled that my father had drummed "strength of will" into my ears from the time when I was a very little girl, and I wondered if he had in his paternal wisdom sensed my coming need for it. This memory, coupled with Gerald's confidence, gave me a spiritual crutch which I was needing badly. It would give me the courage to spend the next few years arranging a defense against the day when, perhaps, I could know something definite about myself.

Mother and Dr. Roehm had long planned for me to go to a conservatory. I hated to disappoint them; I could not face the disappointment myself without feeling wobbly inside. But I knew

[25]

now that music could never be my career. If I were successful, I would be socially conspicuous; if unsuccessful I would be miserable, for I was born ambitious.

Now I had to think of a profession where numbers meant safety, where identity was of little importance—and, to the amazement of my family, I decided on teaching. The one thing about the prospect that heartened me was the thought that since there were so many ineffectuals in the profession it should not be difficult to be successful. With my plans resolved, spiritless, I decided on a large co-educational college several hundred miles away from home.

My mother had gone to infinite pains to start me off to college with attractive clothes; I had a good social and scholastic background—everything I needed to secure a bid to the sorority of my choice. When I was asked to join the sorority, I was overjoyed.

My one eccentricity was my insistence on rooming alone, contrary to sorority custom, for I recalled too vividly physical memories of Ruth. Yet, afraid of my tortuous penchant for introspection, I wanted no time to myself. Having girls just close enough for friends, yet with no chance for intimacy, was a hard balance to achieve, and I managed it only by growing emotionally in several new directions, all of them outside of self. I became more interested in people as such and, once I got the habit, it seemed that my capacity for understanding others had always existed.

By being careful not to cultivate particular friendships, I soon found myself with many, and confidante to so many sisters that I was sometimes hard put to it to keep secrets associated with the right girls. Then, because I was afraid I would not be taken seriously if my friends knew that I was the youngest girl in the house, I added two years to my age.

Spreading out my friendships helped solve the problem of

rooming alone and yet not being too much alone. My room became a natural rendezvous—whether for talking, reading, music, bridge games or midnight coffee.

I ignored with almost fanatic self-discipline those girls who were particularly attractive to me; I did not want my strength tempted. Occasionally, the effort proved a strain that gave me an unpleasant sense of duality and dispossessed me of confidence. But it never occurred to me that I might have any choice.

My music was the one thing that I knew I could always depend upon. Where I did not feel sure of myself in intimate midnight discussions of life and love, I could feel at ease when I was asked to play. My friends wanted popular music, not classical, and, at first a little ashamed, I went back to my childhood trick of playing by ear. Their appreciation often exhausted me, but I was glad to have such an easy means of being companionable. Parlor tricks compensate for a multitude of shortcomings.

Fortunately for my social ambition, I was considered attractive. I dated often; I went to the important fraternity dances. By the end of my second year in college I was amused to learn that I had acquired the reputation of being one of the best "owls" in the house. Translating collegiate slang, this meant that I dated the "right" men from the "right" fraternities. But in justice to my ruthlessness, I must admit that there were boys who definitely attracted me.

My happiness of the first two years buoyed my hopes for adjustment, and when, at eighteen, I was awarded a junior scholarship in English, it seemed to me that I had as much as any girl had any right to expect of life.

If I were to become a teacher, I must decide on something to teach, and I chose languages. Possibly because of my trained ear, languages had always come easily to me. I liked both my French and German professors, and I was at an age when French poetry got into my blood. Nor could I imagine a more ladylike way to earn a living. Somewhat cynically, I settled my major as simply as the telling implies. It seemed to me then, as it does now, that the grim business of providing for three meals a day should be made as painless as possible.

In my junior year, my equilibrium was upset by an ironic turn of events for which I was totally unprepared. During the week of quarterly examinations one of my senior sorority sisters, Grace, asked me to study with her. I was flattered, for I had been rather awed by her cool charm and by her oft-repeated refusals to go out on dates with the boys who invited her. She was the daughter of an army officer, and had the soldier's gift for rollicking yarns. Sometimes, during our midnight sessions, she would tell us stories that would set our blood tingling. While she talked her eyes would become brilliant and her words excited, but when her tale was finished she would withdraw into a cool reserve which I could never fathom. Yet somehow I was drawn to her.

The night Grace came to study with me we read Verlaine and Baudelaire and reviewed notes for several hours. It must have been about 11:30 when we became wearied with our reading and put our books aside to make coffee on the electric plate. Suddenly, inspired no doubt by Verlaine, she began to talk about homosexuality. Obviously, she was trying to sound out my reactions to the subject, and my self-consciously evasive replies made me blush with embarrassment.

"But I mean," she finally asked, "do you feel intolerant?"

She did not look at me. I sensed what was in her mind and was frightened.

"I don't know," I answered. "Maybe I'm just sorry for them."

After long minutes of silence she told me, simply, that she loved me.

"But please, Diana," she said, "I don't want your pity."

GRACE

Had she given me time to prepare for this confession, my interest in her might have been great enough to defeat me. As it was, my confusion was my defense. Extremely sensitive, Grace interpreted my awkwardness for reluctance, and, humiliated for having "misunderstood," she left.

Her avoidance of me for the next few days was not the only unhappy result of this revelation. I was disturbed by her double-edged expression of having "misunderstood," for I was certain my guarded remarks on homosexuality could not have been interpreted one way or the other. I did not know then what I know now—that in spite of subterfuge and cleverness, one homosexual is uncannily apt at recognizing another.

My curiosity was piqued. Grace then, unknown to any of her closest friends, was a lesbian. She was the first I had ever known. Even greater than my emotional concern was my psychological interest in her. Doubtless her lesbianism explained her ability to hold people off. But how did she react to her abnormality? Was she unhappy and rebellious? Had she, too, lived too much around men? Most important, was she ashamed?

My prejudice amazed me. Ignorant of Grace's abnormality, I had liked her. Now, almost before I knew it, I felt distrust, even antagonism. Inward searching for justification did no good; I knew it was beyond the reach of reason. Yet so was pity.

Partly because of my overwhelming feeling of affinity with her, partly because of my guilty conscience, I sent her a note three nights later asking her to come to my room.

At about ten o'clock she knocked at my door. Suddenly regretting my note, I wondered frantically what I could possibly say to her. She came in; she was dressed in red velvet lounging pajamas, her long blond hair more lovely than I had ever seen it. Her eyes were timid, and I knew I must be careful lest I wound her. She never asked why I sent for her; perhaps she knew. Conversation seemed wooden, and I was glad when she finally re-

[29]

lieved the tension by playing some records on my phonograph. I remember that she chose some Ravel. I lay on my studio couch and watched her as she listened. She had high cheekbones, a triangular, interesting face, full of breeding. Her hands folded and unfolded ever so slightly. When the music stopped she asked if she might light the candle on my table. She leaned close to me to put out the wall lamp as she did so. Still she said nothing, nor did I. But the candlelight dissipated her timidity, and she looked at me for the first time. Quickly she came over to me, kissed me on the forehead and whispered,

"It was sweet of you to let me come tonight. Please don't mind my loving you like this. Don't let it matter to you."

Then she left. I realized I had said almost nothing to her. Awkward as I had been, my feeling was one of relief that Grace had not suspected my own vulnerability. In the light of what she had said, I could believe now, surely, that she did not suspect. I was no longer frightened.

She came to see me frequently after this, always late in the evening after I had returned from my dates. Ashamed of my first antagonism, I made every effort to be hospitable without overdoing it, and Grace, losing her painful self-consciousness of the first two evenings, became a welcome, easy companion.

"Forget it, Diana, for my sake," she said once. "I'm not cut out for pathos. I'd shrink clear away if I thought you pitied me."

Though she said nothing more about her feelings, I was sensitive to the restraint that I came to admire as something beyond the need of pity. It was a gentleness, and, at the same time, an indescribable dignity.

Eventually I realized, and it startled me not a little, that Grace was taking the sting out of my prejudices. I had expected and feared I knew not what of her, but except for small attentions which would have escaped ordinary notice, she turned out to be not a whit different from my other friends—though I had no idea at the time at what cost to her histrionic energy.

Twice she gave me Brahms records for my victrola, but I thought of them as hers too, for she loved to listen with me. Those few times when I could feel sufficiently detached to kiss her good night, I was deeply touched by her gratitude, a gratitude that was akin to sorrow. At no other time did she come near me. And yet, tactfully, she never gave the suggestion of humility.

Had it not been for the constant attention of Carl, in whom I became suddenly interested during my junior year, the occasional tenderness I began to feel for Grace might have caused me to declare myself to her. Grace believed that I was in love with Carl, and I made no effort to disillusion her. Perhaps because I wanted to believe it myself.

PART II

Carl

J Meet Carl

CARL was a graduate student five years older than I, the only child of well-to-do parents who were divorced. Both of them worshipped him. I first knew Carl only by sight. Tall, blond, slightly stooped, clean-featured, with the gentle manners of a man much older, he was the enigma of the typical campus which can understand no variation from the norm. He was notoriously elusive with the co-eds, who, because of his good looks and his money, were all too eager to meet him more than half way. He had been captain of the golf team, a member of the polo team, and was a brilliant student of philosophy who confounded his professors with his insouciance. He had, too, a reputation for hard drinking that was the envy of his less sure-footed fraternity brothers. The first time I ever heard his name he was quoted as saying *The Crock of Gold* was his Bible and Thomas Mann his God. I remembered this only because the extraordinary combination seemed the more curious coming from one reputed to be a dissipated playboy. Too, I had heard the story of how Carl, drunk, had called the Dean of Women on a dare, asking her for a dinner date. Though the Dean's position gave her a formidable reputation with collegians, she must have had a sense of humor, for later, when Carl called at her office to apologize, she held him to his bargain. Legend had it that the Dean considered the evening a great success; she had become, according to her own story, Carl's best friend after his polo pony. Since I had seen Carl playing golf with the Dean, a handicap player herself, I imagined the legend had some truth in it.

DIANA

I first met Carl when a sorority sister, who was ill, asked me to borrow his psychology lecture notes. They must, she said, be model notes; Carl had an "A" in the course. When I called him he surprised me by saying he'd taken no notes, but he offered to drop by and explain the details of a coming examination. When he came that evening he was so deep in his cups I had to send him home. The next day I was surprised when he called me for a date. Not especially interested, and having a paper to write, I refused. He came for me anyway. Because I was surprised and amused by his presumption, he became embarrassed. The arrogance I had expected was not there. And somehow, contrary to anticipation, I liked him. I suppose I liked him for what he finally said.

"I can see any number of reasons why you wouldn't want to go out with me, and none why you should. But I've wanted to know you ever since I read your essay last year." Then, as if it were the highest tribute he could think of, "I wish I had written that myself."

My essay, in which I had exhausted a little further the subject of youth's disillusionment, had won an English prize and some little local attention—no more, no less. Of course he exaggerated its importance, but his interest pleased me.

Was it because of this new kind of flattery that I thought I detected sincerity? I don't know. I only know that, woman-like, I liked his eyes, and that I finally asked him to stay.

The next day he brought me a short story he had written. It was my turn to feel inferior. And delighted. I was no critic, but I did recognize a high-keyed imagination and an assured style far beyond any amateur work I had ever seen. I urged him to submit it for publication, but his conviction that he was a ne'er-do-well was too deep-seated for me to reach. He did, finally, give me his grudging permission to submit it for him. And when, within a

month, it had been accepted by a magazine of genuine literary
reputation, Carl was speechless with joy.

I learned to know Carl in the next few months as few of his
campus friends had ever known him. That his devil-may-care
attitude was a defense-mechanism became clear at once, but, unfortunately, it had gone almost far enough to obscure a fine mind
from itself. His devotion to his father, who was remarried, was
equalled by a deep sense of loyalty to his mother, with whom he
lived, and I suspected that his drinking was an escape from her
neurotic dependence on him. And it was true that Carl and the
Dean of Women had become friends. It made no difference to
either of them that their friendship, which defied campus tradition, tempted the campus wags. The Dean was, besides being
maturely attractive, a very wise woman.

Carl was eager to be serious with anyone who would take him
seriously. With his literary début a success, he wanted to prove
to his own satisfaction that he could survive the indulgences of
his father and the smothering of his mother. At the Dean's suggestion, and with my encouragement, he quit an aimless graduate
course—urged by his mother to keep him near her—took a small
apartment of his own, and gave all of his time to writing. Happily, his mother recognized his need for independence, and editors
continued to encourage him. As though he could not bear any
distraction from his new enthusiasm, Carl stopped drinking.
Nothing was ever said about it between us. It just happened—
a choice rather than an effort. I was relieved, for I'd have been
awkward at preaching.

Our relationship had begun on a peculiarly platonic basis. He
had, during the first evening, made the conventional advances,
but in spite of his skill I detected an indifference that, perversely,
delighted me. I suggested amiably that we get along without
pretending. Carl's relief was comical, and he made an unforget-

table remark which was an unconscious commentary on the mores of the younger generation.

"I'm glad you don't mind if we don't," he said. "I'm sick of it."

"I knew it."

For several months following, in spite of our friends' ill-concealed speculation, our friendship was frankly and blessedly platonic. We read together, studied together, rode and swam and played tennis together. Carl, wary of my temperamental game, shared golf only with the Dean. We had breakfast, lunch and dinner together, often in his apartment. We came, in fact, to be known as the "Most Devoted" couple on the campus, as we learned to our amazement from a spring poll of the campus newspaper. And Carl, on reflecting what irony it was that we were so misunderstood, kissed me gaily—for the first time—before a sunroom full of gaping sorority sisters.

I was happy for Carl when, at the end of my junior year, he began to talk about going abroad. He had been to Europe years before with his parents, but he had, as he said, "ricocheted from one country to another." Still held by boyish impressions, he wanted to spend a year studying and living in the places he liked best.

It was about three weeks before he was to leave that I realized he loved me. My first feeling was one of dismay. The only emotion I had ever felt for him was that of the mother who sees her bad little boy trying hard to be good and is finally convinced that he really prefers being good. Carl depended on me more than he may have realized, but I had never considered seriously the possibility of his loving me. Yet, with a woman's uncanny intuition, I knew it. Perhaps before he knew it himself.

I was dismayed because I was afraid. My ego was flattered, but my emotions were confused. When, finally, Carl told me he loved me and asked me to marry him and go with him, I knew what my answer must be.

Yet I could not force myself suddenly to end the happiest friendship I had ever known. I found myself clutching at straws, frantic at the thought of losing him entirely. For days I put him off, one hour unable to imagine getting along without him, and the next seeing marriage in unbearably bold relief. Sensing my distraction, Carl urged me to make up my mind during his absence. He would be gone a year. And so I was to consider myself engaged.

Was Carl's mood infectious that I should become deliciously happy when he gave me his fraternity pin? Was it a contagion of emotion that explained my own pale emotion—the first I had ever felt for any man—as Carl kissed me?

My feeling was, thank God, a triumph of normalcy. A weak desire, yes, but strong enough to identify itself as my first authentic *normal* emotion. It had been sweet, infinitely sweet. When I left him I ran up to my room giddily happy. Oh, dear God, it had happened. I was going to be all right.

When Grace came in I was so radiant she guessed what had happened. Impulsively I told her I loved him. Then, embracing her with so much tenderness that I surprised her, I was reminded that my feelings were too jubilant to be entirely personal. My great joy was that my emotion portended the normalcy which I wanted more than anything else in the world.

I could not sleep that night for wanting to tell Gerald.

2

J Decide About Carl

I HAD NO particular friends during my senior year. Grace had
been graduated, and Carl was in Europe. The new loneliness
was rather a happy change. I had spent three long years trying
to find myself in the sun, and now, with Carl's love, I felt that
a long homesickness had come to an end at last.

Carl wrote amusing letters that were likely at any time to
break into studied grammatical horrors simply because I had said
I was afraid to correspond with a professional writer. Or again,
his letters would reveal a tenderness I had had too little time to
know in the short while we had been engaged. He would send
gifts, anything that happened to strike him—a tiny Swiss music
box, a gay Bavarian smock, a caricature of himself drawn at a
Viennese carnival, an antique French bracelet that intrigued my
sisters. Every package was an adventure; every one, whether it
meant something lovely or something amusing, made me long
all the more to be with him.

Still I wished I could deceive myself as well as I deceived others.
As the year wore on, I had to admit that there were times when
Carl seemed not real to me, when my love seemed a thing of
ideality rather than of reality, a hope rather than a fact. It worried
me that sometimes his endearments would strike me as impersonally as if they had been intended for another. At such times I
would force myself to write gay, affectionate letters, whose appearance of spontaneity was, I hoped, not labored.

Spring came. I had to practice for an inter-sorority musicale,
as well as a play to be given by the French department; so many

senior activities absorbed my time and energy that I did not feel equal to a positive decision about Carl. But I did make up my mind that marriage would be unwise unless my feelings changed.

Carl surprised me by coming back two days early, just before my graduation, to see me play the rôle of Madelon in Molière's *Les Précieuses Ridicules*. Bronzed and happy, he looked more handsome than he really was. In the thrill of seeing him again my doubts went scudding off so fast I couldn't remember ever having felt casual about him. But all our eagerness had to wait on the exigencies of practicing Madelon's French. Carl read cue lines to me all his first evening, playing valet, lackey, father, suitor, and—with grudging spirit—niece.

His definite question was to come soon and my answer, whatever else I may say of it, was to receive all the judgment I was capable of. My mind riveted on unemotional considerations (if such are possible), I sifted impulses from attitudes, cleared away what I *wanted* to feel from what I *did* feel. Yet, no matter what perplexity gathered, my thoughts returned cleanly to a single focal point: there was between Carl and me a communion—clear to the initiated—that could not be confined to definition. It was a possession of understanding, a source of energy or of tranquillity that sprang from undercurrents far deeper than reason. It keyed all my emotions to a faster tempo, all my thoughts. It had order and rhythm and harmony about it.

I had every possible reason but one to be convinced that Carl and I would be happy married—I did not know whether I loved him physically. I had never ached with tenderness for Carl the way I had for Ruth during those fearful hours of one brief night. Still, I seemed to be always on the brink of it, as though a sudden rush of feeling were all I needed to push me over.

The sex relationship, I understood, brought unpredictable and deep psychological changes, and I had read the case histories of women whose apparent frigidity was cured by it. I had heard an older cousin admit that she had learned to love her husband only after months of marriage. My body was healthy and normal, and my attitude toward sex was, I believed, healthy and normal; I imagined a happy sex life to be of such importance to mental and physical balance that I knew I would not want marriage without it.

While, theoretically, the thought of "free love" or "trial marriage" had never appealed to me, I was afraid, practically, that marriage itself would be unjust to us both. Reason told me that, considering my uncertain stage of emotion, the wise and sensible thing to do would be to live with Carl as his wife before I married him.

So long as I had been merely Carl's friend I had been able to shake off thoughts of homosexuality; now I had to think of him as well as myself. Memories of his parents' unhappiness made him look upon marriage with more than usual seriousness; he had never tried to persuade me. In thinking of his attitude and his future even more than of my own, I knew I would despise myself if I married him while I felt the slightest suggestion of risk. At last I could appreciate a family story about Mother's grandfather who left his bride of a year to start out alone against the hazards of the West. His neighbors, who scoffed when he said that leaving her took more courage than taking her, drew a stern reprimand. "This is," he said, "a matter between my God and my conscience. My neighbors may know my God, but they don't know my conscience. It's not near so easy to hide from."

I longed for a confidante to whom I could explain the lingering question of homosexuality, and from whom I might receive disinterested advice that was free from petty attitudes. Yet I was aware that the mere fact that I questioned would be, inevitably and humanly, taken as proof of fear—an injustice to the open-mindedness I felt. I believed that Gerald, could he have been disinterested, would have understood both my unwieldy interrogation and my decision.

I could do nothing but what I did: tell Carl I would live with him indefinitely without marrying him. My excuses were frail but persistent. I even used the argument that mother would disapprove of my marrying so young. Worldly as he was, Carl was disconcerted by my decision, but he acquiesced to the understanding of marriage later.

Carl was working very hard at his writing and he could be completely happy, he told me many times, only when I was with him. Although he wanted to go home with me from school, I thought it best that my family should not meet him. I persuaded him to go on to New York to find an apartment, where I would rejoin him in two weeks. Then, on my way home after graduation, I began to dread telling my family that I had a job in New York.

Instead, I told them that I'd have to go to summer school at Columbia University, in order to get more credits in education; that I had a job teaching French and German in a private school; that I'd get $150 a month, but that I wouldn't get home again until Christmas. To satisfy Mother, I promised that I'd try to find a congenial teacher with whom to share an apartment.

I left home shortly, with advice ringing in my ears and my heart sick inside of me. But I could not wear out my emotions on things I could not help. I needed to turn my heart and my mind toward what lay ahead, my life with Carl.

3

Trial Marriage

CARL HAD WRITTEN that he'd taken a small apartment in the West Seventy's, high and airy, and boasting a view of Central Park. That was all I knew of it until he carried me across the threshold.

I could understand his look of pride. Contrary to the original plan, he had furnished it himself. It was more spacious and more beautiful than I had imagined, even in my excitement. I loved the sherry-colored drapes, the deep maroon rug suggestive of dark coolness. On the wall was a single picture, a Van Gogh landscape. I knew that Carl must have had many a thrill in selecting this little bibelot or that, a cloisonné vase, a white lacquer cigarette box, a slender coffee table. But, most exciting, there was a handsome grand piano, so tempting that Carl had to remind me there were other things to look at.

He hurried me down the hall to admire his study, and there he pointed to his books already classified in their cases, to his great flat desk already littered with work and yesterday's cigarettes, and to a Matisse sketch he had bought in Paris. I was touched to see a picture of myself on the only clean corner of his desk.

I knew it was timidity that made him save my room to show last. For no reason at all I remember the glass door knob. When he opened the door he kissed me and said,

"Darling, this is for my bride."

He had already given the room a charming personality. There was a broad, low French bed with a soft blue brocade covering.

There were ivory venetian blinds and a cool bouquet of lilies-of-the-valley on my bedside table. On the table, too, was my own copy of *Angels and Earthly Creatures;* I had missed it, but how he got it I never knew. Sight of it made everything seem familiar. Then, in a niche at the far corner of the room, I saw a small blond cocker spaniel studying me, his paws tucked under his ears.

"That's Bonk."

Carl smiled at my surprised delight. I called Bonk. He was suspicious of me; after all, he had been there first. But after a moment Carl came over to me and, right there, with Bonk still nipping at my heels, he gave me a square-cut blue sapphire that quite took my breath away. Slowly he put it on the third finger of my left hand.

"All right, Diana?"

"Very right," I said, and tears came in spite of me.

Carl loved me and I felt humble and undeserving. Yet certainly my affection, whatever its shortcomings, must count for as much as my confidence. I would try so very hard to make him glad of my existence. When I started to tell him that, he kissed me and I didn't get quite finished.

I wondered what possible difference there could have been in Carl's welcome had I been his bride. None, I believed. There was even a sober business angle given me before I had been in my new home a day. Carl handed me a large envelope, an insurance policy on his life, with me as beneficiary.

"Just to show you what a practical man your husband's going to be," he said. Then he went on to explain what he had only mentioned to me before, that he had an income from his maternal grandfather's estate, which consisted of a plantation in Georgia and holdings in a tobacco company; and that, in addition, he had invested in his father's advertising firm in Chicago. Now, in the first years of the depression, his annual income was about $20,000.

"That," Carl said, "is all I ever want. My mother and father

[45]

would be together today if they hadn't gotten too much money. Mother could afford neurasthenia, and Dad could afford other women. I've never known whether Mother drove him to other women or Dad drove her to nerves. But anyhow, darling, you'd be bored at a spa and I'd be bored with other women. Which leaves us where we started. There's only one thing that would make me want any more money. Children."

Carl lay beside me, asleep in the early morning, his robe thrown over the back of a chair, his slippers by the bed. Some indescribable emotion pulled at me as I looked at him, and all I could think of was something I had read—of a woman happy that her lover need no longer sigh with unrest; she would give him ecstasy. I understood that now. Suddenly I gloried in an unexpected sense of possession. It seemed to me I had never been so happy. There was no need to question. My place was with Carl.

It did not matter that first physical intimacy had been disappointing. I could not expect a miracle of chemistry to follow the mere act of defloration; I understood that it frequently took some little time for a woman to become adjusted, for two to learn rhythm, to grow together. At least I had managed the first pain. Now I could look forward. Though my physical desire had been passive, my mental desire was swift and certain. Soon I would learn to respond spontaneously. Until I did, Carl must believe that my desire was as natural as his.

In the next few days I wrote to Mother that I'd settled in an apartment in the West Seventy's with a girl I'd known at school. "She's going to Columbia too," I said, "and will be here all winter as well. We can manage nicely together."

Like all young couples, Carl and I planned for our future; and like all plans, ours were just as full of happy nonsense as they were of practicalities. It was now summer, and Carl wanted to spend the coming fall and winter in New York.

"I'm not going to spoil my chances for marriage by waiting any longer than spring," he'd say. "We'll get married in time to spend next summer traveling. But where?"

One week it would be deep-sea fishing off Tahiti; the next, when I'd use my influence, it would be a motor trip through Germany and France. Within a month Carl and I had enough travel literature to start a tourist agency. But practically, because Carl had a growing interest in oriental philosophies as literary material, we settled on a trip to China. The prospect was enough to send our imaginations soaring.

Yet such plans, made so confidently, could never completely escape sudden raps of fear when I'd stop to think that all of them assumed marriage.

My ideas of marriage were, of course, colored by the memories of my father's and mother's devotion, a devotion I had accepted as being natural rather than extraordinary. It was fortunate that Carl's experience had prepared his attitude better than mine had prepared me. I had to learn from him that marriage was a creation rather than a contract, and a maturing adventure such as I had never expected it to be. For the first time in my life I learned what it was to feel *selfless,* to think and be and act for another, and not for myself; to grow inwardly by thrilling to a lover's pleasure or, again, by the hurt of disappointing; to feel my way along uncharted emotional channels as I learned grace in sharing.

Most important, I learned to understand what Carl meant when he said he wanted me to feel a sense of completeness, a sense of common destiny. That sense, Carl said, held two people together. Habits and a thousand intangibles and sharing of common responsibilities went into it, to carry it beyond the narrowness of individual needs. And, in understanding, illusory hopes seemed for all time settled into confidence. I felt that I was becoming a woman.

Carl had his writing, and I went back to music with such vehemence that I rented a practice room in a vacant apartment rather than have him endure my orgies. After several months, when my fingers felt at home again on a keyboard, I began to listen to his suggestion that I study under Lubin, who had retired from concert work and who would, on recommendation, take pupils. Finally I went to see him and enrolled in a four-month course which was, I knew, extravagance of the wildest kind, but such a thrilling experience that I still think of it sentimentally.

Carl was at work on some short stories; within the past year he had written several which, with some previous ones, he hoped to have published in book form. Three had by this time appeared in magazines, and whatever may have been said of them, they had not been ignored.

Some editors had been cold; others had called his work significant. He had a gift for satire, for bold and original imagery, and a ruthlessness of characterization that was bound to produce a definite effect on the reader. But never, in my opinion, would his work be popular. Nor did he seem to care.

Because Carl himself had so much to inspire affection, his brilliant hardness as a writer troubled me. I thrilled at his control over words, at his manipulation of characters, but his meaning and his women frightened me. More and more disturbed by having to continue my pretense, I couldn't help wondering if I were as transparent to him as the women he created.

Carl understood my reluctance to let my college friends know I was living in New York, and I was content to make my friends among his. I was not so much struck by the number or variety of Carl's friends—for he had done undergraduate work in an eastern university and had lived in or near New York since child-hood—as I was by the deep affection he seemed to have inspired in them. There was Andy, a college friend, a soft-spoken blond giant who found college teaching a satisfactory excuse for being lazy; Olivia, Andy's wife, tall, dark, and so beautiful that I thought of her as ornamental; Gregor, an engineer, who had worshipped Carl with puppylike faithfulness since boyhood and who taught me old Russian folk tunes; Myrna, Carl's literary agent, a nervous wild-haired woman of forty-five who knew an astonishing lot of musical lore; and Hart, a bachelor and a friend since prep school, who had too much money for his own good and who drifted from one speakeasy to another.

Myrna took me to afternoon concerts, Andy and Olivia came often for bridge, and Hart loved to surprise us with packages from the delicatessen. But of all Carl's friends, I was to become most fond of Claudia, a widowed middle-aged novelist who had seized upon Carl as a refreshing change from the other young writers she knew—he was having success in spite of normal living. I liked her western sanity and heartiness. I even enjoyed looking at her—a short, squat ash blonde, with a tilted nose, shrewd green eyes, as excited a listener as she was a talker.

I had read several of Claudia's magazine serials in college—lightweight, sentimental stories of popular appeal. Sensing that her name intimidated me, Claudia was not long in putting me at ease.

"I wrote an arty novel once," she told me. "I starved three years to work on it. It's the only decent thing I've ever done. And I got good notices. It brought me $630 in royalties. Or, in case you can't divide, that's $210 per year. Then I got roaring mad and wrote a 50,000 word serial in four months. My God, it was sloppy! And sold it for $20,000. Or in case you still can't divide, that's $5,000 per month. I've got four poor relations dependent on me. Now, what do you think you'd do?"

Although Claudia was ignorant of music, she was passionately fond of it and bullied me into coming to her apartment to play for her, afternoons on end. I recall these afternoons as my first glimpse of unconventionality untouched by self-consciousness. Claudia always loosened her clothing and settled deep in a divan with a bottle of scotch whiskey in one hand and a water tumbler in the other.

"None for you, my pet. Too young," she'd say, pouring herself four fingers. And then, "Now play."

Claudia was the only friend close enough to guess that Carl and I were not married. Somehow I did not mind her knowing, even though she scolded occasionally.

"You two aren't the kind who'd get a bohemian kick out of unconventionality," she said. "Get married. Have children. Have six. What the world needs is less introspection and more babies. From people like you."

I had thought of having children long before Claudia began to mention it, but she gave impetus to the idea. For weeks I thought of it, and tried to catch some of Claudia's maternal spirit. But I lacked the final courage. I did not really want a child. And bringing a baby into the world, hopefully, just to see what effect it might have on me, was a thought too baldly clinical.

4

I Begin to Feel Normal Love

C
ARL AND I had friends, tastes, interests, and even work in
common, for I helped him correct proof, type, and (delighted beyond all reason whenever he trusted me) do research
in the libraries. We had, further, a freedom from financial worry
which, I have since learned, was a blessing I was unprepared to
appreciate.

With so much security and so many mutual interests, I would
never have believed that my inadequacy in sex could, slowly,
almost imperceptibly, mean a shift in the balance of our whole
relationship. Though I had of course read that sex was the cement
in the foundation of marriage, I had regarded it as part of the
whole affection, sufficiently separate to succeed or fail on its own
plane. And, I had believed, in the event that it failed with Carl
and me, we would at least be no worse off.

Such optimism had come from plain ignorance. Experience
was to teach me that separating the physical and spiritual was
as impossible as any sharp demarcation between intellect and
emotion. One overlapped the other: each touched the other at
so many common points that the two were often indistinguish-
able, and each drew on the other for sustenance. Where one was
deficient, the other lost its balance. And I feared I was losing my
balance to fear and guilt.

Fictitious happiness got mixed up with the real. Endearments
of the first few months grew into guilty reassurances of the next
few. I could learn what marriage ought to be, and even what a

[51]

sense of common destiny was, but I was afraid I could never learn to feel for Carl what I had felt for Ruth.

Now, as if I had seen her a week before, the memory of Ruth streaked through my thought like a draft of cold air. Again and again I thrust away doubts by telling myself that I wanted too much of life not to be satisfied with what I had. And with suspense that tore at my nerves, I worked up enough courage to keep on hoping. I knew this was my one chance to live a normal life.

At Christmas time I went home to spend the holidays with my family, who of course expected me to have a vacation from school. I must make good my pretense of attending classes, so that they would not worry. My younger brother, John, was home too, and with him his fiancée, a dark, lissom, attractive girl named Eulalie, but whom we all called Lee and whom I liked immensely at first sight. I soon discovered that the feeling was mutual.

When I returned to New York Carl did not meet me, though I had wired. I took a taxi, thankful that it was evening and traffic fast in spite of rain.

The door of the apartment was unlocked, and Claudia was on the divan, reading, with Bonk in her lap. She almost crushed me with her hug.

"I've been nursing and making soup," she said. "Carl's got a streptococcic throat, and along with it the disposition of a bull ape."

I was afraid that he was more ill than either he or Claudia would admit. His voice was thick, and though the lamp was shaded, I could see that his eyes were brilliant with fever.

The next morning he was not improved, and the doctor advised a hospital. Feeling too wretched by now to protest any further, he asked Claudia to stay with me, and left with the doctor.

In ten days he had to have a blood transfusion, and two weeks after that, another. For three more he was desperately ill, and during a part of that time I was allowed to see him only a few minutes each day.

At the end of six weeks he came home from the hospital, pale and very weak but in high spirits. I must have surprised Carl with my devotion when he came home. A smile, a gesture, the affectionate care of helping him through convalescence—they came with a spontaneity I had not guessed natural to me. Perhaps it was the affection that follows on a wave of grave anxiety. Perhaps I had missed him for too long, ever since I had left him to go home, two months before. No matter the cause, I remember the two weeks following Carl's homecoming as the happiest period I had ever known with him, and the only period in which I forgot guilty answers and guilty promptings; they did not exist.

It was exciting to feel myself growing emotionally, when every indication seemed a happy portent toward a selflessness I had often felt approaching but never quite enveloping me. At last I knew what it was to tell him I loved him without wondering if I meant it—triumphantly, even eagerly. And, though I had never questioned Carl's love for me, I felt a heightened pleasure in being so sure of it, as if, during the months before his illness, I had been in the tension of a dream and its meaning had not broken through.

"I Am a Lesbian!"

WITH A LITTLE foresight I could have told that this happiness was not destined to last. But not until Carl became well again could I see what had happened to my affection. When I did see, it was with a feeling of self-revulsion that was as unexpected as a blow from behind.

It was as clear as if a psychiatrist had drawn a chart. Without knowing it, I had taken advantage of Carl's convalescence. Spiritually, I loved him dearly. So long as he was passive, I could respond to him in my own way. There was nothing to humiliate or depress me; I did not have to pretend. There was no need for self-interrogation, no cause for remorse no feeling of strain. I was complete simply because I was not asked to give what I could not give.

Now Carl was well and my relief was over, almost before I had sensed it as relief. His love for me destroyed it, and my feeling of uxorial obligation. It was bitter to realize, heart-breaking to admit, but I could no longer play ostrich with myself. In my efforts to love Carl normally I had to abuse my instincts, for I was not a whole woman. My affection for him was the affection of extraordinary friendship; that I knew. But I had to face the truth: it was not the love of a woman for a man.

It had taken abstinence to show me exactly what I was or was not capable of, and, having known the perfection of friendship, the imperfection of normal love became intolerable.

I had hoped to the point of prayer that consummation would

bring a change in my imperturbable emotions. Not once in eight months had physical intimacy meant anything to me but the giving of pleasure to Carl. Giving my body was for this reason not without its compensation, but the very words "desire," "passion," "ecstasy," were but fugitive words to me, symbols of unsounded experience.

I had become a slave to dissimulation. Afraid of hurting Carl by my frigidity, I had pretended. Now I tried to convince myself that he did not sense my melancholia, that I was exaggerating the significance of the marriage bed. Yet I knew in my heart that he did sense it, did not want any sacrifice of me, would not want me at all if I once suggested by word or action that I felt like a martyr.

I thanked Heaven that even in my sharpest moods of intolerance I never weakened into shifting the responsibility of my failure to him. He was never demanding, never selfish, nor did his failure to detect my dissimulation indicate insensitiveness on his part. My ability in deception was foolproof.

Soon the corrosive influence of continued deception began to affect even my friendship for Carl and, indirectly, my mental health. In spite of myself I began to brood in anticipation, and to give excuses—petty illnesses, headaches, anything to avoid humiliation. Then I would go to lie alone, fighting remorse, my body turned to stone. Sometimes I would get up in the small hours when Carl was working late, make sandwiches and take them into his study as an act of penitence. But the fleeting relief I first found in such hypocrisy began to turn sour. All the conscious reasoning in the world could not stem my steady growth of self-disgust.

He was, of course, puzzled by something intrinsically wrong. His face told me. Why, I marvelled, did he not see the real reason? Surely I could have been neither so clever nor so consistent as I had meant to be. Surely, in the months I had been with him there had been slips, when my own selfishness betrayed me, when my eyes could not agree with what my lips said.

There remained the possibility, of course, that Carl did know, that he was being as deceitful as I. That possibility I must not ignore. Perhaps, like myself, he too was hoping and waiting to protect me. If that were true, his recent nervous reticences were understandable. Yet I could not be convinced. Chivalry had its limits; if not chivalry, then pride.

Carl did the worst possible thing to aggravate an impossible situation: by trying to reach across the abyss that was dividing us, he revealed his dependence on me. In gentle ways, in the sudden warmth of his hand against mine, in impulsive talk of our forthcoming honeymoon in China, even in planning his work, his dependence made itself more and more apparent. Occasionally he startled me into wondering if his subconscious mind were not making accusations against the day when I was bound to hurt him.

One evening at a dinner party, Claudia, lamenting the inconvenience of making her living in a man's world, asked Carl how he could work steadily when necessity played no part in keeping him to it.

"I write for money," she said. "But you make no sense. You've got an independent income. You may be an artist, but you're too normal to plead art for art's sake. And you'd be the first to admit that there are a thousand ways to work off energy with less wear and tear on the disposition. Tell me, why, how, can you do it?"

"I've asked myself that same question so many times," Carl laughed, "that I'd like to fool you with an arty answer. It's got something to do with the ego, of course. But the fact is, I wonder if the real reason doesn't go back to something no more noble than rank sentimentalism? Most men are worth no more, you know, than the faith their women have in them. But damn few of them will ever admit it."

"You're giving Diana a pretty compliment," Claudia said. "And, I might add, responsibility."

Carl, who seemed to have surprised himself by suggesting more than he'd intended, turned to me. What he had said, we both knew, amounted to one of those rare flashes of insight that only a third person can uncover in an intimate. Hesitant now, he tried to right himself, his voice showing his impatience.

"It's my fault, not Diana's responsibility," he said. "But you wanted fundamentals. Damn you, Claudia, for being so hard to lie to."

This depressing discovery frightened me out of waiting longer. Now I knew: there was the answer to my question of how greatly Carl would be affected by the consequences of having loved me. Too late I realized so much that had been unguessed months before.

I had to give up. I hated myself, I pitied him, and I was sick with remorse. There was, I knew, nothing to do but tell him everything. Anything short of the truth would leave him no defense; and the most tormenting of my thoughts was how to protect him. For his sake the blame must be placed squarely where it belonged.

Two evenings after Claudia's question, Carl and I were reading together. He put his book down, went back to his study, and returned with a steamship schedule. Several times lately he had mentioned that we should make our reservations and attend to our passports. He sat down again, patted Bonk, asleep at his feet, and asked with unnerving suddenness,

"Diana, when are we going? Everything's up to you."

His tone was serious. I knew that he was also asking when we would be married, that he meant to have an answer, and to have it now. I was sitting on the ottoman near his chair. I kissed him and I felt him move very close.

I heard my voice, very low. "There's nothing I can do except hurt you."

I felt the pressure of his fingers on my arm. A sense of impotence such as I had never felt settled on me. But I had to tell him. Now.

I told him that I could not go to China with him. I stopped, as if that were the real issue. He said nothing, and finally I told him that I hated myself for having to hurt him, that it took almost more nerve than I had. He waited for me to go on. The pressure of his hand was shifting from finger to finger with monotonous rhythm.

"I've wondered sometimes if you haven't known," I said.

"No," he answered. "I haven't known. I have sensed something. But I haven't known."

"I do love you, Carl. I'll always love you. There are things between us that nothing can ever touch. But there's something that matters so terribly. . . ."

I had to stop. My eyes were burning, my body shaking so violently that Carl put his arm around my shoulder, as if to steady me. I moved away from his arm. I could not stand his sympathy. I wanted to run, to hide, never to have to face his eyes again. The silence seemed so articulate that I wondered how it could be that he did not guess.

"I had thought I could say it, Carl. I'd made up my mind to be logical about everything. Now I can't think of how it went. All I can think of is that it means giving up, once and for all. Please help me."

"It isn't very easy to help you say you won't marry me." Carl turned his head away from me as he spoke. "Is *that* it?"

Finally I nodded.

"I AM A LESBIAN!"

"Then why in God's name do you keep on saying you love me? Tell me, Diana. Don't lie to me. Tell me. Do you?"

Somehow, perversely, it helped to know he was impatient with me. "Yes," I said. "But not the way I've tried to make you believe I did." It had to be now. I had started. "I've tried to make you believe I loved you with my body too."

And then I shall never forget what Carl said.

"Diana, you are beautifully passionate!"

The full extent of my deceit assumed the proportions of horror. He hadn't seen, hadn't guessed at all. It was incredible!

I had to steel myself. I couldn't stop now. I had to tell him. "I've never felt anything," I said. "Not once."

Carl jerked my arm painfully, made me look at him.

"It didn't mean anything. Not once," I repeated. "I thought I could go on for your sake. But I can't. Don't you understand that, darling? I can't!"

I begged him not to blame himself. I was frantic. "It's all been my fault," I kept on saying. Carl stopped me.

"My God, Diana, why didn't you tell me? Of course it's my fault." His face had gone white.

I knew the tremendous pride a man feels in his masculinity. Suddenly I could see that it kept him from understanding me. Now there was no choice. He would not understand until I had told him in words. I hadn't thought it would be so hard.

Then it was that I had to say: "I'm not really normal."

"Not really normal." That didn't mean anything. Who is really normal? I was still hedging. I got up and walked over to the piano and stood by it, but I hadn't the slightest idea why. Maybe it seemed a little easier, not so close to him. Finally I turned back toward Carl.

"I'm what people call a lesbian," I said.

A euphemism. I'd lacked the final nerve to come right out with a decent honesty, "I am a lesbian."

"I am a lesbian," I said. My words died in a whisper.

It was over. There was Bonk, still asleep, as if nothing had happened. How blunt I had been, how brutal! I had meant to make everything so clear. And I had even kissed him first.

Carl sat without a word, looking down at Bonk, thinking God only knows what. I couldn't even tell if he had heard me. I had hardly heard myself.

Slowly I realized that I wanted him to forget for one minute that he was understanding and sympathetic, and treat me as I deserved. I hated him for his self-control, for refusing to give me any justification for what I had done.

"Don't be so damned quiet!" I almost shouted. "Didn't you hear me? Do something! I don't care what. You couldn't hurt me more than I've already hurt myself. Go ahead. Or do I have to say it again? I'm a *lesbian!*"

Carl waved his hand in my direction as if to quiet me. It was a limp, heartbreaking gesture.

Finally controlling my own thoughts, I knew that he was making no effort to be understanding or sympathetic. He was not able to think at all. His face was still white, he sat motionless, and I had the feeling that he was mercifully insensible. For the first time in my life I wept for sheer shame. I doubt if he even knew I wept.

I went back to him and sat down, needing the steadying balance of words.

"I love you," I said, "the only way I know. And so much so that what I feel is always getting mixed up with what I want to feel."

Then I told him about Ruth. Gerald's denial. Grace. But not as I had planned to tell him. I had planned to tell him about the book and to lead up to these other things. I had wanted so terribly to make it clear to him.

At last Carl lighted his pipe. I was glad he no longer was so very still. I went on as if speed were imperative. My thoughts were thick. I finally told him how I had hoped, even expected, that a relationship with him would stimulate my latent sexual nature.

"Being able to marry you would have meant everything I've hoped for. Everything."

Words had become helpless and empty. I sat exhausted of sense and feeling. From a curious distance I heard Carl saying clearly:

"Leave me by myself for a little while, Diana."

I left him and went down the hall to my room. Bonk followed me halfway and then went back to Carl. Mechanically I undressed and got into bed. I lay still, shrivelling inside. After a while I heard Carl pass my room and go into his study, then return to the living room. I tried to think what he might be doing, what he might be thinking.

Had I ever doubted Carl's love, his answer that night would have convinced me forever of its reality. He came into my room, carried Bonk to his niche, and then he threw his robe over my chair and came to my bed. He took me in his arms and held me as one holds a hurt child. He said only one thing to me:

"Go to sleep, darling."

6

I Leave Carl

THE NEXT MORNING the sight of Carl's twisted smile gave me resolution. The least I could do for him now was to leave as quickly as possible and swallow my bitterness alone. I told him I was leaving that day.

Urging me not to be impulsive, Carl spoke of the happiness of our early platonic relationship and valiantly suggested that on a new basis our relationship might bring happiness to us both. I realized that he was reasoning emotionally under the stress of my leaving. He couldn't really want me now. Our old relationship would be impossible for him as well as for me. It was far better for me to go at once. I couldn't stay and see our affection drying inward from the edge, like a little pool. I had had a humiliating lesson in experimenting with human nature, and I wanted to leave before Carl began to despise me for it.

It was hard to speak as dispassionately as I wanted.

"I have lied for too long, Carl. I have lied to myself just as much and even longer than I have to you. Now we both know. And it almost makes me a different person. A person I've got to learn to manage. A person I've got to get used to. You couldn't, dear. Even if you could, I wouldn't want you to."

Carl laid his hand over mine. gently. I tried to keep my voice from trembling as I drew him to me and whispered, "If I had to find out, darling, oh, God, how glad I am that it was you!"

I was thankful when Carl finally left me alone to do my packing. He had not been gone from the apartment an hour when

[62]

I LEAVE CARL

Claudia came. I shall always believe, in spite of her denial, that Carl had told her to come. Yet she pretended to be shocked.

There seemed nothing sensible to say in explanation.

"I've tried and tried and it didn't work," I said. "I'm a fool, Claudia. And the quicker it's over the better for Carl."

Claudia helped herself to Carl's whiskey, but, to my surprise, handed the drink to me.

"Not too young any more, dear," she said. "You're pale. Drink it and maybe you'll get some sense to go with your nerve. Or maybe it's nerve to go with your sense."

For a long time Claudia said little else. She knew as well as I that any question would be an unfair thrust; but, as the minutes passed, her sympathetic silence seemed more and more penetrating. The thought that Claudia was seeing right through me came with surprising calm. Whatever she would say to the truth, I could be sure her judgment would be free of littleness. What she finally said was direct, and I recall it as if she were warning me of homosexuality itself—as indeed she may have intended.

"I'd give anything in the world if this hadn't happened," she said. "Six months ago I'd have bet my last dollar on you two. But lately I've seen it coming. I'm full of intuition, you know. That's the only thing I'm good at, seeing things that aren't any of my business. And I know you've reached a limit. But listen to me. I've seen more than that. I didn't live with you day and night for six weeks for nothing. Carl's nurse didn't have any harder time taking care of him that I had with you. You don't have to tell me. I know.

"But what I really want to say is this. Whatever your reason is for giving up, don't let this get the better of you. You've got to be mature enough to have a spirit of compromise. Compromise doesn't mean you're licked, you know. It's simply smart managing of experience. I think you've got imagination enough to get on to that. And don't worry over what's better for Carl. He'll be all right. He'll work out of it. Unless I'm badly mistaken, this looks more like your problem than his."

Suddenly I was in Claudia's arms, weeping as I hadn't wept since I was a little girl.

"I'm glad," she said. "Now this will be over before Carl gets back."

Then I said a rather peculiar thing to Claudia, and I have wondered since just how much sense it made to her. "Try if you can," I said, "to make Carl see that he lost nothing, really. He just drew a blank. He didn't have anything in me to start with."

Carl returned to the apartment only in time to have tea before he took me to the train. Neither of us could make any effort to talk. Bonk brought his red rubber ball for Carl to throw to him, but Carl only shook his head. He looked done in.

Our ride to the station seemed to take hours. Bonk went along, too. Carl got on the train with me, and there he gave me a hastily rolled package, the original pencilled manuscript of the story he had shown me the second day I knew him. I wanted to tell him how very much this meant to me, but I could not trust myself to speak.

Soon it was time for him to leave, and I saw tears in his eyes.

"Diana," he said, "we must write to each other every now and then. There's too much. . . ."

I kissed his eyes, his cheeks, his mouth, oblivious to everything but the overpowering necessity of having him know something of my remorse. With impulsive suddenness Carl held me close for an instant, and then almost ran from the car, forgetting Bonk on the seat. I tried to call to him but he was gone.

A blessed feeling of unreality saved me. It seemed a long time afterward that I opened Carl's manuscript, which I knew was the first in a collection of his short stories to be published the next spring. On the inside of the roll was a red rubber ball. Bonk

[64]

sprang out of my arms and grabbed it happily. Attached to the manuscript was Carl's dedication. It read, "To D——: Thanks for your existence."

I could not go home when I left Carl; it was not yet the time of year for school to be out. Though he had bought my ticket to Kentucky, I stopped off in Charleston, West Virginia, and planned to pass a month in a third-rate tourist home (I had seven dollars in my purse) before I dared go home "at the end of school."

I found a room with an iron bed and a wicker rocker for $2 a week, in advance. By the end of the first week I had succeeded in selling the rest of my Pullman ticket for $8, to an elderly travelling man I boldly approached in a hotel. He seemed amused when I pointed out his saving of a few dollars.

Meantime, it would have been impossible to drop out of existence for a month, without either Carl or Mother discovering it, had it not been for Claudia. She bribed the apartment janitor to intercept and forward Mother's letters to me in Charleston, and I in turn sent my replies to Claudia to be mailed in New York. Then, the second week, as if the waves of my anxiety had carried clear to her, Claudia sent me $25. "It's not going to hurt you to stay in a room that has portable plumbing," she wrote, "as I imagine you're doing. But you can't do without food, and don't try. It occurred to me that you might need this. Take it and let me know if it's enough."

In that month I saw no one except my landlady, and then only to beg for clean sheets; went no place except to meals, and slept day and night like one drugged, simply because I didn't have the courage to get up. But by month's end I could go home with some composure and tell Mother that instead of returning to my job the next fall, I had decided to go to a woman's college and take a Master's degree. When she asked about Carl, about whom

I had told her at Christmas time, I could explain what I'd already begun in letters. He had turned out to be a disappointment; it was not his fault. We simply did not get along. Now I was going to forget him.

"I'm glad you're level-headed about it," Mother said. "Your father always used to say there's only one thing worse than trying to fool others. That's trying to fool yourself."

PART III
Jane

Nancy

THE HUMILIATING failure of my experience had been complete; I had reached bottom trying to convince myself that I was essentially normal. In my search for deliverance I had learned a magnificent lesson, deceptively simple: that a "normal" relationship with a man was unendurable. However great my remorse, I knew that I would never have been convinced by any lesser experience.

With this acknowledgment of my homosexuality I discovered myself; now I had something to go on. It was like being born all over again, and the relief I felt astonished me. I had, so to speak, nothing left to be worried about. My fears were all confirmed.

I am sure now that it was the calming sensation of anticlimax that enabled me to be objective in evaluating my new self this summer at home. Once more obstinacy was to characterize my thinking. I was determined to respect myself for what I was, lesbianism be damned. First I was an individual; second, a lesbian. I was twenty-one; my mind was quick if not profound; I had discriminating tastes, a certain amount of looks and charm, a good background, and a family to which I was devoted. I would be equipped to earn my own living when the time came. Fortunately, Mother hadn't yet felt the depression; I could take my training how and where I wanted. I had always made friends easily; I could continue to do so. I would live as a woman and not as a bad imitation of a man. No one need know of my emotional inversion. If homosexual love ever came to me I would accept it. If it did not, my life would not be frustrated. Love, I would remember, was only one of many things, and sometimes a very small one. I would work hard, play hard, and have a full life. There would be no more cold-blooded rationalization. I was sick of that, and of thoughts made of hopes and never of honest logic.

Whatever there was of soundness in my attitude came from hard common sense inherited from a mother and father who had no patience with quibblers and who had wisely taught me the value of vanity. My vanity as an individual was a precious thing. It could not allow for any martyr complex—and I imagined self-pity to be the easy pitfall of the homosexual who is hyper-sensitive to an antagonistic world. Self-pity either thwarted honesty with one's self or it engendered defiance. Nor did I want to embrace my nature, proudly, as some homosexuals do, as a protest if not as a conviction. That seemed weak to me, a childish defensive evasion. Somewhere between martyrdom and false pride lay a sane middle road. I think a healthy attempt at self-appraisal put me on it.

I read everything I could find in English, German and French which might increase my understanding of myself, and what I couldn't find in libraries I sent for. Laboriously, often with a great French or German dictionary, I read Hirschfield, Freud, Jung, Westermarck, Krafft-Ebing, Gide and Ellis, and I accepted, piecemeal, what was compatible with my own observations. I no longer thought of homosexuality as a moral issue, but merely as a condition within the range of sexual variations. By considering my own case history I could put no stock in the theory of con-genital homosexuality. The psychoanalytic theory, which leads the emotional cycle from autosexuality in childhood through homosexuality in adolescence to heterosexuality in maturity, seemed much more sensible and clear-cut. I was glad for my natural conclusion on this point. At least I had something to be thankful for—decidedly it was less unpleasant to feel like a case of arrested development than it was to admit to being, like a two-headed calf, a freak from the womb.

It satisfied me to accept Jung's simple statement that homosexuality was a relic of past culture periods; just as our bodies retained reminders of old functions in old-fashioned organs, so did our minds show the marks of the evolution passed through. Gerald had spoken of these "archaic inclinations" in referring to adolescent crushes. My lesbianism, I was convinced, was the result of environment peculiarly fitted to foster whatever inclinations to homosexuality I had had as a child. The latent germ of homosexuality had been nourished by my constant association with boys instead of girls. I had played with boys, studied music with boys, even lived with them. And the germ had been too well nurtured to atrophy under the artificial stimuli I had resorted to. I could see it all clearly now. Understanding was comfort of a kind.

Most of my reading was not only enlightening but *humanizing*. Whether I could or could not agree with psychologists on some of their observations, I did take the attitude that the homosexual was a fellow human being whose behavior was no better, no worse, than that of the heterosexual. What disturbed me, however, was the occasional pulp magazine article on homosexuality. Such piffle—written, I gathered, by washroom savants —was not only uninformed but vicious, for it amounted to half-truths either glorified or grotesque or sentimentalized, and in any case it was as unacceptable to the homosexual as it was to the normal man or woman. But it did teach me that of all curiosity about types of "queer" people, none was more generally unenlightened or more eager than curiosity about the homosexual.

In my new openmindedness I realized how utterly blind to homosexuals I had become, how by some trick of will I had shut them from my consciousness. And, like the reader who meets over and over again the new word he has just looked up in the dictionary, I now recognized homosexuals I would never have noticed before. Doubtless my environment the fall after I left Carl had a great deal to do with this; I had decided to go to a large woman's college in Massachusetts for a master's degree in German. The number of lesbians I met there impressed me not only because my consciousness of them was sharpened, but because they were unmistakably frequent.

I had a room in a dormitory where most of the graduate students lived—a pleasant, livable room overlooking a spacious campus where life hurried by under my window all day long. With my new consciousness I had an ideal post for observation.

My reason for changing from a co-educational to a woman's college was negative. I did not want to meet any men; I was through with pretending. It never occurred to me at the time that I was straying right into the Elysian fields of the lesbian. Gradually I understood why that was so. My own reason was common —lesbians naturally prefer to be with their own sex. But, more interesting, segregation of the sexes tends to make practicing lesbians out of girls who have potentialities; time and again I've seen this happen, both as student and teacher.

I thought of these students as active and passive lesbians. My attitude toward those I considered active lesbians was unreasonable and unjustified. I felt superior. I disliked them for using their abnormality as their claim to uniqueness as individuals. I disliked them for their defiance in making themselves conspicuous. I disliked them for mocking society and themselves at the same time from behind an awkward guise which not only offended society but gave themselves dead away. They were the ones who were ostentatious in mannish gesture, who walked with brusque gracelessness, who smoked and drank with self-conscious bravado, who indulged in transvestitism and wore shirts and ties instead of blouses, and slacks instead of skirts. Male attire on a woman always struck me as a puerile gesture intended to appease one's self while thumbing one's nose at society, and ended only in smart-aleck unconventionality. Even to the point of being rude I avoided women who affected men's clothes.

Active lesbians taught me a lasting lesson: the grace of a lie and a new admiration for hypocrisy. I never heard acquaintances mock them that I did not cringe and vow to myself that no one would ever have such easy clue to my own lesbianism. Society, I learned over and over again, is omnipotent. It was smarter to indulge its ruthlessness—if only for the sake of comfort.

Some girls I took to be passive lesbians—those younger undergraduates who were perhaps submerged in helplessness as I had been—and with them I felt a perfectly natural affinity, a spiritual kinship that respected and sympathized. They were not apparent homosexuals: but they had latent characteristics which, in the thousand little crotchets of time and place that make up experience, would veer them either to the right or to the left. They had no betraying mannerisms and no one but a lesbian of their own kind would be likely to suspect that their delicate innuendoes were suggestive of familiar bewilderment. Naturally, the passive lesbians far outnumbered their older sisters.

That year I looked upon lesbianism largely as an interested bystander, far too busy with my dissertation to have time lag or to feel lonely. The only immediate temptations were too impossible to consider seriously.

There was Nancy, who lived across the hall from me, an affected, rather greasy and coarse-looking creature who was going through a belated period of culture pains. For all her parade of emotional facets I could not decide whether she had no brain at all or a sensitive one beyond my appreciation.

It was about mid-year when she began to leave poems on my desk. A certain lushness thwarted their melancholy, but their personal tone embarrassed me. I knew I had a problem on my hands. Toward spring, in spite of all I could do to prevent it, Nancy declared herself. It was the first time I had ever heard her talk naturally.

"I'm an ass," she said. "I know it. But that's all the fun I have. The only real thing about me is what I feel for you. For a long time I didn't understand what it was. It scared me. Then I finally caught on. I've never loved anyone before—please be kind to me."

I did not tell Nancy I understood. There was no point. But I did make the mistake of being too sympathetic; when she had looked at me and said "Please be kind" I had been choked with pity. I didn't know then what I know now—that a certain type of weak-kneed lover will feed on all the pity he can inspire. Homosexuals are, I have observed, only slightly more susceptible to this weakness than normal lovers.

Nancy's attachment became annoying. She would bring gifts, too extravagant for good taste; I hated to hurt her, but I finally had to tell her she embarrassed me. Then she asked if she could sit in my room while I studied. It seemed a small thing to refuse. But her silent intenseness charged the whole room until I could not study, until sheer nervousness made me frantic. Finally, after weeks of enduring her obsequiousness, I asked myself why I should be more tolerant and more patient with an unwanted lesbian lover than I would have been with any unwanted man. I knew why, of course, but the thought finally gave me the courage to tell her I could no longer even be kind.

One evening she came in while I was at my desk and stood beside me for minutes, her resolution mounting. I was on the verge of sheer panic when she finally broke the tension by bending down and kissing the back of my neck. It infuriated me. I didn't take time to think. I told her to get out. She did, hastily. The next morning I found a note under my door, and what it said taught me something about inherent lesbian ego. "I can bear for

[74]

you to hate me so much better than I can bear for you to forget me."

Within a few weeks Nancy was leaving poems on another girl's desk. But I haven't forgotten her.

The day after my graduation I went home to join Mother and Gerald for a hurried trip west to John and Lee's wedding. Then, one week later, I sailed for Europe to put in a year or so of study and travel before settling down to teaching. I was going first to Berlin, then to Paris; how long I would stay in either place depended on the unforeseen.

I was approaching a future whose peculiar loneliness I could already understand. Willing as I was to take my chances against hazards that were defined and clear-cut, the indeterminate problems of belonging to a third sex appalled my imagination. I couldn't even guess, beyond the obvious, what those problems amounted to.

What was lesbian love like? Its intellectual pleasures were easy enough to guess at, but what physical pleasure did women achieve of one another? I wanted intelligent knowledge of it, for I didn't have much faith in the pretty little legend that nature would show the way. Love is not a matter of blundering on to ecstasy; it demands intelligence, skill and patience. Vaguely I wondered how I would learn to know all the things I needed to know.

Understanding the homosexual character, and my own, was one thing; seeing it in relation to the normal world, quite another. Consideration of what could possibly be a livable compromise brought nothing but questions. But life lay ahead of me, and my hunger for it was greedy. In my own time I would find my compromise. Somehow, somewhere, I hoped to find happiness with a woman who would love me as I loved. There had been Grace; she had been delightful and feminine and companionable. I prayed that there might be another.

2

Elise

IMMEDIATELY out of the remote woman's college and into the world again, I was faced with a problem entirely new to me, like it or not—and on shipboard it was a double dose. In spite of my ambitions to get along without men, I was to find it impossible. It was not that I was irresistible. But the depression was on, and travel was not normal; there were very few women on board.

Unfortunately, I had a sense of humor and a womanly figure that made it difficult to keep relationships with men on the platonic level. Heretofore, imagining I wanted their attentions, I had not realized to what lengths they would go for a woman's favor. Now that my indifference was genuine, they seemed helplessly alike, monotonously single-minded, and gullible to the point of senselessness. It was a shame, I thought, that I had no aptitude for enjoying a game of hypocrisy; I would have been the inevitable winner.

I did not want to make myself unattractive to men and retire in gloom from a social world I really liked. Nor would I ever again serve emotion without sharing it. I had had my lesson. I was willing to make necessary genuflections to convention whenever I had to, but never beyond the limits of casualness. I didn't know what to do, but clearly I had to do something. I was two days out at sea—just about the time an unchaperoned girl on shipboard needs to be resourceful—when I had an idea. It was a simple matter to put back a ring on the third finger of my left hand. For the purpose it served, I was glad it was Carl's ring;

[76]

he would, I knew, understand. It explained everything that needed to be explained, and, except for the gentlemen who turn philanderer with their first whiff of salt air, it was a happy ruse.

A French doctor was amusing, an American aviator was a bore but a good dancer, and a Dutch chocolate salesman loved to talk about his American fiancée. With these acquaintanaces I could sense something about myself that was typically lesbian—I had a natural capacity for friendships with men. It had always been true, but I was only just beginning to appreciate it.

Perhaps this lesbian idiosyncrasy is a compensation, for the normal woman has neither psychological aptitude for, nor interest in, any relation with men that is not based, fundamentally, on the biological urge. The lesbian, on the other hand, has every reason to feel a spiritual affinity with men, and her friendship for them is based on a recognition, however remote, of common sex interests. I wondered, at the same time, what happened to the lesbian's point of view when she looked upon a man not as a kindred spirit but as a potential rival. I don't know by what conceit I believed I'd be able to exempt myself from such jealousy, but it may have been a sense of the ridiculous.

I was interested only in Rolf, an American-born German violinist of twenty-eight, who, I heard, had been trained in Germany and was contemptuous of American musical life excepting, of course, its financial return. His table in the dining salon was not far from mine, and I had first noticed him because of his air of aloofness. He was lanky, pale, extremely nervous, and I was certain he was a homosexual. I had often wondered why the average male invert had so many more tell-tale marks than the average female invert—the flightiness of his hands, the refinement of his mannerisms. Perhaps it seemed so because in this age of pajamas it was less conspicuous, and certainly more attractive, for a girl to appear a tomboy than for a man to appear a sissy. A tomboy might be cute; a sissy remained just sad. I never had known a male invert well, and I couldn't decide whether Rolf attracted or repelled me. But I was curious.

I was alone in the salon one morning, idling at the piano, when he came in and asked me to play some Beethoven and then some Chopin. I did not know the Beethoven at all, and I had not played the Chopin in several years. Naturally I refused.

"I understood you played quite well," he said. "Perhaps I should have asked you for 'Kitten on the Keys.' Or the 'St. Louis Blues.' "

His tone infuriated me. I turned back to the piano and played "Kitten on the Keys" all the way through, glad, for once, of the training my sorority sisters had given me. But they had never heard me play with such élan as I played it now.

I don't know what I had expected Rolf to do, but I felt extremely foolish when he laughed and apologized. There could be no doubt now; I hated him.

That afternoon I saw him walking the deck alone. He was not at dinner, nor did I see him the following day at lunch. I heartily hoped he was seasick. The next evening at dinner he smiled at me, and I was surprised that he could smile so pleasantly. I noticed that he had very little to say to his dinner companions. I could not remember having seen him talk with anyone more than briefly.

That evening he asked me to stroll with him on deck. We had talked for perhaps an hour when he looked at me with uncomplimentary incredulity and told me with some bitterness that he loved me.

I was equal to no more than a startled expression, and something about as devastating as "Do tell!"

"We land tomorrow," he said. "You go to Berlin. I go south to Munich. This is no more sudden to you than it is to me. But don't misunderstand. American women leap to conclusions. I love you, yes, but that is all there is to it. Americans begin to think of marriage the second they feel gooseflesh. It's really touching."

I had talked with Rolf twice, and both times he had been deliberately unpleasant. I had never had anyone make me so angry so quickly—nor draw me so irresistibly against my will. I disliked him and resented him, but when he showed me to my cabin and made not the slightest gesture of affection, I was more curious than ever. Plainly enough he wasn't being gallant because of my ring. And if I was wrong about his being a fairy, so were all his other companions. The only thing that was clear was that nothing about him made sense.

The next morning, as we neared Cuxhaven, he came to my cabin to offer to help me in disembarking. He was grave and unusually pale. I started to tell him I had made my arrangements, but something dissolved my intention. I knew that in spite of my resolutions I would go right along with him all the way to Berlin. He saw to my baggage, my tickets, even anticipated my questions with the expertness of the experienced traveler, and finally reserved our seats on the boat train to Hamburg, and then again on to Berlin.

On the train his manner was friendly, but so impersonal that I began to wonder if I had not dreamed his bewildering confession. He betrayed no more than an initial shade of self-consciousness. He talked of Berlin, interrupted himself to explain everything of interest in the countryside en route, and tried to prepare me to understand the aggressive spirit of post-war Germany—all in such good humor and with such intelligence that the six hours passed quickly and I began to be glad that he had asked if he could see me later in Paris. He was coming to Paris after a year in Munich. I hoped we would meet again.

We reached Berlin in the early evening, and Rolf continued to be gallant. I was still a little surprised, but thankful; except for an address or so in my purse, I knew nothing of the city. He suggested a *pension* in the Charlottenburg which he had known as a student, and, after introducing me to the Café Victoria and a strawberry drink called *bowle,* we took a taxi down the Unter den Linden to see the place.

Going on into the house, Rolf warned me, too, of the *treppen-hausfenster,* but when we climbed the darkened stairs, the sudden view that rose before me was no less startling: a large, stained-glass window on which were depicted a young girl, a swan, and clusters of water-lilies, all done with cheerful abandon in orange, greens and blues. With the ambiguity of the Mona Lisa, the face of the girl looked alternately blank or impish, and, though Rolf professed to prefer the mammoth vermilion roses in another win-dow, between the second and third floors, I was sure they had no legend to match that of the first window—whatever that may have been.

On the third floor, we were soon facing Frau Seubert, the pro-prietress, a tremendous woman with a warming smile. Rolf spoke to her in German.

With a kind welcome, Frau Seubert accepted me into her *pension.* I could never have resisted her smile. Nor the windows. Quickly I settled on a large showy room that seemed too full of furniture, and, leaving Rolf to tell Frau Seubert about the Indians in America, dressed to go to a night club, the Pompeji, with him.

I had hoped that Rolf would not become sentimental; the hope was pointless. Had he been showing Berlin night life to a nice maiden aunt, his manner could have been no more solicitous. He danced well, and though I was keyed to expect a mild insult every time he opened his mouth, he maintained such amiability that by the end of the evening I was ashamed of my instinctive distrust. He said good night very formally and repeated that he was already looking forward to seeing me in Paris.

He came to my *pension* the next noon to say good bye before he left for Munich. Why he bothered I had no idea; he was clearly finished with being charming.

"I hope you'll decide to leave Paris before I get there," he said. "If not, then I hope I can't find you. You wouldn't fit into my scheme of things." Then, half under his breath, "But, of course, damn it, I'll hunt you up the minute I arrive."

I can't say that he said good bye. He merely walked away. And I knew no more about him than I had forty-eight hours before. For some few torrid minutes I vowed I'd never see him again.

I had come to Berlin to perfect my German for teaching and to study music for pleasure. But when my piano teacher, Professor Burghardt, assured me, with no logic whatever, that I belonged with him rather than at the University of Berlin, I was so glad to be convinced that I couldn't even feel guilty about neglecting my academic German.

I was learning how to be independent, and, whenever I was lonely, there were hospitable acquaintances at Frau Seubert's— one of them, Monika, was also a student of the music academy —with whom to learn the art of idling in beer gardens. Monika, unimaginative, good-natured, rather pretty, greeted me every morning with a crisp, startling "Damn it to Hell!" which some-body had told her meant "Good morning."

The *zeitgeist* which was so strongly felt during this period in Berlin was difficult to become accustomed to, for I had neither inherited nor acquired any taste for politics. I had come to Berlin able to play Beethoven and to quote Goethe, but I knew little about the Treaty of Versailles. Intellectually, I was lost, for at that time, in the tense year of Hitler's ascendency, the German people were talking economics, not art. There was no place for a disinterested stranger who had no idea how bread could be the issue. Youth everywhere was aggressive, vociferous. A student might be without money, friends or a future, but he always had a political philosophy. I was forced to admit that my American unconcern must seem, in fact was, shocking.

I came home one afternoon in mid-December to find Frau Seubert awaiting me with an air of delicious expectancy. Another American girl had moved into the *pension*. The American girl was, she said, in her early thirties, a tall brunette, and she held herself very straight.

Frau Seubert's description had sounded a trifle austere. I was afraid of a schoolteacher. When I came into dinner a few hours later, I was delighted to find a chic, self-assured New Yorker, vivacious and friendly, and as glad to find me as I was to have her. Even her name was interesting—Elise.

After dinner she invited me to her room. The first thing I noticed was a large photograph on her desk of a blond woman whose eyes were soft and melancholy and whose mouth had such gentle lines that I could not help remarking. Elise looked pleased.

"That's Katherine," she said, "my English friend. It was her cousin who sent me here. Yes, you can tell even from her picture. Katherine is the gentlest person I have ever known. I often wonder how she can stand me."

What Elise said made me feel lonelier than I had felt in months. For a year and a half I had lived away from friends, behind a barricade of philology, politics and piano, and at an age when loneliness was not natural. I told Elise I envied her her friends. I had not meant to be tactless. When I saw the expression on her face, I wondered. One may simulate sadness, joy, interest—but not nonchalance. Yet I told myself my thought was ridiculous even before it was formed.

The next evening, glad of an excuse to escape Frau Seubert's noodles, Elise and I walked to the Telschow for dinner. It was nice to be able to talk with her alone, to feel American again, to laugh again. When she told me she was a "converted" lesbian and that Katherine was her lover, I was not as surprised as I might have been.

Perhaps the very transitory nature of our acquaintanceship had invited quick intimacy. Whatever the reason, Elise told me of her conversion from normal to homosexual indulgence, and what struck me most of all was her utter lack of regret, her contempt for shame. I had never known a convert before; her reasons interested me.

She had been in love with a married man whose wife's religion did not permit divorce, and was his mistress for two years. For over a year the liaison had been happy, and then she had become pregnant. The horrible experience of infection following an abortion changed everything. Fear began to appall and devitalize. After months of hesitation Elise had finally left her lover for the sake of her mental health. She had gone to England for a long vacation, and there she had met Katherine, whose tactful advances had slowly disarmed her of prejudice against homosexuality. Katherine was aware of Elise's indecision and had bided her time with sympathetic patience. At last Elise accepted her. Now she was in Berlin waiting for Katherine to join her for Christmas after a visit with relatives in Wales.

Within a very few days I knew that Elise was emotionally interested in me. Our isolation, my loneliness, had made us too quickly acquainted; everything seemed slightly fantastic and unreal. Physical desire, I felt, should be the result of friendship, not the cause of it. I resented the thought of desire for a woman who was a comparative stranger, and with childish irritability I wished that Elise was less attractive.

Further, Elise was hard. Though I had no way of knowing, I supposed that her hardness was recently acquired. Perhaps she was more bitter than she knew. Certainly there had to be some explanation for the transition from Elise as a sensitive mistress to Elise as a calculating convert. In spite of her claim to happiness, I sensed a cynicism that made me fear for Katherine.

"I am," Elise said, "all finished with the idea that the way people act has anything to do with what they believe."

I would not have been human had I not resented her attitude. Being a lesbian by choice—incomprehensible choice to a lesbian! —could not be the same as being one by nature. Elise had a secondary defense which neither Katherine nor I could have. Synthetic scruples, and very possibly a slight contempt, would be her natural concession, the most she would be capable of. And I doubted if the scruples amounted to much. It was perfectly clear that, to Elise, lesbian love was not an end but a mediation. But like all converts, whether in religion, politics or sex, Elise was ardent, and the challenge of her eyes was goading me. By now my strength was nothing but a matter of dumb fright.

At midnight, a few days later, Elise came to my room. She wore a mandarin robe with great lavender dragons on the back and sleeves. I shall never forget the dragons: they had fiery embroidered eyes. I felt about five years old, cowering before a fear I could at last name. I was glad when she found my room too warm and removed the coat, leaving only the soft yellow pajamas that were so becoming against her loose brown hair.

With a frantic feeling of forestalling something I both feared and wanted, I talked of many things for an hour—my classes, my family, my hatred of practicing gutturals. Elise was polite but bored, and her eyes began to question me. She was sitting on my bed, and at last, after a desperate silence, she looked at me and smiled, and with exasperating self-assurance held out her hand to me. After a moment tense with hesitation, I went to her, half unwilling, with the tiny remnant of will I still had left.

She got up hastily and turned out the lamp. It was very dark at first. Then a thread of light came through a crack in the door and fell in a straight line on the rug. Elise quickly disrobed and lay beside me. Minutes must have gone by before I looked at her. Her body was startlingly white. She had not spoken. Finally she turned to me and whispered something I did not hear, and placed my hand on her body. I trembled and half sat up; Elise laughed a little, and I was embarrassed. Then she pulled me down to her, kissing me very slowly, and the fullness of her lips excited me as she lingered, tantalizing. My breath caught and I moved away from her. I had never felt like this before. She patted my hand and made me feel over-young. I felt her tugging gently at my robe and then I realized what she had whispered. She turned me gently to draw it off. Her fingers were on my breast, caressing, soft as warm water. Her hand went to my throat and then swiftly she lay full length beside me, and kissed me again. Suddenly an overwhelming tide of passion dragged at me and I threw my arms around her and held her body closer, wanting her but not knowing how. She buried her head on my breast. Exquisite pain held me, and I could not move. I was not frightened now, only hurting, hurting all through my body for wanting her still closer. I had not known there would be a pain like this. Frantically I hoped she would not know; then that she would.

Then suddenly there was a terrible, convulsing pleasure when she touched me. Miraculously, all past and present left me. I knew nothing but the touch of Elise, until I could stand no more and roughly pushed her away.

I was released of all feeling, submerged in a glorious lethargy, timeless and in a dream. I could make no effort to open my eyes. I hadn't expected it to be something like dying.

I do not know how long I lay there. I opened my eyes at last to see a flood of light come in through the door from the hall. I knew that Elise was leaving me. Dully, I wondered why.

The next afternoon I had just returned from class when Elise came in hurriedly to tell me she had received a wire from Kath-

erine, saying that she was coming the next day. She kissed me
and smiled at my quick expression of dismay. She made me look
at her and then she said:

"Diana, I am glad, so very glad. Please be glad too."

I told her a little wildly that she had been my first; that she
could not leave·me, could not. Very gently she told me she had
known, and that she had known all the while that Katherine was
coming so soon. Now I knew why she had left me. For Elise that
had been a gesture of fidelity—lesbian fidelity. I had made no
difference.

Impulses swarmed at me so fast that not even the thought of
Professor Burghardt was enough to save me from a very foolish
move. I left that night for Paris, two months earlier than I had
intended. I finally went to sleep on the train, the rhythm of the
wheels clicking off *"Das macht mir nichts aus! Das macht mir
nichts aus!"*—a lie if wheels ever told one.

3

Jane

I REACHED PARIS in time to spend a godforsaken Christmas in
a small hotel near the Palais Royal, so lonely I even began to
look forward to seeing Rolf. Four days later, exhausted by hunting
a *pension* where I could rent a piano, I was delighted to find a
small apartment up five flights of stairs in an ageless apartment
house on the Boulevard St. Michel, almost opposite the Luxem-
bourg gardens. It had a large living room which sprawled, un-
carpeted, around a corner into a tiny kitchen, which in turn
widened suddenly into a bedroom where—if I leaned out the window just right —I had a view of the Seine. And I was far enough
away for the Seine to be worth the trouble. My dishes were
nicked, my couch squeaked, and the wash stand wobbled, but
there was a piano, a surprisingly good one.

I had not been in Paris a week when I asked Mother to send
Bonk to me right away, feeling foolishly sentimental over having
missed him so much in Berlin. Bonk was, in his own right, a
spirited, gay companion, but he meant a great deal more. As
the symbol of Carl's understanding the existence of Bonk would
tolerate no moods of regret.

I was no more than settled in Paris when I realized that the incident with Elise had, for all its humiliation, given me a kind of
assurance that I had needed desperately. Before Elise I had not
known whether women could have sexual gratification of one
another. I had been afraid that frustration was the inevitable
end of lesbian love, that passion was denied though desire for it

[87]

challenged; that life did, in the last analysis, play a scurvy trick on homosexuals. Elise had completed my knowledge.

At last I began my second-term studies at the Sorbonne. I had studied French from the third grade; I was much better prepared for the Sorbonne than I had been for the University of Berlin. Now I would begin preparing for a degree. I felt that with my master's degree in German and a degree in French from the Sorbonne, I ought to be able to earn my living teaching one or the other or both.

I could not have found more friendly neighbors with whom to become acquainted—Marian, an earnest and talented student of voice from Minnesota, who was appealing in her homeliness; and Edith, a pretty English schoolteacher of real charm despite a hardened cleverness, both of whom lived in the apartment above mine. Though they were in no way alike, I liked them almost equally, and our companionship began casually and naturally.

One afternoon Marian showed me a letter from her older sister, Carol, asking her to meet a former college friend of hers, due in Paris from Cherbourg Saturday evening. It was now Friday and Marian, excited, wanted to plan a small party for her guest's first evening. Marian had never met her sister's friend, Jane, but she had seen her picture. She planned to bring Jane to my apartment after helping her find a hotel.

"Carol said I'd either hate her or be crazy about her," Marian said. "That she could be meaner than Hell or a perfect dear. At least she sounds interesting."

About nine o'clock Saturday evening Marian and Edith brought Jane, an extremely tall woman in her late twenties; I remember she wore a biege tailored suit with a single white sweet-pea in the lapel. She was not pretty, but her appearance was commanding and her personality positive. She had wilful hazel eyes, dark skin, a delicate, prominent nose, and the most frankly sensual lips I had ever seen. They fascinated me. Her voice, husky-timbered, was low and vibrant, and she had the faculty, rare in women, of laughing pleasantly as well as genuinely. She wore a ring with a solitary ruby of quaint cut. Her dark brown hair was worn in a simple old-fashioned roll low on her neck.

I wondered if Marian and Edith noticed that Jane looked at me inquisitively several times during the evening. I was acutely conscious of it, but in all honesty I admit that in spite of the kindness in her eyes I was a little frightened, and very curious. What was her background? Why did she come to Paris alone; why did that seem so mysterious in Jane when I had just done the same thing myself? Why was her face intensely vital one moment and a mask of dreamy indifference the next, except when she looked at me? What was there about her that drew the whole room to her, all of us, with a quiet magnetism of which she seemed unconscious?

We had planned a gay evening. Unfortunately, I became as tongue-tied as a boy on his first date. Now I can remember little of those hours except Jane—how Jane crossed her knee, how Jane laughed at Edith's mimicry, how Jane smiled at me as I poured her wine, how Jane was attentive to the little Russian girl who came up from the apartment below because she was lonely. I remember how, when Jane left with Edith and Marian, the most commonplace good night took on a new significance as she said it.

"I'm so happy to have met you, Diana. I want to know you better."

How foolish of me to remember that! Of course she would say that. She had been my guest. Dozens of people had said the same thing to me at one time or another.

And yet I was almost expecting the note, the *petit bleu*, I received the next morning. I believe I had known it would come, and just what it would say:

"My dear, will you have tea with me this afternoon? Jane."

And though Marian and Edith had asked me to go picnicking with them to Moret, I couldn't resist making excuses. At five o'clock I went to Jane's room in the Hotel Grillon. She wore a green velvet negligee, and perhaps it was the color which made her eyes seem more green than I had remembered them. In spite of myself I was again excited. Jane was a woman of tremendous force; her personal charm was strong as magic. Doubtless this strength came partially from a majestic physical presence.

Over cups of tea and *petits fours,* we talked far into the evening. Jane had come to Paris ostensibly to study painting, but it was evident that her interest was that of the dilettante. Of independent means, she was able to indulge her taste for travel and study with no thought but for pleasure. She would be in Paris, she said, until she tired of it.

I have often wondered just why it seemed that Jane and I had so many immediate and common interests, if few common points of view. She had been too absorbed in the outer world of color and form to care about music, and I had been too taken up with the inner excitements of rhythm and melody to care about visual art. I learned almost at once—and this surprised me—that Jane was deeply religious; I had all the aptitudes for religion, but remained immune. Jane shared none of my headlong sympathies and prejudices. I imagined she was not impulsive; except for her sensual lips, she even looked stable. Yet we were drawn to each other.

Though we lived in different quarters of Paris we managed to see each other every day. Showing Jane Paris was fun, and already I had learned it well enough to be confident. It was spring now, and I could see how Paris in the spring could be inspiration enough for a dozen troubadours.

We would take cocktails at noon at the Ritz, or go down the Seine on a barge, or tramp cobblestone streets in the Montmartre, or spend hours in the Dingo Bar over red checkered tablecloths

—doing all the standard things. Jane filled the need for close feminine companionship I had shunned almost as long as I could remember, and quickly I learned to depend on her interest and sympathy as necessities. I was no believer in miracles, but I soon felt the extraordinary sensation of having known her always. I, who had for so long held friends at a distance, now felt the splendid nearness of understanding. Jane's rare ability to give the meaning of joy, gaiety and intelligence to the commonest things which held none of these qualities in themselves, stimulated my comprehension of the world about me and became a part of the spell I felt in her presence. Within a few weeks I couldn't even remember what Paris had been—what I had been—without her.

But I was troubled by my friendship with Marian and Edith. One day I had them and Jane to tea, and they didn't get on well. Jane didn't fit in with them; she hadn't since the first evening. I don't know by what peculiar cross-current of feeling it happened, but in spite of all my efforts to find a conversational stream, it would dry up before it got started. Edith was antagonistic, Marian timid, and Jane too polite. I never tried again. Jane had turned out to be my friend instead of Marian's, and natural jealousy of situation was too much for me.

The closer I was drawn to Jane the more the question of her normalcy baffled me. The occasional feeling that her interest in me was more than mere friendliness was inexplicable and without evident foundation. I dared not believe that I could recognize her in the act of shielding herself; wishful thinking was tricky. I asked myself if the slight pressure of her hand as she told me good night could have meant anything. Or the way she smiled at me or looked at me, in a special, personal way. Sometimes it was an amused look, often merely an interested look, and again, when I said something to displease her, she'd call me *mon enfant,* and look at me with intense hurt in her eyes. But I could tell nothing.

I wondered if I could do without seeing Jane every day; I could think of nothing but Jane; I wanted nothing but Jane. Then for days I thought of telling her I loved her and putting myself at her mercy. But I remembered Nancy's "Please be kind to me," and disgust with myself rejected the impulse to be servile. Only a reckless hope that Jane might not scorn my love kept me from throwing discretion to the winds.

I had tried anesthetizing my emotions by every means but the obvious one—study. For four days I took the academic veil, morning to midnight, with an expenditure of nervous energy that, had I stopped to think, meant bearing a little more than I could bear. I fed Bonk but I did not eat myself; I read in the libraries the whole day and evening, leaving only when they closed, and took notes that I would see the next day without recognizing. But at least I stayed away from the telephone.

I was taking a course in the history of French art that required gallery-visiting—and nothing could give me less succor at the moment than the sight of a dish-faced Watteau shepherdess. The miles in the Louvre itself inspired only a hankering for roller-skates.

One evening I fainted in a subway station, and as I fell I cut my head on the corner of a bench. I was waiting to meet Jane when it happened, and by the time she arrived I was being attended by some ten Frenchmen, who were making a major scene out of a minor scalp wound *"de la jeune Allemande."* I had come to in the manner of a drugstore novelist's heroine, murmuring quaint mysteries of the subconscious. In this case it was *"Das macht mir nichts aus!"*

Jane, alarmed at sight of such a bloody forehead, took me home in a taxi, bandaged my forehead, and put me to bed. I had a fever and my head ached terribly, but Jane was so sweet that I knew I could endure anything if only she would stay with me.

She read to me for an hour, but I didn't hear a word. My

heart was beating so hard I was afraid she must hear it. Finally, when she stopped reading, I dared look at her. I couldn't even smile. I wanted to hold out my hand, and involuntarily my arm moved toward her. But a tide of helpless imperatives dragged at me. Fear surmounted courage, even desire.

Silence seemed to stretch on forever. I closed my eyes, as if against it. I heard Jane move. She put down her book and came over to me. She sat on the edge of the bed and finally I felt her fingers tracing the lines of my bandage, very lightly. Then they went away. I could not even breathe for fear of shouting out something—I didn't know what. Almost angrily I opened my eyes. I hadn't known that she was bending toward me. Or that tears were in her eyes.

Swift and sharp came the incredible realization that Jane, too, was afraid. I couldn't try to speak. I reached for her hand; she whispered one word: "Child," and quickly took me in her arms.

Thank God, I knew I would not be alone this night.

Frustration

I was happy to the point of giddiness. At last I knew what it was to love and to be loved! And those lovers' assurances were mine, mine to speak happily, to listen to greedily. Those assurances that I had known only as guilty promptings were now spilling over each other in monotony so lovely it hurt a little, as ecstasy can hurt. Never had I dared dream such joy as this.

Jane and I agreed that we wanted to share an apartment. Now we would wait until I had taken my examinations. I was studying night and day and though I could not be with her regularly during the last week of school I heard from her often. As I'd sit by my little *poêle* studying and trying to keep warm in a cool summer, with Bonk at my feet, I would hear the *concierge* shuffling up the stairs with a note from Jane, with perhaps some fresh fruit or *chocolate glacés*. One night there was even a rubber rat for Bonk. "He's mine, too, now," she said. No matter how often the little notes came, each one seemed sweeter than the last.

"Please hurry and study hard and want to get back to me. I love you. Your Jane."

One midnight I got a note by taxi—"Darling, without your hand in mine I was afraid. Your Jane."—and in spite of a formidable amount of reviewing, I couldn't resist getting dressed and going across Paris to her.

In five days more, my examinations over, Jane came and took me to see "some rooms," she said, in the Rue des Sts. Pères, about halfway between the Quai Voltaire and the Boulevard St. Germain. It was a charming studio-like apartment, all spic and span

FRUSTRATION

and ready to move into. Jane admitted that she'd gotten it ready as a surprise.

We quickly settled down to living together, exactly five weeks from the day we had first met. And though Jane had said, "I'm afraid you won't love me so much when you're with me all the time," the hundred little intimacies of keeping house together only gave me a more mature conception of what she meant to me. To be loved, to be shamelessly spoiled by a charming woman whom I worshipped—this oasis in my desert of years was a magnificent antidote for the ugly duckling obsession I had long endured.

Jane and I had a beautiful companionship, we loved each other, and knew exactly what we wanted: the opportunity to live together without question of criticism, without interested opinion. We wanted a normal domestic life and we wanted our happiness together. We asked nothing of anyone. We hurt no one. We were mature, free, and perfectly sure of ourselves.

But social intrusion began to tug at our consciousness. We were deviators from conventional morality. We had signed no papers for clergy or state; we were social outlaws. Our relationship must be clandestine: there could be no joy in sharing the knowledge with family or friends, no hint of anything more than ordinary affection. We must get used to hypocrisy and camouflage that degraded and humiliated. We must have courage to steel ourselves against coarse remarks made by unsuspecting acquaintances who tarnished homosexuality with their light contempt.

Adjustment would require extraordinary tact and adaptability, and above all, a sense of humor profound enough to be a sense of proportion. During my first months with Jane I had to learn to be a consummate *poseuse*. For there were Marian and Edith and a half-dozen other acquaintances with whom I had been friendly before I met Jane. I had sensed Marian's and Edith's very personal curiosity even before Jane and I took our apartment, and I was in constant fear of self-betrayal.

It was imperative that no one suspect our liaison, and at the same time it was awkward that it could not be assumed. For Edith and Marian continued to ask me to join them at tea or the theatre, not bothering, after the initial polite gesture when we had first moved, to invite Jane too. Jane was no longer gracious to either of them; for some reason I could never explain, she had disliked Marian from the first. Her jealousy of my friendships frightened me and made me miserably conscious of her inability to understand unemotional friendliness. Yet I could not feel free to accept an invitation which did not include Jane. No more would a bride leave her husband to join a group uncongenial to him.

I missed my friends. They had been such essential companions for me in Paris before I met Jane that Paris itself seemed unfamiliar without them. I had hoped that they'd find her congenial. But lesbianism meant jealousies and now, recognized by Edith and Marian, estrangement. I could never think of them without feeling humiliated and resentful.

It was with slow, fearful incredulity that I realized something now that I would never have believed without experience: it was far easier to live with a man out of wedlock than it was to live with a woman in lesbianism. Perhaps it was, simply, that the regularity of the normal world was steady enough to wink at an irregularity that ran parallel with its structure.

Yet I loved Jane enough to endure scorn and disapproval. Valiantly I told myself that complete independence with Jane was what I really wanted, independence of friends, of Paris, of everything but our lives together. Valiantly I told myself that isolation was the only answer to lesbian happiness, studied casualness and persiflage in my manner with her the only answer to the questions of our acquaintances, our neighbors, even the *concierge,* and the public we could not ignore.

So, before many months, we were entirely friendless and independent to the point where we could have dropped out of Parisian existence and nobody but Bonk and the *concierge* would have missed us. This was better, I said to myself, than feeling continually threatened by other people's contempt or indifference when there was no way of fighting back.

It will not be difficult for the normal to understand that the homosexual can feel no part in the surge of an immense social destiny. Whatever that feeling of social destiny may amount to, whether it is called herd instinct by the sociologist, or community spirit by the mayor, or fellowship by the preacher, it is the normal individual's kinship to the world about him. And it is his secondary defense against the terrors of loneliness.

I sensed it flowing all about us, so keenly that it might have been something animate. It was exciting to hear, moving to see —but it belonged to the normal world. Trying to get close enough to feel it coursing over me was as useless as straining to see the invisible. Yet nothing could keep the sound and the sight far enough away from them not to matter. They always mattered. And they always hurt. This is the peculiar loneliness of the homosexual.

I had expected a sense of isolation in the third sex, but I was not prepared for its chronic painfulness. No less surprising to me was Jane's apparent obliviousness to it. There was no sign that it hurt her, and the one time I mentioned it to her she seemed not to understand. I did not press the point. Neither Jane nor I had ever actually spoken to each other of emotional inversion; and perhaps it was better, I thought, to continue to ignore the fact that we were different. I was willing to take my cue from her, and I assumed that she, being the older, had learned better how to temper herself for resistance. At least I contented myself with that explanation, and envied her such seasoned immunity.

What happened to my own attitude was natural. Needing a defense, I began to sidetrack my awareness of exile by vague sentimentality and spiritualizing. Jane was the only refuge I had ever known, an escape from the eternal solitude of self. With her I was feeling what I had wanted to feel with Carl: an inter-communion and a sense of one-ness. This must be my compensation.

Stored deep in my consciousness, my last harrowing resistance to lesbianism had been freed by Jane's need of me. I had justified myself, and I would try to belittle the price I had to pay. Accepting lesbianism and my circumstances without fear, without distaste, would be my ultimate freedom.

The sharp desire for ecstasy was a longing neither of us had ever known before. I would not have believed, in the enchantment of first intimacies, that our physical relationship could change with such imperceptible subleties that my illusion would turn into apprehension before our first year was out. Yet, inside me, confidence was being shaken. Something was wrong, a vague something I did not at first understand. To be tantalized without achieving sexual fulfillment began to be a recurring disappointment that bogged me in an old confusion I had hoped never to have again. I had expected concern for achievement to be a mutual problem in smoothing a hundred temperamental differences; in this I had been wrong. It was once mutual; it became entirely mine. Temperamental differences were not smoothed by time; they were aggravated.

Though it took me months to interpret what was happening between us—months of blaming myself and excusing Jane—the maladjustment seemed simple to explain once thought could struggle beyond the knots in my emotion. Love could not be

[98]

grudging; love was ruthlessly practical, really, for it demanded freedom. Or it could be very cruel. The plain truth was that Jane, for all her initial eagerness, had not found herself capable of passion. She was neither insensitive nor unsympathetic; she was physically and mentally awkward because she was a prude.

She would have protested, even been alarmed, had I told her she was a prude. She thought of herself as a woman not to be awed by the conventions—as a sophisticate. Her manner and her conversation were convincing enough, but even Edith would not have believed me had I told her that Jane was full of the most ordinary scruples. I would not have been surprised if my great-aunt had said that she'd rather I didn't keep brandy in my room. "I don't care what anybody else drinks," Jane had said, "but somehow I don't want you to even have it around." And I, who'd grown up accustomed to the presence of liquors, had been—because it was she—a little charmed, even relieved, to run across such a quaint reluctance among the arty Americans in Paris.

It was by this same reasoning that I'd been touched by Jane's religion; I'd already become so bored by the self-conscious decadence of Americans in Berlin and Paris that I'd reached the point of not caring what a man believed, if only he believed *something.*

Trivial as the brandy incident had been, I could see it now as a clue to a system of right and wrong that had nothing to do with reason. Jane had the instincts of a sybarite, the inhibitions of a god-fearing provincial. Between the two was a hiatus I could not measure.

She acted in half-measures. Her perspective, her sense of values, were chained by a decorum which overbore her rich feeling for life and left psychically incapable of exposing herself to fullest experience. Nor had she any criteria to go by in matters of sex. She didn't even know that to realize the peak of experience, sex had to be mutual.

For her sake as well as my own, I prayed that my ideas about her might be wrong. I could feel her growing away from me, and instinct told me that it was in spite of herself. Her incapability meant occasional anguish that was almost torture, and I would lie stiff with fear that the desire pounding at me would betray itself. I'd rather not have her touch me at all than to face the possibility of being taken to the edge of ecstasy, and let down with a suddenness that shattered my nerves. For her sake I could have pretended, but I'd never be caught in that kind of lie again. It seemed to me then, as it still does, that the lover should not have to articulate his needs.

It is amazing how hope can persuade the mind into accepting a situation which is dotted here and there with just enough happy color to give the whole a deceptive shade. Dimly, I sensed ecstasy often enough to keep my hope alive. My will was imprisoned by my love.

One summer night everything changed with vicious suddenness. Every second of the scene remains with stubborn firmness in my mind. The conscious effort to forget it has only made it more deeply rooted.

Jane was particularly affectionate and desiring. She put my hand on her breast and pulled me down with my head on her arm, and I knew she wanted me to kiss her. The faint aroma of her body was eternally sweet to me. She held me close to her, as I loved her to hold me, and I noticed that her breathing was heavy, excited. I could feel her heart beating wildly as she pressed me to her. Then with a violent contraction she took my hand, and I let it lie where she placed it on her body. . . . I did what she wanted that night.

For a long time afterwards she lay silent, and then she began to sob hysterically. I was frantic, afraid I had hurt her. I couldn't get her to speak to me.

Minutes later, calmed now, she turned from me and said in a toneless whisper, "I didn't want to! I didn't want to!"

I shuddered at what I had heard, not daring to understand what she meant. Finally, hurt and frightened, I took her hand. She held it very tight and then she took my face between her palms and looked into my eyes. Hers were still limpid and soft when she whispered, "Please, let's not any more. I can't stand feeling so ashamed the next day. Please. . . ."

Mechanically I kissed her and mechanically I promised, not knowing what I was doing or saying, my thoughts paralyzed. Jane finally went to sleep, holding my hand while I peered into the darkness, lying on one elbow, seeing nothing, feeling nothing, only hearing over and over again a thousand terrible times, "I can't stand feeling so ashamed," until I was almost mad from the rhythm of it.

Out of my rigid thoughts came one that saved me. I was so very glad I had let Jane be the aggressor from the very first. I was so very glad I had even let her fumble for me awkwardly before I had shown her. Never, I was satisfied. had I ever forced myself on her. Never, until she said "I didn't want to! I didn't want to!" without warning, without preparing me, had there been any indication of reluctance.

After that I did not touch her. I did not want to sleep near her. All happy symbols of affection were gone for me. When she kissed me good night and lay near me I began to hate her for her self-possession. I didn't even dare take her hand. Once I even tried to sleep on the chaise longue in the living room, but Jane told me I was being foolish. Dully, like a person stripped of will, I went back and lay beside her, worlds away. Night after night, long after she was asleep, I ached to touch her, with emotion that mounted fiercely for being forbidden. If in her sleep she touched me, or flung an arm across my body, I trembled for wanting, nerves tingling up and down my spine. Sometimes I would move far away from her, not trusting my impulse to take her roughly in my arms and be damned with the adolescent hang-overs of Sunday school class. Chilled with the horror that Jane had vilified what I looked upon as a natural impulse, my mind began to recoil from the servitude I was facing—frustration of the most senseless kind.

5

Rolf

I CAME HOME late one afternoon from class, and from the hall I saw Rolf sitting in a low chair by the window, trying to entertain himself with Bonk and make conversation with Jane, who did not bother to hide her annoyance. It had been more than a year since I had seen him; I had almost completely forgotten him. I was surprised by his pleasure in seeing me, but he left shortly, intimidated by Jane, when I promised to have dinner with him that evening. I had, in fact, been so glad to see Rolf intimidated by anything that I did not remember in time that I'd vowed never to see him again.

I shut the door after him with fear in my heart, for Jane had gone with brusque suddenness into the kitchen. I dressed for dinner, angry with Jane's jealousy and her rudeness to Rolf; at the same time I felt guilty about leaving her alone for the evening. Before Rolf came I tried to kiss her. She turned her cheek, but not from anger now.

This was the first time I'd gone with a man since I'd been with Jane. But Rolf was different; I didn't think of him as really counting, for I was still certain he was a homosexual. Yet I could not bring myself to tell Jane that. Thought of mentioning homosexuality, ignored from the first, seemed harder as time went on. I promised not to leave her for long, regretting now that I had told Rolf I would go at all.

He took me to the Tour d'Argent, a tiny and very old restaurant over by the Jardin des Plantes, and as he ordered, I wondered at the change in him. He was, he said, very conscious of having been more rude to me than to any other woman he'd ever known. That was such a back-handed superlative that we both laughed.

"I told you I loved you," he said. "I meant it. But I neglected to say that I also hated you. You made me feel like an ass the minute I met you when you ripped through 'Kitten on the Keys.' For two days you ignored me more convincingly than I'm used to being ignored. Then, to round things out nicely, you beat the hell out of me at cards. I hate women, Diana. But I loved you because for some reason or other I could forget you were a woman. You gave me several bad weeks after I left Berlin. Then one morning I got up and I didn't love you any more. It was marvelous. Now I feel merely apologetic, of course. But I'm really a nice sort when my teeth aren't on edge."

"I loved you because I could forget you were a woman." Rolf's suggestion, natural as it was, assured me of his homosexuality. Cautiously I invited his confidence. Then I learned a surprising thing which has been true of every homosexual I have known since: in direct contrast to the ordinary lesbian who will make every effort to conceal her nature from her closest friends, the homosexual is eager to talk of himself to any listener who seems sympathetic. Rolf's effort to explain himself was without apparent embarrassment. Perhaps his frankness was admirable, but it quite took my breath.

"I was in love with my mother until I was sixteen," he said, with no effort to euphemize.

Slowly I was able to reconstruct from his suggestions a boyhood and youth with a very young and lovely mother whose husband's business kept him away from his family a large part of the time. The mother absorbed her son to compensate for her loneliness. Constant companionship during Rolf's boyhood had grown to slavish companionship during his youth until his mother, finally realizing his lack of balance, had urged him to go out with girls as his friends were doing. It was too late. He could not adjust himself to girls his own age.

"When I was about fifteen she tried to give me some social graces by teaching me how to flirt with her," he went on. "I was awkward and scared, of course. She'd take me to hotels for dinner and smile at me across the table just as if I were her date. Christ, she was beautiful!"

I knew that modern psychiatry was giving the Œdipus complex more and more significance in explaining homosexuality. Rolf finally admitted to its inevitable climax—jealousy of the father. From that point I drew my own conclusions. Rolf had finally found relief in a homosexual relationship.

He was highly intelligent, sensitive, and cynical. I understood his mature contempt for women. There was probably nothing personal in it; rather, it was masculine rankling at the hurt of appearing too much like them. Some quirk of fate had made me attractive to him, and he resented me. I could not blame him, but the very fact of his resentment attracted me; this was something new in men. I had been used to admiration; now it was challenging for a man to dare me to interfere with his scheme of things. Rolf was so arrogant and sure of himself, so confoundedly smug, that I needed no more impetus than his final "I'm glad I've rid myself of thoughts of you" to set my purpose firm. I would enjoy hurting him. I'd never felt this way before, but Rolf had a genius for bringing out the worst in me, as I did, apparently, in him.

I was sure of something which Rolf did not know; I knew why I had attracted him, just as he had attracted me. There was enough male in me to meet on a common basis with the female in him. That affinity he felt but did not know.

It did not occur to me at the time that my sudden foolhardy whim to subdue him was traceable to my frustration with Jane.

DIANA

The psychical necessity to do something to assert myself had become, unrecognized by reason, the first predatory instinct I had ever felt in my life.

I passed several afternoons with Rolf the next week in spite of Jane's jealousy, but I was annoyed with his indifference. It was not easy to admit to myself that the longer I knew him the more he baffled me. Though he continued to be more friendly than before, intuition told me he was pretending, that he was contemptuous of himself for wanting to be with me.

I knew I was hurting Jane deeply by seeing Rolf. It had galled her that he had even taken an apartment close by. She was no longer merely angry; she was vindictive. And I was sorry. I had overreached myself. We were having trouble enough without my doing anything to aggravate the situation. I knew the lesbian relationship had to depend on mutual trust, fidelity. I knew it must ward off conventional intrusions or perish. No trifling with Rolf was worth the hurt I saw in Jane's eyes when he would bring me home and she'd be waiting for me.

I told her I would not see him any more. Two days later she gave me a tiny package she had saved, she said, until I was over Rolf—a beautiful ring of five chain emeralds of a curious triangular cut, set deeply in yellow gold. On the inside of the delicate band were carved the initials—"JE—DF." I looked at her in helpless joy, but she guarded my lips with her finger and wouldn't let me try to speak.

I was young; I did not realize that people would not always react as I intended them to. I was spoiled; too often I had had my own way. When I told Jane that I would see Rolf no more, I sent him a note the next morning and expected it to end all questions. With inexcusable high-handedness I gave him no reason other than a crisp something about needing more time to study. Nor did I think anything of it when no answer came.

[106]

Jane and I were content again now that our independence had triumphed over the first threat to our security, and I was thankful that her jealousy had died so quickly.

Then, in a week, Rolf met me one evening as I left the apartment alone. I knew he had seen me from his window. He wore a white angora turtle-neck sweater and maroon Russian-looking house slippers that strapped twice about his ankles—very impressively continental. Almost without looking at me he took my hand and begged me to come and talk with him. Compelled by the tone of his voice, I walked with him to his rooms, curious and excited in spite of myself. The front room was strewn with sheets of music, empty brandy bottles and cigarette butts. Rolf apologized curtly and cleared a chair for me. Then, towering over me, he said with husky abruptness:

"You've made me love you. You've got what you wanted. It was one hell of a game."

Suddenly I realized he had taken my note only as a challenge. I tried to explain; he paid no attention. He lifted me to my feet and kissed my mouth, holding me so tight I could not move my arms. His roughness hurt me. I pushed him away, furious and revolted, but he was unperturbed. I knew he was a little drunk. His lips were loose and wet. He kissed me again and then shoved me back into the chair.

"Damned little bitch!" he said, smiling at my fury. "Like all women. Scared of fundamentals."

Of course anger would not placate him. It would do no good to tell him that his touch repelled me. With a tremendous effort I tried reason. He was pouring drinks and I took advantage of the brief distraction. It was an unmerciful but frantic inspiration which made me ask if anything about me reminded him of his mother. The question took effect.

He abandoned his effort to speak lightly. "Your mouth," he said. "The same kind of lips. Voluptuous. Selfish."

I had touched a vulnerable spot. The first reason for his interest in me, the only reason he had ever looked at me a second time!

He drank two fingers of brandy and came over to me, his defiance gone.

"Why," he asked, "did you want to humble me? You didn't really want me."

Rolf's penetration was devilishly upsetting. I felt as cheap as a tart. There was no point in lying now. It was easier to speak simply. I told him men had been too easy; he was at least different.

"I see," he said, and with ironic formality he went to open the door for me to leave. "Women," he said, "have the damnedest ways of amusing themselves."

A nasty rebuttal froze in my throat, and I walked past him without meeting his eyes.

The tempestuous interlude with Rolf sent me back to Jane shaken and very much wiser in humility. My sense of humor saved me from continued anger; I knew I had laid myself open to everything that had happened. What had dumbfounded me was his penetration. No normal man, with as much cause, could have been so sensitive to my lack of physical desire. Rolf had known even before he touched me. No normal man had ever guessed ruthlessness so quickly. And so I first learned from Rolf what I have observed since many times: that the male homosexual, by virtue of the female in his nature, has extraordinary acumen in understanding women.

I had read explanations for the frequent harmony between homosexuals and lesbians, for the third sex met, psychologically, on common ground. I had even seen case histories of marriages between them, where both husband and wife found in each other full spiritual and physical satisfaction. But I was quite sure that no homosexual could have more than intellectual appeal for me.

Rolf's touch, even discounting my distaste for his shocking manners, had been singularly revolting. Where proximity with a normal man was simply a bore, proximity with a homosexual made me feel sick. Quite unreasonably, it seemed vulgar and unclean. The first thing I wanted to do when I got home from Rolf's was to cleanse myself and do anything, frantically, to get rid of his touch. I am reluctant to admit to retching.

Knowing that it would only upset her, I did not mean to say anything to Jane about it. But she guessed something had sickened me and finally I told her, late the same evening, without sparing myself. I had expected her to be angry. Instead, she had an almost anguished desire to escape the thought of Rolf's embrace. I can never forget the pain on her face as she kissed me.

"Never anyone else, dear, never," she said.

So I learned, bitterly, that Jane and I must shut out everyone for our happiness. No women friends. No men friends. No intrusions.

After Rolf, Jane changed. The possible fear of losing me, present if unreasonable, may have been accountable, but it was more than a matter of emotional mood and circumstance. Jane wanted me to love her again, wanted me with desire that denied shame. But tension was no less so far as I was concerned. I did not want Jane in spite of herself. That sort of desire repelled me with its weakness—as if I were the instrument for passion instead of the cause. Wisely or unwisely, I told her so and left her to herself. My love for Jane was forgiving and God knows it was patient. But I would not have it abused. Either Jane would learn to want me without an atom of regret or our lives would be apart.

She asked for more time. I was afraid of time. I was afraid of everything now. Our whole relationship was in the balance. Integration could not be achieved with Jane's attitude *à rebours*. Had she been undesiring or impotent my feeling would have been merely one of regret, but shame was an emotion against which logic stood mute and disconcerted. The struggle must be decided in Jane's own mind. When I refused her I understood fully how I humiliated her; I was beyond caring. I moved to the chaise longue, and stayed there.

〜〜〜〜〜〜〜〜〜〜 6 〜〜〜〜〜〜〜〜〜〜〜

Jealousies

I WAS WRITING letters at my table one evening when Jane asked me who had given Bonk to me. It struck me as peculiar that her tone was so imperative, and also that she assumed he had been a gift. Perhaps Marian had told her.

"A friend," I said. "A very dear friend."

"Man or woman?" she asked.

This seemed ridiculous, but I answered in a flat monosyllable.

"Did you love him?" she asked, and I answered, "No."

Jane was sitting on a high stool absentmindedly scraping bits of hardened paint off the sides of her easel. They were dropping to the floor and Bonk, optimistic, was sniffing at each one. Two little pieces of red had landed behind one ear, and stuck like confetti. I called him, and he bounced at me, wagging his tail affectionately. Had I had the intelligence to realize the extent of Jane's mood, I'd never have chosen that moment to laugh and grab him up to me. He was still trying to lick my face when I heard Jane say, "Diana, I'd rather you got rid of Bonk."

For a moment I couldn't take her seriously. She repeated. "I don't want to think of anyone else's ever having loved you, ever having given you anything. That's not much to ask."

My evasive reply had the effect of making her all the more jealous of this unknown friend. But I had sworn for Carl's sake, if not for mine, never to mention him, and my past with him in no way overlapped the present with Jane. I scoffed at her for being ridiculous.

[111]

DIANA

"The one thing I have ever asked of you, Diana," she said. "Please! If you love me, I'll not have to ask you again."

Edith had said once, "Don't let Jane overbear you. She's imperious." But I had never seen her like this. I shook my head.

Jane sprang to her feet and left the room, her face drawn with anger. The bedroom door banged so loudly behind me that I jumped. I wished I didn't have such a masculine horror of scenes. It must be a relief to slam a door like that. But any quarrel I participated in was bound to lack color. Twenty minutes later she came out, dressed as if she were going to dinner, and passed through the living room without looking at me.

I waited until amost eight o'clock, but she did not come back. Finally I prepared the cutlets we had planned for dinner, and with some satisfaction I gave Jane's share to Bonk. I would give up my friends if I had to, for Jane. There was reason in that. But I would never give up Bonk. That made no sense.

I was in bed when she returned, quite late. I could not guess where she had been. She said nothing, went into the bedroom, and soon I saw the light go out.

A long time after midnight I heard Jane open her door and walk toward me. She sat down by my side. Jane had only to touch me and all my resistance melted away, as if the wave of tenderness carried away last precautions. "Diana," she whispered, "I don't want to be mean to you. Please don't ever let me. Love me enough so I can never be."

Even in her embrace I shuddered a little, wondering why she would say that.

By this time, having completed my course in literature, philosophy and history, I was putting in long stretches on philology. My special thesis, on tracing the genealogy of several hundred words from the Latin down through the centuries to modern French or English, entailed research in such techniques as morphology, phonology and semantics, and the mammoth dictionaries in the library of the Sorbonne and the Bibliothèque Nationale seemed to weigh more day by day. Elusive as some of the word histories were, it gave me a kind of esthetic satisfaction to do such dusty digging, the only successful approach I ever made to an honest science. In July I was to take my examinations at the Sorbonne, this time for a degree. I had thought myself prepared until the time came. They were such a frightening experience I am still intimidated at their mention. During one terrible minute in the orals, I could not make a sound either in French or English. When everything was over I went home and wept. But I had passed.

Jane, meanwhile, was elated that one of her paintings, a moody seascape begun in Brittany the previous summer when we vacationed, had won gratifying recognition from critics. I was interested that the seascape was referred to as "masculine"; I had long observed that the essential Jane was much more masculine than her studied character betrayed. The inference was, I thought, significant. But if Jane gave it a thought she never indicated it.

Partly to celebrate our success, partly to celebrate our first anniversary of living together, we decided one evening to go to the Casino de Paris. So happy to have our first care-free evening in months, we sat through the whole revue like boarding school girls on vacation. Then, getting off the bus near home, we decided to have a *liqueur,* and we were walking over to the Boulevard St. Germain when I heard the strains of a tango orchestra coming from a little side street. That was enough. In a few minutes we found ourselves going down an adventuresome darkened stairway to a café new to us but welcome in our mood. I pushed the door open and Jane followed me in. A three-piece orchestra was at the opposite end of a long, narrow room, dimly lighted. We made our way to a small table at one side and ordered. Slowly I realized what we had come into. I had heard there were many such places in Paris, but I had never been in one before.

Women dressed as men were dancing to the rhythm of the tango with women partners, some of whom were dressed in feminine clothes. The grace, the decorum, the nonchalance of the couples amazed me. The floor itself, of lightly shaded squares of glass, through which the only light came, added to the charm of the muted and voluptuous music. Transvestitism, as always, got on my nerves, but I was nevertheless fascinated. A deep sense of having been here before held me, in spite of the novelty. At once this tucked-away refuge assumed significance. The outside world didn't matter here, nor even its whispers.

Jane, admiring a Renoir nude on the wall, had not yet taken in the situation. I looked at her, and finally I saw her jaw set in inflexible scorn. I was surprised. She picked up her gloves, put a five-franc note on the table and turned toward me. I told her I wanted to stay.

"You have a morbid curiosity," she said. "These people are depraved. They're homosexuals!"

Jane got up, walked hurriedly toward the door and left. After a few minutes of indecision, I followed. I had to run to catch up with her. We walked home fast, without speaking, my anger almost choking me with the question raging to my lips. When we were home I asked it, bluntly.

"What in the name of God do you make of you and me?"

Jane would not answer. The fact that she ignored me only made me the more angry, but still I was incredulous.

"Are you denying that you're one of them?" I asked. "Or that I'm one? Are you saying *we're* depraved?"

I had finished when Jane broke in, furious, her face flushed. "Diana, shut up! You don't know what you're saying!"

I did shut up. I couldn't have spoken another word. Jane, now moving with tense calm, went into the kitchen, patted Bonk and gave him a scrap of meat, and then went into the bedroom to undress. I got up and closed her door myself. A feeling of degradation surged over me, as if I were a strumpet and Jane had just found it out.

I sat that night, long after Jane had gone to bed, and tried to arrive at some kind of explanation for her extraordinary remark. I could not make the mistake of comparing her attitude in any way with my own. My conclusions on sex had been a matter of compromise from first to last, for every moral and intellectual principle I knew had led me to feel shame—and yet I was enamoured with all the richness and sweetness of physical life. In lesbianism I had had to learn an inner resilience; I had learned better than to judge myself by normal conventions, because that would have limited my capacity to experience. My love for Jane was in accord with an essential beyond the reserves of sense. Jane might have called that essential God.

I would have given my soul had I thought I could make her see my point of view, but I had already lived long enough to know that one's code is not transferable. It goes clear to the bottom of the heart, a highly selected and personal set of feelings of no use except to one's self.

If Jane did not admit to homosexuality, what was my rôle in her life? Was I to be merely her "child," as she often called me, someone on whom to lavish her maternal complex? But no, there was much more than that in her love. She had a passionate nature which could ascend the heights of sexual emotion. Something in her past must explain her, something I did not know. Having no patience with the idea that emotional inversion is inborn, I assumed Jane's homosexuality to be largely the result of her height which, during adolescence, had made her timid and awkward with boys and, no doubt to compensate for this deficiency, aggressive with girls. She had often hinted these things, and when she went from high school to a girl's boarding school, I imagined the balance had tipped decidedly toward homosexuality. A further

[115]

and no less important influence in Jane's background was her adoration of her father, a worship that amounted almost to father fixation—and particularly important here since Jane, an only child, felt apologetic for not having been born a boy.

It was with slow, excruciating shock that I realized that Jane, whom I had seen as a mature woman whose struggle against her nature was a seasoned accomplishment—to the extent that I had envied her superior "protection" against a feeling of isolation— had deceived herself. She judged herself by normal standards, though she lived as a lesbian. Cool appraisement of her failure to have made any conciliatory transition from the one mode of life to the other made her, to my mind, almost contemptible. Or was it pitiable? In either case, plain interpretation was unavoidable. The subconscious, with its power of wishful thinking, had its triumph. Jane was strong-minded, sentimental. She believed what she needed to believe. Self-justification measures itself by need, and Jane had substituted her heart for her brain. What she had done was evident; how she had done it was a feat that only the refinements of higher psychology could explain. I had heard of homosexuals who never learned the grace of admitting their abnormality to themselves; I would never have been convinced before this.

Gradually my anger became pity, an emotion no less profound for being within an inch of disgust. Yet, despite the fact that all happy symbols of affection were gone for me, my love remained. It was not admiring now; it could not be proud. But I couldn't imagine its being any less. My immediate and my only hope would be to help her to a happy acceptance of herself.

That night, the night of our first anniversary, I finally went into the bedroom, hours after Jane had turned out the light. I spoke her name. She had been waiting for me.

Probably I sounded more far away than I felt.

"We are starting all over again, from the very beginning," I said. "That's the only thing I do understand."

Then I left before I could finish. I'd intended to tell her that I did not want her love until I could be proud. But my thoughts had been stronger than I.

The Café in Paris

TWO DAYS after our visit to the lesbian café I wanted to return alone without telling Jane. My first brief glimpse of frankly lesbian women *en groupe* had made me conscious of a tribal similarity I had never before suspected. I wanted to discover those points of common likeness if only to avoid them. Though their resemblance one to the other was entirely spiritual, the thought of an inherent lesbian individuality bothered me.

It was a rainy afternoon at a late tea hour. As I went down the circular stairway, sudden timidity almost turned me back before I could push open the door. I could not explain my fear of the women I saw there, but I sensed their guarded interest in me as I made my way to an inconspicuous table.

Five or six couples were dancing to the music of phonograph records, some few groups were idling in booths, and two women were alone reading. The entire room was not as large as it had at first appeared, and its atmosphere of indolent sensuousness soon calmed me. The hush of night formality had given way to easy sociability. These women, younger than the night clientele, looked my own age and were, obviously, American and English.

I was relieved that none of them were dressed as men, although most of them were mannish in bearing as well as attire. It struck me that the English girls were more earnestly mannish than the Americans who looked, in contrast, only tailored and tomboyish. It was not prejudice which made me observe their certain talent for smartness which the English girls lacked.

An onlooker ignorant of the character of the place would not have caught the significance of the four photographs of young women on the wall, close to my table. Two of them I recognized as American actresses. I was amazed at the boldness of a *propriétaire* who would dare defy the secretive habits of lesbians. Remembering the collegiate penchant for hanging pictures of famous sisters in sorority chapter rooms, I caught myself thinking of them as prominent alumnae.

As I sat sipping tea and occupying myself with a book, a rather strange thing happened: a sensation of almost blood-intimacy came over me and for the first time in my life I had the feeling of being a part of a group of fellow human beings. No normal person could understand the relief I experienced as I looked about me and saw the vividness of faces that knew, as I knew, that here was a haven where social prejudice was only a bad dream of the other world. No pressure here or that constant feeling of separateness; no dread here of shame, not even the mask of bantering smiles. Here I could lose a little loneliness with creatures whose hopes and understanding and passions were my own. Here for an instant I could feel beyond the pain and pale of moral judgment.

These girls were individually vivid and intelligent-looking. The thought had never occurred to me before, but now I wondered why I'd never seen either a drab or a stupid-looking lesbian, and I imagined several reasons. First of all, a stupid girl probably would never ascertain her abnormality if she were potentially homosexual—a fact not at all strange on second thought. Further, the girl who did come to understand her inversion was likely to have character in her face, if no degree of beauty. The very fact of her abnormality assured her of that; her expression would be crossed by a subtle something, according to the measure of her disillusionment. No woman could adjust herself to lesbianism without developing exceptional qualities of courage.

I became interested in an American girl of about twenty-five, whose eyes betrayed a trace of boredom as she danced with a tall blonde. I would not have noticed her apart from the others except for her feminine appearance and the fact that she was, unmistakably, trying to flirt with me. It had never occurred to me that lesbians flirted with one another, I'd never seen it before and I felt a little silly and embarrassed. Yet she excited my curiosity. She had an interesting face—cold and smooth and restless. At last, when she was seated opposite me, several tables way, I managed a smile that I hate to recall for its childish self-consciousness. It must have been effective. Almost at once she came to my table, introduced herself simply as Elizabeth, and asked me to dance.

A stubborn prejudice made me refuse. I had never liked the sight of women dancing together, and lesbian couples, while aping normal privileges, only seemed to emphasize their abnormality. I was glad that Elizabeth took no offense, and accepted my invitation to join me.

Her first formality was charming. Our conversation began quickly over mutual interests; I learned that she was accompanist to an American contralto now in Paris, that she was training for concert work herself. Then, after a pause, a slow smile illuminated her dark eyes and I yielded to sudden excitement as she simply looked at me with questioning candor.

"My friends are suspicious of you," she said. She had to explain no further. I understood. I was new here. I had them at a disadvantage.

I'd not suspected the group animosity of lesbians, but this evidence of their eternal desire for secrecy should not have surprised me. I felt as gauche as if I had walked into a private lodge meeting. Then, suddenly, their suspicion became insupportable. I was moved by a quick desire to prove myself, to make them know, to make sentimental appeals so they would know. Prejudice was no longer important. Impulsively I took Elizabeth's hand and asked her to dance. She smiled, understanding, and led me to the dance floor. As we passed her own table, Elizabeth nodded, still smiling, to her friends there; though I had said nothing I interpreted her nod as an official stamp of approval. Then, in the first overt admission of my own nature, my face went hot with self-consciousness. Elizabeth, seeing my confusion, pressed my arm and whispered, *"Il faut du courage."*

In a little while I was myself again. Elizabeth's friends began to ask for dances, and I had the extraordinary sensation of feeling like the belle of the lesbian ball.

At first I wondered why Elizabeth asked what kind of cocktail I would like, and hovered near me like a zealous escort. Later, from what her friends told me, I understood, very much amused, that Elizabeth was merely being cautious.

I hated having to dance. But I was learning, a little more from each partner, what I had come to find out—something of the class idiosyncrasies of lesbians, what it was that gave the whole group a subtle mark of similarity. In my eagerness to learn I went on abusing my prejudices.

Without exception my partners gave me the impression of being wild and strong and a little devil-may-care. The more I saw of them the better I could understand. Everything they did seemed vital, every move intense. Their faces were mobile, their eyes sensitive, their conversation spirited, their understanding facile, their sympathy quick. Nor was their spiritual nature any more intense than their physical. Their laugh was a little abandoned, their gestures expansive, their energy nervous and suggestive of strength.

After I'd had time to understand the reasons for these impressions they made perfectly obvious sense. Of course the lesbian's reactions would seem more vigorous than those of a normal woman —her emotional range is wider, is masculine as well as feminine. This fecund sensual nature is exactly what gives her distinction from normal women, and what gives lesbians similarity.

The intensity is understandable. The lesbian is forever conscious of her destiny. Lack of social purpose inspires a self-awareness that naturally intensifies thought and action. No matter what she does in life, society always sees her as a frustrated woman. Her armor may be strong, her philosophy pliant, but the social scheme remains a jump ahead of any compromise she makes. The effect does one of two things, depending on her spirit: it swerves her into silent submission or brings out the intensity of a woman affronted.

I was relieved when at last Elizabeth rescued me from a large-boned English girl who was becoming sentimental with English awkwardness. With scarcely a word Elizabeth led me up a short flight of steps and into an alcove. It had not occurred to me that a lesbian café would have private rooms. Elizabeth lighted candles and all I could make out was a small narrow room, furnished well but simply, with a low couch and a coffee table. Almost at once a *garçon* brought in a bottle of brandy, glasses and incense. I noticed his care in letting Elizabeth select the scent she preferred for the incense burner that hung from the wall. The thought of aphrodisiacs crossed my mind and I wanted to laugh before it occurred to me that perhaps I should be frightened.

When the *garçon* had gone out, Elizabeth held a candle close to the wall and pointed to some writing.

"Wouldn't you like to make a contribution?" she smiled, handing me a pencil from the table.

Curious, I got up to read. There, handwritten on the wall, were a dozen aphorisms and fragments of poems, some faded by time, some in bold script, some in dainty. The type of sentiment almost all of them carried interested me. The first I read was Edna St. Vincent Millay's "Prayer to Persephone." Next to it, scrawled in a different hand, I read: "The wise want love; and those who love want wisdom." Farther on was a sentiment written by a lachrymose admirer of Paul Fort: *"Mon Dieu, qu'il est doux de pleurer sans raisons!"* On the opposite wall, printed in heavy black, and outlined as if it were intended to be the motto of lesbianism, I read: *"Tout comprendre, c'est tout pardonner."* I recognized the next lines, from Byron's *Manfred,* and I assumed they had been written by an English girl:

> "Thou lovedst me
>   Too much, as I loved thee; we were not made
>   To torture thus each other, though it were the
>   deadliest sin to love as we have loved."

But most interesting to me was the last I saw, written with a black pencil that must have been in a stoic mood; even the printing looked determined, and there was a heavy, round period at the end of the second line, as if for emphasis:

> "Then I said: I will eat of this sorrow to its last shred,
>   I will take it unto me utterly.
>   I will see if I be not strong enough to contain it."

I should have liked to have known the woman who wrote that; I think I would have admired her.

Again Elizabeth asked me to write something but I disliked the flavor of exhibitionism and made excuses. My reluctance aroused her curiosity. She sat down beside me and asked me a surprising question.

"Do you mind telling me," she said, "if you are one of us or a spook?"

I was embarrassed to be ignorant of lesbian jargon. Elizabeth had to explain what she meant by "spook":

"A woman who for some reason or other strays into lesbianism as second best. And stays because she likes it better."

I reassured Elizabeth, inwardly exultant that my lesbianism was so well disguised.

"Once a woman is a spook she almost never prefers a man

[123]

again," she went on like a teacher. "She may marry if she wants a home and children, but chances are she has a lesbian lover."

Then the surprising opinion I have heard many times since: "Women make better lovers."

Elizabeth's tone left no room for argument. Reasonably, I resented this smug attitude. I knew the legend "Once a lesbian always a lesbian"; I had always wondered to what extent lesbian conceit was responsible for it. It was natural that lesbians should be proud of converts. The thought that an occasional woman stayed into their ranks was support to a pride that had little to lean on. And it was true that woman's nature favored her avoidance of the common mistakes of male lovers—haste and selfishness. As significant for some women, too, was the question of a happy intellectual level. The educated woman often wanted, but seldom got, the intellectual respect accorded her male consort. This irritant was not a factor in the lesbian relationship.

"But isn't it true," I asked, "that converts would be women who were either too weak or too scared? Women who are psychologically or physiologically unfitted for normal love?"

"Yes, of course," Elizabeth said. "Lesbians are mostly spiritual. The Greeks, you know, called them 'Uranians,' after 'Ouranos,' which meant 'Heaven,' because their love is a lot more emotional than it is physical. It's nearest the spiritual ideal."

I was struck by the defense mechanism which bound lesbian love all the way through. Unable to conform to the conventions, lesbians took the obvious course of exalting their feelings. That was clear enough. Yet Elizabeth was not idealizing so grotesquely as it might at first appear.

Lesbians idealize because they have to. The homosexual relationship does not have what marriage has to hold it together: property, family, frequently even profession. It doesn't have the blessings of church, law and state; if love goes, the relationship is ended with no more papers than it had to begin. Sentiment has to take the place of all these privileges. It is needed as compensation.

But Elizabeth had not brought me into the alcove for conversation. Soon she began to make love to me, and the ease of her approach was startling. Her eyes were brilliant, her hands beautiful, and their warmth on my arms more exciting than I had expected. Still impersonally, with the mood of the voluptuary, I encouraged her. I was almost fascinated by technique more artful than any I had ever known. Elizabeth was touched by that rare charm that sometimes makes a woman radiant in emotion, and when at last she turned my face and kissed my lips I knew my experimenting had gone too far.

Too excited to think, I do not know how I came to lie in her arms. I hadn't thought I would want to. I had not meant to. Elizabeth was talking to me, whispering and leaning over me.

"Tell me you will go home with me. Tell me I won't lose you as suddenly as I've found you. Diana, we could be so happy for a little while. Until I sail."

Her voice was too seductive, her phrasing too practiced. Chilled now, my mind cleared and desire died. I got up, a little rudely. Without emotion I accepted the fact that I had come into the alcove with Elizabeth wanting something to happen. It had, and I had behaved shamefully. Curiosity had been satisfied with a vengeance. Now I wanted only to go home to Jane, where I belonged.

I had not seen clearly before. My attitude of impersonality quickly changed with Elizabeth's glibness. I looked at her, her eyes shining with invitation, and I knew it would not be easy to tell her I had tried for an instant to see if I could match her own spirit. Now, depressed, I feared as something personal the spirit of the place I first thought of as a haven. Lesbianism became hateful for its lack of discipline, its prodigality of intimacy and sensuality. I even began to hate the ridiculous symbol of the incense pot.

I wonder now what I had expected in the first place. Perhaps I had hoped merely to get away from the ever-present contrast of myself with the normal, to become a part of whatever there was of soul and intelligence of my kind. But it hadn't worked. The illusion of one-ness had gone as quickly as it had come. The salvation of transient love, of desire for the body as a last resort, could not be mine; I could never become a part of that grand looseness with which these girls assuaged their natures.

Elizabeth was still lying where I had left her. I told her I could not see her again. After a long minute she looked up at me, and the quiet regret in her face gave the impression that she had known all along.

"Is your lover here in Paris with you?" she asked.

I nodded, feeling like a child caught sneaking. And then Elizabeth became angry.

"Then why did you come here? Were you just in a playful mood? Or could it be that you are honestly as ignorant of the mart as you seem?"

From Elizabeth's sarcastic remark I learned an astonishing thing. I had not known before that lesbians had both "rendezvous" and a "mart." The former was merely a meeting place for lovers, the latter—the café I had unwittingly chosen—an open house for lesbians who were, as Elizabeth bluntly put it, "single."

I began to despair of ever learning the complexities of lesbian social life. But, disillusioned by my first glimpse of it, I could not persuade myself that my ignorance made much difference.

New York

THE HUMAN HEART refuses to allow dread conclusions as long as a shred of hope remains. I must look forward, I concluded, and have courage. Hope itself engendered courage. I remained apart from Jane, and she understood that I did not want her to approach me. Though I ached with emotion that only grew for being forbidden, I would not go near her until I was welcome for what I was, not in spite of what I was. Presently, not suddenly, I understood that her anxiety was as great as my own.

External forces can sometimes end dilemmas that seem, in the abstract, impossible of lasting solution. Out of a clear sky in late August I received a cable from Dr. Gaffron, my old German adviser, telling me of an instructorship in the French department to begin the middle of September for which he was recommending me to his associates. I had written him in June, but he had replied that he anticipated no vacancy. I had about decided to stay in Paris another year and was awaiting word from Mother to tell me what to do. Now my surprise was no greater than my indecision as to whether to be glad or dismayed.

I cabled the French department, and within two days I received a reply, offering me the job. The offer was unexpected luck, for I was inexperienced. But what about Jane?

Although her father, harassed by the depression, had already asked her to come home, Jane had let her plans wait on mine. As she reluctantly advised me to accept the offer, questions from all sides heaped upon me. Should I try to persuade her that she would be happy with me in a small college town? Again, if I did, what possible excuse would she give her family for remaining with me under such circumstances?

But the crucial question was: Should I take Jane with me even if she did decide she wanted to go? Though trying to imagine that life without her was as unreal as imagining life without air, I had to force the light of objectivity on to my problem. Brave rationalization and braver hope were about exhausted. I was tired of being indulgent, tired unto death of being strong. Perhaps I would be happier in the long run if I were to leave Jane. I had invested heavily in good training. I was ambitious and wanted to start my career well.

We decided to sail home together. I still did not know whether she was coming with me or going home to her family. The day before we were to leave Paris I talked with her without any show of emotion. I told her, as though I were a third person speaking, that I could face the thought of trying to live without her better than I could face the panic of frustration.

"It took me years," I said, "to build up a defense that you blew to bits in one sentence. I love you. I guess I always will. But you're ashamed of me. And I'm not any good at long-suffering."

Jane wept. I kissed her tears away with maudlin impetuosity, and then grabbed Bonk and took him for a walk, staying away as long as I could stand it. When an hour was up I almost ran back to the apartment. I found Jane packing our clothes. I needed no other answer.

"Darling," she said, "who'd take care of you if I didn't go with you?" Her gentle question told me that her emotions had made her decision; but I still wasn't convinced.

On the boat two days out from Cherbourg, she crawled into my narrow berth at dawn and whispered to me until I awakened. I clasped her to me so naturally that not until I was fully awake did I feel astonishment that Jane was holding me. I looked at her, afraid to try to read the expression on her face as she leaned to kiss me. But I had not misunderstood. Over and over again I heard her voice, husky and tense, "I've missed you so much," as if she were saying it for me too. "Whatever you are, whatever I am, I love you."

I did not know when her trained conscience had surrendered; I was too excited to bother about examining cause and effect. But fear of Jane had become a habit not easy to break. I still needed to know that her triumph was a spiritual release from which there was no turning back.

We landed in New York on a Thursday morning. Jane had planned to take the first train to Detroit to spend two weeks with her family before meeting me at school, and because I did not have time to go home before school opened, Mother was coming Friday noon to spend the week-end with me. Thus I had arranged to have Thursday afternoon and evening free. I wanted to see Carl and Claudia; I had promised to let them know when I came home, and although Carl had understood, Claudia had scolded me for not calling either of them when I had sailed more than two years before.

Tender spots were healed now, and I had sent Carl a wireless from the boat telling him when I would be in but asking him not to meet me. Then when we landed Jane very suddenly decided to spend the day with me in New York.

"*C'est notre lune de miel, mon enfant,*" she said. Agreeing, I wondered at the eternal euphemisms of lesbians. Somehow it was so much easier to say, to listen to, in French. "Honeymoon" made one think so instantly of normal sanctions, normal blessings, rice and laughter. But in spite of my pleasure with Jane's sentiment, I was convinced that an evil genius was doing its worst.

I was going through with my plan, Jane or no Jane. Waiting

until the next day to see Carl would be no solution. I wanted not to raise any question in Mother's mind, and I'd rather have Jane angry than Mother hurt.

I telephoned Carl from our hotel room, and it was hard to keep my excitement down when he told me that he and Claudia had been sitting by the telephone waiting for me to call. Claudia even yelled into the phone, "Hurry up! My pudding's burning!" and Carl explained that she was cooking lunch for us in his apartment. I had no choice now. I was told to bring my friend along.

Carl said he would drive to the hotel for us, and Jane, no doubt wondering how angry to be with me, and curious that I had often mentioned Claudia but never Carl, seemed nevertheless pleased at the prospect of meeting them both.

I had thought with just what degree of affection I would greet Carl in front of Jane—again a compromise. And then Carl came. I should have known better. He held his arms wide and, with merry abandon, swept me clear off the floor. I couldn't imagine what illusions Jane might have left. Now, even before I could introduce Carl to her, Bonk sprang out of his chair toward him. The picture of Bonk's tail wagging at the sight of him gave me a start. I was quite sure by now that Jane had no illusions left. Bonk was in Carl's arms when the two met.

Jane refused Carl's invitation to come with us, though she had told me she would go.

"If you don't mind," she smiled. "I'd love to, but I've been seasick and still feel shaky."

Such pleasantness was more disturbing than the expected scene would have been. Besides, she had not been seasick. I left with Carl, held in the suspense of not knowing what Jane could be up to.

I had wondered desperately if Carl would assume that Jane

was my lover, and how he must feel when meeting her. I had not a doubt now that he did know, but he chose the easiest way for both of us by asking perfectly natural questions—when we had met, what did Jane do in Paris, where did we live. Finally, just before we reached his apartment he said, "Just one thing more, Diana, before we go in. Are you as happy as you look?"

Our eyes met, and for some reason I spoiled everything by coming near to tears.

"Yes," I said.

Carl now lived on Morningside Drive, and I recognized only two pieces of furniture from our apartment—his work table and my piano. I had to play Claudia's old Irish lullaby twice. I was sure that Claudia stayed only because she knew that we were imploring her not to leave us alone with our aching memories. News of each other and scraps of nonsense were far better. But my hours with them are of no importance to my story; the important thing was Jane.

When Carl took me back to the hotel at five Jane was asleep. She had left a note on the dresser. "Hurry up and come back and wake me! I've got something to tell you!" I went over and kissed her cheek. Instantly she awoke and crushed me to her.

"Sweet, you'll be so proud of me," she said. "It went all over me when Carl came and I could tell he'd been something so special you couldn't possibly want me along. Listen. I'm not jealous any more! That's what you wanted, isn't it? You said once it didn't make sense for a lesbian to be jealous of men instead of women. I even surprised myself at first. I'm just finding out how different I am."

For the briefest second I felt a thousand years old. I couldn't say anything, but I knew what she meant. That was the first time Jane had spoken of herself as a lesbian.

Suddenly she took my face between her hands and looked into my eyes. Hers were brilliant with emotion and when she caressed me I began to tremble, nerves tingling up and down my spine. Something was happening to Jane, something unlike anything I had ever known in her before. Whatever it was, it paralyzed my thought, drew me into excitement that almost suffocated me. Then she kissed me in a way she had never kissed me before. When I looked at her, startled, she laughed a little. Her eyes had changed. They were hard as ice, and they looked through and far beyond me. Her mouth was drawn a little at the corners, even grimly, as if she were deep in keeping a resolution. For some reason I could not name I knew I was frightened. There was no tenderness in this unexpected Jane, only sensuality. Lust no love

I have thought of this moment many times since as one of Godsent clairvoyance. But it faded rapidly. It meant nothing five minutes later. Lovers are not only blind; they are stupid.

By the time I met Mother Friday noon I had taken a room in an efficiency hotel, bought enough groceries to frighten her, and thought of all the things I was hungry for from home—angel cake, tomatoes, her own oven-baked beans, and coffee that wasn't black chicory. Mother hadn't exactly counted on cooking molasses and beans during her holiday in New York, but she laughed and forgave me my opportunism.

She had two surprises for me: the first she had just learned herself—that John and Lee were going to have a baby. The second, which my family had wanted to keep from me until I came home, was a sequence of such distressing news that I was spared comprehending everything at once. The bank of which my father had been president had suddenly failed two months after I left Berlin; the bank securities that he had left Mother— dividends from which had constituted a comfortable income— were now worthless; the allowance she had been sending me for over a year had come from two sources—a recent mortgage on our home and from Gerald.

The crash had come the semester Billy got his degree in law and now, as clerk in a large law firm, he was earning apprentice wages. John had been able to finish his last year in liberal arts; since graduation he had taken the only work he could get, as clerk in a dry goods store. Gerald, having gone into private practice, collected barely enough to support Mother, keep the house and help me.

"I would have told you, dear, only they all kept saying it would do no good and you'd worry. We knew this degree meant everything to you, and that you had to have it to teach. Gerald determined he'd get you through."

In sum, Gerald had deprived himself for me, Mother had no income, and John, who had planned to go on for his Ph.D., had no money for his new responsibility of fatherhood.

"Gerald was always a little impatient with John for getting married before he was through school," Mother said. "Then, of course, he thinks John's a man and better able to take care of himself than you'd be. But now that you're home, he'll help him."

Mother had hinted not one of these things in her letters. That the depression might have a deep personal significance had never entered my mind. I would have imagined that Gibraltar could be no more solid than my father's bank; it had been in the control of our family for three generations. I had supposed it would always be, and indeed Billy had taken many business courses with the natural idea of becoming a banker when the time came.

I almost resented my family's desire to spare me. It was a little humiliating to think that my brothers had treated me with such deference to my femininity.

Vaguely I told Mother the same thing Jane had decided to tell her family—that she was going to work on a master's degree in art in the same college. That seemed logical. We both knew our parents would never be likely to find out the college had no graduate department in art. Lies—revolting lies—the inevitable deception that forced us to live in two worlds.

9

Accusation

W E BEGAN our year with the same lie. Jane was not really interested in further study. It may have been to ease her conscience that she enrolled in two courses, one in history and the other in art. Too, her original plan, of keeping house while I worked, seemed too suggestive. But inured to lies by now, I was facing more sure, more settled happiness than I had ever known. All my life I had done nothing but take. Now I could give, give myself, my money and my love. It was sometimes so hard to contain the joyous new feeling of purposefulness that my mind set down reasons for my happiness, as though to apologize.

I looked forward to teaching with an idealism that, in retrospect, seems exactly as young as it was. My ambition had two faces, both lined deep by my experiences as a student. I wanted to have the humanity so many of my own teachers had lacked, and I wanted to be stimulating. I'd have fascinating, dynamic material to work with—my own field of interest, and human beings. If I weren't good enough to transmit vital material vitally I'd give up and peddle shoestrings before I'd end by peddling platitudes.

I liked being practical. My salary of $1,500 would be adequate; if I were cautious about living expenses, I could send John a third of my check each month. It was sporting of Jane not to mind my plan to economize for this brother she'd never met but whose picture she liked because, she said, his eyes were like mine. We took the drabbest apartment we looked at simply because it was the cheapest, and while I spent the first few days in faculty meetings, Jane had the walls painted gray-green, made clever

[135]

brick-red wool curtains, and then, because she couldn't find a yellow to blend, dyed material and made slip-covers for our furniture herself. Our three rooms were so transformed that we almost couldn't enjoy them for thinking we'd cheated the landlord.

Any fear I'd had that Jane might not be content in this little Massachusetts town was quickly set at rest. The thought that I had once lived here seemed, to my surprise, enough to give her a feeling of belonging.

I was amused when, the first week, two girls met me on campus and tried to interest me in their club, not realizing that I was a teacher. I believed the students liked me, and the faculty was genial. Dr. Charpin, the chairman of the French department, gave me a desk in a large, pleasant office with four other French teachers. Ideal classroom hours left most afternoons and all weekends free for conferences and research. Besides my class in composition and conversation I taught two sections of grammar, first and second year, and a survey course in French literature. I had been teaching two months when Dr. Charpin told me that a colleague was retiring at the end of the year, and that I would inherit her course in the nineteenth-century novel on the condition that I proved my fitness as a teacher of literature in the elementary survey course.

"Teachers who say they prefer the technical language courses," he said, "are usually admitting that they're insufficient as interpreters of literature. You've indicated that you'd welcome the chance. Go to it."

I liked Dr. Charpin's frankness. The prospect of teaching some of my favorite French novelists—Stendhal, Merimée, Daudet, Zola—drove me along at a feverish pace, but Jane helped me prepare notes for lectures and grade tests so willingly that no amount of work seemed too heavy. With such help in routine business, I had time to read with the idea of preparing, meantime, a few research articles that would contribute to this career I was so serious about.

Jane's triumph turned out to be a release from which there was no turning back. She had called herself a lesbian and she meant it. The physical evidence of her change was the natural one, a feeling of inchoate ecstasy to be able to meet the challenge of sex and know the climactic experience of love which marks the difference between frustration and fulfillment. For the first time there was no feeling of strain in the desire to grow together, no feeling of fear. Jane's passion was an expression of love that I cherished with all my heart.

Her remarkable feat in having twisted shame into pride—a matter, really, of conquering her habit of acting in half-measures —was not without its price. In telling me of her sensations in lesbianism she sounded self-conscious, like a little girl speaking of her beautiful new stepmother. Deep inside me I was sorry that her newly drawn symmetry admitted the slightest bit too much pride, as if she had a new prestige. But regret scurried off shamefaced when it dawned on me that the rapture I saw in Jane now was drawn from outside herself, from me. Not only did this realization fill me with tenderness without an end; it made me feel strangely responsible.

This consciousness of responsibility was too heavy to settle into a happy satisfaction; sometimes it struck me as downright grim. It was the one thing that made me fear for our future. I was no longer free to make plans; I had to make a living. I could not follow Jane; she would have to follow me. What would be her excuse for staying with me the second year? What would be mine for having her?

Happiness has a way, however, of begging off tomorrow's worries. I placed faith in the goodness of whatever fate oversaw my personal life; and in my professional life it was enough that, right after the Christmas holidays, Dr. Charpin asked me to take the novel course the following year. So in my little world I was getting along. It had its limitations, but I was in a mood to deny them.

Several teachers lived in the same apartment house, but Jane and I had been careful not to risk hasty intrusion by encouraging callers, nor did I stop to realize what a disastrous mistake I was making in giving repeated excuses to colleagues who invited me to bridge or tea. It did not occur to me that it was important for a teacher to take part in the community life of a college; I stayed away from the Saturday faculty teas because Saturday was the only day I felt free to use a piano in the conservatory. My absences would have been excused had I been gracious enough to bother about making up for them in some way. But my fellow teachers seemed academic and dull and I evaded them, sure that I bored them as much as they did me.

Seclusion with Jane in Paris had spoiled me. I had found in Paris that a normal social life did not work out; it should have occurred to me that seclusion, our solution in Paris, would not be so simple in a small town.

I didn't even have a guilty conscience when, one afternoon in March, I found a note in my office mail box from the dean, asking me to call that same afternoon at 4:30. I had received several such notices during the year, all about committee work that Dr. Charpin had turned over to me. Any foreboding I might have had made no impression after the message I'd just received from Mother that noon. John and Lee's baby was a girl, named Diana Randall for Lee's father and me. Indeed, when I walked to the dean's office I told him of my namesake, and I remember he laughed when I said that now I'd be obligated to be fond of her even if she turned out badly.

ACCUSATION

The dean led me into his inner office and gave me a seat at his long polished table; then he sat at the end facing me. Though I'd been in his office many times, I'd never even seen his inner sanctum. I was a little curious at this stiff formality. But I liked the dean, a kind and jolly family man of fifty, an eminent scholar whose work I admired, and I believed he liked me as a teacher.

His grave embarrassment in asking his opening question was suddenly, to my horror, clue enough.

"I do not ask this personal question," he said, "because I want to. I am obliged to. Do you mind telling me how long your friend —I understand she is an artist—has been with you?"

My thoughts fought to make sense. I answered his question in too great detail and he interrupted to give me a cigarette. My hand trembled so violently I wished I had not tried to light up myself. I realized too late that no teacher had ever dared smoke before him. Then I knew he meant to be kind, and this made it harder.

He didn't know how to go on, but I knew what he wanted to say.

"There has been some criticism," he said finally, not looking at me.

I refused the thought that appalled me, and expressed regret, asking foolishly if there were complaints about my work. My voice was high, and hearing it so unnatural unnerved me. Mercy made him come right to the point.

"The teachers resent your lack of sociability," he said. "I believe you should know there have been innuendoes here and there about your friendship."

Now the dean looked at me. I had to meet his eyes. Stark fear crowded out embarrassment. For a second I couldn't speak. Then a calm, an emergency calm, blanketed my thoughts, and I could answer at last, steadily. I expressed regret that my friendship had been misunderstood, for I was aware of the implications.

Carefully, I explained that my first position necessitated orientation that took extra work and time from activities, that I had not realized that campus sociability was so important.

"We're considering contracts for next year," he went on. "In view of your training and in view of your work we do not want to let you go. Dr. Charpin recommends you highly. It isn't often we can find a good teacher who is so well liked by her students."

He suggested a compromise. I was to live in a dormitory on campus next year and ingratiate myself with the faculty. The dean made it clear without mention of Jane's name that it was not the custom for teachers to share their dormitory suites.

"Maybe you'd rather tell me tomorrow," he added. Only then did I realize I had not replied to his compromise.

"No," I said, "just give me a moment." He left me alone for about five minutes. I could hear him talking with some students in the outer office. I was so tense my hands were stiff. Of course I had been all kinds of a fool in my wishful thinking, and now I was discovered. Dishonor and shame pressed in on me—such anguish as I had never known.

Somehow, in spite of shock, my problem fell into two clear-cut questions, one opposing the other. Was my responsibility to John greater than it was to Jane? The depression had put better teachers than I on the dole; the dean didn't have to tell me that any other job for next year depended on chance. What about family loyalty, ambition, even my namesake? What about the fact that, bluntly, a husband would stand by his wife in any emergency such as this, or a wife her husband?

With that question I lost my helplessness. The dean's visitors were gone now. I called to him. I knew what my answer would be. I needed no more time.

"I can't come back," I said. "Gossip grows. I'm afraid of it. I've made a mistake, but not the kind I can get over by staying here."

ACCUSATION

It was bitterly satisfying that he reassured me, urged me to remain, even with a salary raise. I could not reconsider. My life was with Jane.

I haven't the slightest idea now what platitudes passed between us as I left his office, except that he said Dr. Charpin would not know of our conference, and he offered at once to recommend me for another position. I recall having to smile at students as I went down the hall. I recall greeting colleagues too effusively as I left campus and walked slowly home to Jane.

I could not tell Jane. She was so proud of my work, so zealous of comments she heard from students about my teaching that I could be less self-conscious about everything if she didn't know. Naturally, she was surprised when I began to talk about finding another job for the coming year. We had already made plans to take a larger apartment the next fall. Sensible excuses for my change of mind were hard to make, but I couldn't hurt her with the truth. Finally, used to indulging me, she gave up trying to persuade me to stay.

The afternoon following my talk with the dean I found in my mail the carbon copy of a letter he had already forwarded to teachers' agencies in Chicago and Detroit. I read: "Miss Frederics' excellent record as a student promised the quality we have found in her teaching," and so on, a painstaking letter of unqualified endorsement designed, I thought unkindly, to ease his own conscience. The cruelty of his generosity was the last straw. I wept until Jane shook me by the shoulders.

10

Betrayal

EARLY ONE EVENING the first of May, Jane received a telegram from her mother that her father was critically ill. "Angina pectoris," the wire had said. I knew what that meant.

Jane had not said anything. The shock had been too great. She had sat on the bed with the telegram in her hand, helpless, while I packed her bag for her to leave on the first train for Detroit.

She wired simply that her father's condition was slightly improved. The third day she wired for me to send her things, and that she would not return for the last weeks of school. Daily hasty notes spoke of a long period of convalescence for her father, during which she would stay with him.

"I must, dearest, I must," she wrote. "But my home doesn't seem my home without you. Is it terrible to say that I'm homesick even now for you?"

Then in several weeks came a long letter explaining that our plans to be together during the summer must be dropped. "Promise me," she said, "that this will make no difference to us. Tell me that you'll want me next fall wherever you go."

It was a bitter disappointment, but I answered sympathetically, knowing she was disappointed too. In a few weeks, at the end of school, I tried to arrange to see her for a few days, but she could not leave home to meet me, nor ask me to come for fear her father would be disturbed by an outsider.

I went home restless, with nothing to do, no prospects of a job, and further upset when Jane said she was too busy and too worried to write regularly now. But I must be patient. I wrote daily letters of encouragement. I knew her father must come first, but I hadn't thought angina pectoris was a matter of weeks.

Jane had been away from Detroit too many years to have friends there; she was lonely for companionship. Naturally, I was pleased when she began to mention the kindness of a young married woman, Louise, who lived in the apartment above hers. Jane enjoyed Louise's little girl, Betty, a child of five; she even had Betty draw a pig on a letter to me. Then she wrote that she was going to Toronto for the week-end; Louise was driving her. I felt lonelier than ever, for Jane had said she would call me Saturday evening, and I was afraid she would forget.

I stayed home Saturday evening, but Jane did not call. I wished she had told me where she would stay in Toronto. It would help to know whether to imagine her at a hotel or at a friend's home. She had not mentioned a friend.

June passed dully. Mother was my only pleasure, but she worried me by her concern over my health, blaming wakeful nights and loss of appetite on accumulated fatigue of years of study. Poor Mother! I couldn't tell her anything. I couldn't tell her that Jane didn't realize how lonely I was, or that she should have written more. I was glad John and Billy were not home now, for they might guess; and that Gerald was far too busy to notice.

The first of July a teacher's agency in Detroit wired me to come for a personal interview with the president of a coeducational college. Happy over the first prospect of a job, thrilled that I could see Jane, I called her for the first time in two months. Her voice sounded so natural, so sweet, I almost wept for joy. She couldn't ask me to stay with her because of her father, but I would take a room in a suburban hotel near her home. And I made plans to stay in Detroit a week, wanting while there to see a teacher of French I had met in Paris and with whom I had corresponded about plans to collaborate on a textbook.

DIANA

As soon as I arrived I telephoned Jane from the hotel. I was annoyed when she explained that she had to spend the afternoon with her father, but she asked me to come to her home for the evening.

I met the president of the college in the afternoon. When he told me my former dean was a close personal friend and that my application had been discussed between them, I flushed miserably, wondering what he might have been told. So self-conscious that I was inarticulate, I wondered, when he gave me encouragement, how I could have made a favorable impression. Evidently the dean had been humane, and once again I was thankful that I'd had grace enough to end the year with my temper in my pocket. My fear left only when the president told me that my training suited him perfectly. Now I wanted to hurry through long hours until I could tell Jane about my prospective job near Detroit.

Jane saw me from the courtyard and ran to embrace me. It was good to hear her whisper, "I love you!" I had almost forgotten how lovely her eyes were when she smiled. Her hair was changed from the quaint knot to a braid around her head; for a moment the change upset me and I felt shy until she took my hand and laughed at the face I made.

She had been sitting in the courtyard of the apartment house with her mother and father. They welcomed me warmly, and I knew I would like them both. Then, in the half-light of the evening, her chair pushed slightly outside the circle, I saw Louise. I knew it was Louise even before Jane introduced us. She took my hand with a cordiality for which I instinctively liked her. Her first words startled me.

"I hoped you weren't as lovely as Jane said you were. Now I'll have to hope you're not as clever."

Louise was naïve. I wondered what she knew of me.

During the next half hour it seemed to me that every one of

the group was, by some inadvertent design, bent on making me miserable. I hadn't expected to see Jane's father up, active, and, though I hated to be unhappy because he wasn't sicker, this surprise disconcerted me. Then Louise passed me a package of mints, saying she and Jane had gotten them at the matinee that afternoon. My heart almost stopped—yet I knew I could not have heard her right. Later I was confused when Jane's mother showed hurt surprise that I intended staying the week in a hotel, and even offered the use of the car if the distance to the teacher's house was what kept me from staying with Jane. My embarrassment was relieved when Louise's husband, Paul, came and the subject was dropped. I had been able to tell nothing by Jane's expression, not even when her parents, saying good night, had spoken of seeing me in the morning.

I liked Paul instantly, as I had liked Louise, but in my impatience to be alone with Jane I could think of nothing to say. Jane walked to the door with them as they left and I saw that Louise, in the light for the first time, was surprisingly pretty. Her round, sweet face reflected a generous and impulsive nature. She struck me as the most artless-looking woman I had ever seen. I noticed Jane take her hand as Paul turned from Louise to pick up his evening paper. Jane walked back to me, stopped for a moment, then looked full into my eyes and I saw what I needed to know even before my question was out.

"I do love you, Diana. I'll always love you."

But she had spoken reluctantly. I was frightened. Quickly I asked if she had gone to a matinee in the afternoon. Her impatient denial relieved me.

I don't know why I asked Jane if she wanted me to stay the night as her mother had insisted. Perhaps I needed to hear her say she wanted me.

"If you want to stay, Diana. Of course I'll be glad to have you."

The crisp indifference of those words terrified me. I spoke

before I knew what I was going to say. I asked Jane what Louise meant to her.

"She is sympathy, Diana. I couldn't have done without her. But she doesn't matter to us."

She did not look at me, and my fear was no less. It was like her to personalize Louise with one word, "sympathy." She had once told me I was gaiety and companionship and intimate understanding. There was a long silence before I could manage the obvious question.

Jane answered wearily, "Yes, I love Louise too."

She got up to go into the house, and held out her hand for me to follow. A distant consciousness told me I had no pride, but I could not help myself. Reason was a blindness. Stiff, hating myself, I followed without a word, not even knowing what I hoped for.

Jane took me to her room, laid out linens for me, and from a drawer handed me, without apparent recognition, the pajamas I had given her our first Christmas. I got into bed. Jane had not spoken at all. She leaned to kiss me lightly on the forehead, said good night, flipped out the light, and started to leave the room.

Quickly, my head reeling in anger, I sprang out of bed. She had answered every question in my mind. I started to dress in the dark. Jane, hearing me, came back and tried to restrain me. Her voice was tense.

"Diana, don't be an impetuous fool! I didn't know it would make this much difference. I'll sleep with you. Now get back in bed and be a good child."

Jane made me feel like a brat, and I hated her power over me. Furiously I pulled away and went on trying to dress. Anything to get away from her. She took hold of my arms and pushed me on to a low window-seat and then held me close to her, her arms full around me. I could not free myself. She tried to kiss my mouth several times, but I turned roughly from her. She kissed the back of my neck and whispered soothingly, time and again, that she loved me. At length she lay her head on my shoulder. "Oh, darling," she said, "this couldn't have happened. Not to us."

My anger died as quickly as it had come, and suddenly I felt only foolishly repentant. Jane took hold of my arm and led me back to bed. Then she walked around to her side and settled inches from me, without speaking a word. I lay tense, sick with apprehension, afraid to breathe for fear of tears. Interminable minutes passed in the darkness, minutes of threatening silence. Then Jane, leaning clear over my side of the bed, which was near the wall, tapped with her ring on the radiator pipe leading to the room above. Eight clear taps, spaced and vibrant.

Her message was simple to anyone who knew the old story of the lighthouse keeper who flashed his lights to his sweetheart on shore, flashed them as many times as there are letters in "I love you." Jane had told me the story herself, long ago.

The answering taps were staccato clear.

11

Louise

THE NEXT MORNING is indistinct in my mind. I had not slept; all night I had lain awake listening to Jane's deep breathing. She had been a little restless. I was dizzy with emotional fatigue and my heart ached to the point of physical illness. Since that night I have understood the harsh realism of the French idiom which uses the word "heart" to speak of nausea—*J' ai mal au coeur.*

I do not recall how I managed to endure a family breakfast. Afterward I made my excuses to Jane's father and mother and tried to leave at once. On the porch Jane told me I was being melodramatic.

"I could have stood a clean cut so much better," I remember telling her.

Her mother called my name from inside the house. I went back in, but Jane did not follow me. Her mother took me into the back bedroom. She was a tiny, wiry woman with kind but analytical eyes, and a perfect foil for Jane's father, a tall and large man with considerable slow charm.

"Diana, dear, you mustn't mind Jane." Her mother came right to the point. She had realized more than I had supposed. "Jane's always just had one friend at a time, as long as I can remember. I've talked and talked to her. But nothing does any good. I remember Gwen cried and Carol talked with me about it and then just got mad and let Jane alone. She just wraps herself completely—but she's so terribly fond of you. She's been with you longer than with anyone else. And you must just be patient. Jane will get bored with Louise. She's sweet, but that's all there is to her."

I wondered how much Jane's mother knew, and suspected that her confusion was genuine. I was glad she was not asking advice, but merely telling puzzling facts out of kindness. There was sudden, selfish comfort in thinking of Gwen and Carol. I had never heard of Gwen, but Carol, I knew, was Marian's sister. Now I understood why Jane had never been more than civil to Marian.

At that moment I heard Jane laughing out in the courtyard, below our window, with Louise. She was holding a pretty, frail blond-haired little girl.

"That's Betty, Louise's little girl," Jane's mother said.

Our conversation died. There was nothing more to say when Jane's mother concluded, "I've never understood Jane." But she had made me feel that she liked me, and in her artless simplicity I didn't mind her sympathy. Tears of release came to my eyes when she patted my arm. I knew she understood when I so awkwardly said, "I'll just go."

"I'll tell Jane good bye for you," she said. "Everything will be all right." She said it several times, asking me again to be patient.

I was not more than a block from Jane's home when a car stopped by the curb and Paul asked me if he could drop me at my hotel. He said, surprisingly, that he had planned to overtake me as he went to his office.

"I'd like to talk with you some time about Jane," he said. "You know her better than I do."

Paul knew too. I felt suddenly as if my problem were dwarfed by the side of his. He had social position, a home, a child to complicate matters. I was glad to be able to talk with him. He asked me to meet him for lunch.

I had been back at my hotel an hour when the telephone rang.
I was lying down, still a little nauseated. I expected it to be Jane.
It was Louise. She said she wanted to see me at once, and sounded
so worried and distressed I told her to come on up. What, I
wondered, anxiously, could she possibly want of me?

In a few minutes she knocked on my door, and I knew she
must have called from the hotel office. She was dressed in blue
and white, and in spite of her breathlessness she looked charming.
I resented being drawn to her when, practically, I should have
hated her.

She explained that to get away from Jane she'd said she was
going to her mother's home across the city. She sat on the bed
and took off her hat. Nervously she passed me a cigarette.

"My dear," she said (she had called me that the night before),
"I felt so sorry for you last night I could have cried."

I wondered what Jane had told Louise, what Louise referred
to.

"Jane has told me she never has loved anyone so much as she
loved you. She still loves you. I'll never mean to her what you
have."

What was in Louise's mind? Why this extraordinary confession? I was too dull to figure it out. Suddenly, as Louise went on
and on, it seemed unbearably painful to be talking about Jane.
There was a limit to my endurance. I wanted nothing more than
to be alone, away from everybody who had ever known her. I
wanted detachment. What had been between Jane and me must
remain ours alone. Abruptly, I told Louise I could not stand
listening to her.

I might as well have spared myself the embarrassment. Louise
went on, ignoring me. Finally I understood what she wanted.
She was afraid. Naïve and sweet, she had seen Jane ruthless.
And she was afraid. The whole melodrama took swift and ridiculous perspective. I loved Jane. I had been succeeded by Louise,

who loved Jane. And Louise, seeing the very process of my humiliation, needed to be reassured.

"Louise, don't you see?" I asked, with the release of truth exaggerated beyond reality. "Don't be so serious. Here we are, all adults. We have brains. And look at us! For God's sake, where is our dignity?"

Louise replied that I didn't understand how much she loved Jane.

I tried not to sound too unsympathetic, for she had brought me balance. I could never have seen without her; Jane would never have admitted that Louise had taken my place. It even occurred to me that Jane might herself believe the charming platitudes about loving more than one at the same time.

I told Louise I hadn't known about her until last night.

"I know that," she said. "I begged Jane to tell you. I would have felt better myself. I've seen your letters in her mail box next to mine every day, you know. I felt sick and guilty all over every time I saw one. I thought she was going to see you yesterday afternoon, but she said you'd be out last night."

Then, slowly, not to be surprised by anything now, I asked Louise if Jane had been busy in the afternoon.

"No. I thought she was going to see you until she came up to the apartment about two and asked me to go to the matinee."

I had heard Louise right when she passed the mints. Jane had lied. "Diana," she had said to me so many times, "there's nothing in this world I value more than honesty." And she had used her father as an excuse.

"It was selfishness, really, my caring how she treated you," Louise went on. "I couldn't stand for her to lie to me as she did to you. I couldn't stand it."

I was afraid Louise was going to cry. I tried to think of something to say to throw her off.

"I can't be natural with Paul. I can't eat. I can't sleep. Sometimes I'd give almost anything I ever expect to have if I'd never met Jane. I love her so much it makes me ill to think of losing her. But I will. And I've been so jealous of you I've cried myself to sleep nights. Yesterday she called me 'Diana' five times."

I was shocked by such admissions. A young married woman with a child, with such a complete lack of old-fashioned stamina —it was beyond my experience to grasp. But even greater than my contempt for Louise was my contempt for Jane for having violated a home. Louise was a fool, but Jane was neither a fool nor a weakling.

My voice was more severe than I'd ever heard it when I told Louise I had little sympathy for her.

"Diana, you can't say anything to make me feel any worse than I do. I know I'm weak. But I haven't the nerve. God, I'd give anything if I had the nerve. It's so hard on Paul. Everything is so perfect when I'm with Jane I forget how horrible it is, really. And weeks ago, when I began feeling like this, I told Paul I wanted to visit my sister in Philadelphia. I thought I'd be all right if I got away for a while. But it wasn't any use. I wrote Jane every day, I wired her, I phoned her. I hated myself, but I couldn't help it. And then when I got back Jane took me to Toronto for five days, just to get away. She was wonderful to me. I don't think I've ever been so happy in my whole life. Paul didn't know about us then. Jane doesn't know that he knows anything yet. She can be so sweet, so very sweet. Sometimes she makes me feel like such a child. She's really a wonderful person, you know."

I was equal to any number of dead words. I remember replying that Jane was very strong in will and energy. That she should have a brood of six to spend that energy on. Or a steady job of some kind.

"I've been thinking of getting a job for myself, Diana. Only there aren't any now. I don't have enough to do. Paul keeps a maid for me. I don't have anything to do, really."

Suddenly I wanted to ask Louise if she were actually as free from guile as she seemed.

"Yes," she smiled. "It isn't very smart, is it?"

She didn't mind my question. I asked another, though I had no right to. Did she love her husband?

"Oh yes! I can't imagine trying to live without Paul."

I had thought of myself as something of a student of human nature, and yet within twenty-four hours I had done little but feel helpless in an extraordinary emotional maze. I felt as naïve as Louise seemed. Louise, I had thought, was simply an unsatisfied wife. A suburban housewife, who got into trouble because she didn't have enough to do, a sentimental little pea-hen who had the emotional control of a ten-year-old. Her husband, poor devil, was in for it. I did not tell Louise, of course, that I was going to meet him.

"We try to be frank with each other about this," Louise said.

She went to the telephone and ordered drinks sent up. "I hate myself," she finally said. "So much that it's sometimes pathological. I'm not fit to be a mother. I'm no wife at all any more. And yet Jane won't promise to go away with me. She says she loves me, but she won't do anything to hurt her family. God, I'd do anything, anything if only she'd go with me. Right now I'm begging her to go to California with me for the winter. One day I think she'll go and the next I'm afraid something will happen and she won't."

I wondered if Louise would leave her little girl for Jane. Though she took my rude question with honest grace, she did not answer. The drinks came, and she gulped down her whiskey without taking the glass from her lips.

"Jane would like to have Betty too," she finally said. "She adores Betty. But Paul would never let me have her. And Jane is afraid he would understand why we went away and tell her father. She'd rather die than have her family know. Paul really does understand, of course, only she's not sure. Jane is right. He'd do anything to get Betty back. He's told me he would."

Louise was trembling; tears were rolling down her cheeks unchecked. The whiskey had made her able to cry. There seemed nothing more I could say to her. I remember seeing the picture of Louis XV on the wall for the first time. How mockingly self-possessed his face was! I hadn't noticed the Gideon Bible before, either. Too familiar. Louise was sobbing, on the verge of hysteria. I shuddered.

"It wouldn't be so awful," she said in a half voice, "if Jane didn't still love you. I've thought of suicide. I've thought of it until I'm almost crazy. But I haven't the nerve. You don't know to what depths I've gone. . . ."

I almost shouted at her to stop.

"I've got to tell you. You don't know what hell it is. I go down twenty times a day to borrow sugar or salt, anything to get a minute with Jane. I've lain on the floor of my bedroom above hers just to see if I could hear her footsteps when I'm not sure she's home. I beg her to leave her key out under the mat so I can go into her room for an hour in the morning before anybody's up, so Paul won't know. Then I'll lie awake all night hoping and praying it will be there. Sometimes it isn't, and then I almost go crazy."

Undoubtedly Louise was a masochist. Jane liked the feeling of power. She made Louise feel young, too, though Louise was her age. Here was a woman of good breeding, wallowing in a psychopathic debauch and calling it love. I wondered, not irrelevantly, why Jane sometimes failed to leave the key. And how thick the rug was on Louise's bedroom floor.

Louise held up some small, folded notes from her bag and handed them to me.

I took the notes. They were in familiar handwriting; the

daintiness of Jane's script had never failed to interest me for its studied femininity.

"My darling," one said, "please hurry down to see me! I'm loving you and wanting you every minute. Your Jane."

And the other, "Sweetheart, without your hand in mind I am afraid. Your Jane."

"Don't you think that's beautiful?" Louise asked softly. "I've never had anything she ever said to me affect me quite the way that did."

"Yes," I said. "It is beautiful. And effective."

Parting

I MAKE NO APOLOGIES for my muddled logic the week following the night in Jane's home. If what I did seems unreasonable to me in present detachment, I must remember that I hadn't the mercy of detachment at the time. The mechanism of shock, of enduring more than I could endure, had unbalanced me. I could not admit that Jane and I were finished. Not when my successor appeared to me moonstruck and sickening, not so long as I had any reason to believe Jane might still love me. Now the only thing to do was to act, act somehow, anyhow, to rid myself and Jane of this thing that had happened to our love.

Paul and I, in sympathy for each other as victims of a curious complicity, became immediate friends. His hopefulness about the outcome of his own dilemma gave me a certain support. But, most important, he became interested in me.

Paul was, to my great surprise, unaware of my own lesbianism. His suggestion that I, too, must be upset by the homosexuality involved relieved me of my first self-consciousness. If his first assumption of my normalcy was a gallantry, my own instinct to deceive was designing enough to quiet his suspicion.

Like all cynics, Paul was sentimental. The hour for a woman's sympathy was favorable. While ostensibly making every effort to save his marriage, Paul remained the essential male. He was blond, lanky, attractive, and women were no doubt easy for him. Friendship with a woman who understood his unhappiness would bolster his injured ego. In realizing this attitude, I gradually made

Paul the tool of a fantastic hope that seemed, at the time, reasonable: through him I might save Jane and myself.

The one thing to accomplish immediately was to frighten Louise back to her senses. A friendship with Paul, were it to arouse her jealousy, would solve my problem. Her situation was an impossible one, a temporary one, and a careful by-play on my part might send her back to her husband.

I moved to a hotel downtown and made plans which seemed inspired. From every point of view the end seemed to justify the means. So, with aplomb a seasoned strategist might have envied, I set my course. The only doubt I had was of my own cleverness.

In three days Jane had made no effort to see me, nor I to see her. A note from Louise had been forwarded from the other hotel, telling me Jane was hurt that I had left without saying good bye. "I don't like feeling entirely responsible for this," she wrote. "Please call her. She won't even leave the house, waiting for the phone." I did not answer the note, nor did I call Jane.

The third evening Louise asked me to dinner. Paul, though she did not know it, was in my hotel room at the time she called. He rescued me from harrowing indecision by signalling that I could not refuse. On second thought I realized that Louise, guileless to the end, had indeed done the one thing which would at this stage bring my own hopes to a climax. After three days of lunches and dinners with Paul, the psychological moment was at hand. His state of mind was exactly right. What he had begun as frank philandering had reached the point where, confused, he was beginning to ask about our own happiness. The fact that I had not let him make love to me made him even more eager.

Knowing Louise's disregard for the conventions, I should not have been surprised when Paul told me the other guest at the dinner for four was Jane. This coup astonished me at first, until I realized it was not a coup at all, but an impulse. I had to re-

member, in trying to understand Louise, that she was a masochist
—and a sentimentalist.

Paul had come for me in his car, and his last words before we
reached home had been, "See how they act together. See if you
think it's hopeless." I saw Jane as I came in, and I knew I did not
imagine the quick expression of pain on her face as she touched
my hand in briefest greeting.

Perhaps I remember this dinner so well because I have never
told anyone these things. After the first few minutes general
conversation died through self-consciousness. At the table Jane
nervously ignored me, Louise had no thought for Paul, who
talked only to me—and I tried to fit into a labored rôle without
letting Jane's voice and Paul's attentions distract me. And though
the presence of Jane made it hard for me to remain detached, this
hour was one in my life when, out of humiliation and cruelty
and confusion, there came a need to be cruel myself.

It was so much wasted effort. Except for a gay remark early
in the evening about Paul's apparent infatuation, there was no
indication that Louise even noticed. The remark was too offhand
to have any meaning. So far as Louise was concerned, my evening
was a maddening fiasco.

But there was Jane. She had seen. She was surprised and angry
with me. From the beginning she had felt the sympathy between Paul and me and had resented it boldly. Her antagonism
toward him made me wonder how long such a tense situation
could last without breaking. It was like Jane to tell me, as I left,
that she was coming to see me the next evening. Her tone was
almost a slap in the face.

Idiotically, her anger made me happy.

Paul rang my hotel the next morning and asked to come up
at once. He ordered my breakfast sent to the room and then,
without any show of feeling, he began to talk of Louise. Since

I had not told him of her visit to my room, he assumed I had not known the extent of her affair with Jane until the night before. Now he spoke more freely.

"At first I didn't take it so seriously," he said. "Louise kept saying she'd get over it. I had faith in her. She got over another woman several years ago, just two years after we were married. But this has gone too fast. This is bigger. Louise has lost her nerve.

"Then I decided to try patience. I'd let her and Jane get their fill of each other and maybe it would die a quicker death. They're not suited. Jane was just lonesome and Louise was handy. Louise was impressed with her. I can see that. She's a handsome woman. But they're not getting over it. Now I've decided I'd better go on and send Louise to California this fall to get her away from Jane. She wants to go. I've an idea she thinks it might solve the problem if she could get far enough away from Jane."

For the first time I realized the enormity of Louise's deception. I've wondered many times since: should I have told Paul what Louise had said to me about California? I did not because it was a confidence, and because, paradoxically, the thought of her deception strengthened the feeling of justice in my own.

My breakfast came and Paul arranged my table himself, and then he came over to me and sat on the floor near my chair.

"Diana," he said, "you're the one complication I wasn't prepared for. I should be thinking what I'm going to do with Louise, not you. Or what's going to happen to Betty. I'm crazy about Betty. I'm the one who insisted on having her, you know. That was when Louise was infatuated with this other woman. I thought it would help, and it did, for a little while."

After a long silence Paul looked up at me. "Diana, if we go on liking each other, and if we can see our way clear—that is if we should decide it's the thing to do—don't you think Betty ought to go with us?"

Now I had to tell Paul I could never love him. His ignorance of my lesbianism made any answer dishonest, and I knew he suspected me of sparing his feelings. The unexpected trust he wanted to give me in Betty had, more than anything else, made me loathe myself for these lies. It seemed unnecessarily dramatic, when he left me, to refuse to see him the following day before leaving. Half unwillingly, I gave in to his suggestion that he come to my room again the next morning before he went to his office. As he closed the door behind him, I could not keep back tears of remorse. The poor devil had enough lesbians concentrated on him without me.

Nothing had gone the way I anticipated. Louise, the one person who should have been affected, was untouched. Paul was hurt, and Jane was angry. Now, in a flash of perspective, I realized to what reckless lengths I had gone. In weary self-contempt I was ready to admit that from the first I had been a fool. I could hope for no more now than a peaceful finale with Jane.

The moment I saw Jane's face I knew she must be ill. She denied it. Finally, relenting at my concern, she admitted she had been having chills and fever. I made her lie down.

The anger of the night before had gone out of her voice. I wondered at her change of mood and hoped her matter-of-factness was not misleading.

"Don't complicate a mess any further, Diana," she said. "I'm sick of it. That's really all I wanted to say." Then, with painful casualness, she asked the question I feared.

I hated lying to Jane, but I had no choice now: for Paul's sake as well as my own. I told her I had seen him twice; he had taken me to lunch. If Jane knew that Paul had not spent the last three evenings at home she apparently failed to connect those absences with me. I knew Paul had given clever excuses, had called Louise during the evening, and had not stayed late.

Jane accepted my denial without expression. Then, to my amazement, as naturally as if nothing at all had happened, she held out her hand to me. Yet I couldn't go to her. When I tried to tell her why I could not, I felt my voice weakening. Determined, I shut my mind against the entreaty in her eyes.

"Child, come here." She spoke softly.

No. She could plead, command, call me "child," in a voice that was almost voluptuous. I could not go. I no longer dared to look at her.

"Diana, don't do this to me."

Still I sat dumb. Then I looked at her to speak. The sight of her face was more than I could bear.

Jane grasped me, trembling, pulled me down beside her. Then the excluding instant was past and she held me away from her, her eyes shaming me.

"I thought maybe you were using Paul to hurt Louise because you thought she had hurt you. Don't you know she couldn't hurt you, dear? Because I love you. She knows I love you."

Jane kissed my cheeks, turned my lips to hers, and the panic in her breath gave me a second's false impression that I was the stronger of the two.

Soon, in rediscovery of Jane's love, I was beyond the pain of doubt. Even the meaning of Louise faded as Jane begged me to be patient with them both until she could let Louise down gently.

"I was miserable, Diana. The whole thing went further than I'd intended. But I'd be afraid to hurt her too much now. She's been good."

With happiness in her eyes, Jane said, "Now tell me about where we're going to live this fall."

Jane asked me to wire her when I learned definitely about my position. Then she would drive to the town, close by, and make our apartment ready by September. Dimly I sensed that she knew our love as a changeless thing. I had never known before the strange passion of forgiveness.

Jane felt wretched. She still lay on the bed. I knew I should ask her to stay the night. Although I couldn't bear the thought of her leaving me, I could say nothing. When Paul called early the next morning she would know I had lied. Jane herself climaxed this anxious thought when, over late coffee, she asked if I didn't want her to stay. As she telephoned her mother that she would not be home, I prayed for a miracle, that somehow Paul might learn overnight that Jane was still with me.

The telephone was by Jane's side of the bed. Granted that Paul would call before he came up, I began to worry that Jane would reach for the phone. I recall my irritation that I couldn't think of an excuse for changing sides with her—such a little thing, so important now. I dared not think of the possibility that Paul might not bother to call first. Grimly I decided to stay awake all night. I was a deep sleeper; were I to be asleep when he came, he might ring, knock or call my name several times before I could answer. Awake, I could at least have a chance.

I undressed, kissed Jane good night, and lay down beside her. For hours after she was asleep, I lay fearful, turning often, pressing my nails hard into my palms to keep awake. Then I got up and tried to smoke a cigarette, but Jane missed me and I had to go back. And the next thing I was conscious of was the ring of the telephone. Frantically I climbed over Jane and answered.

"Diana, I've got a surprise! Can I come right up?" Paul's voice seemed to ring out over the room.

I had prepared too many careful answers in advance to have a single one ready. All I could manage was a brittle request to call again at ten and I'd attend to the matter.

If Jane noticed my confusion she was kind enough not to wonder aloud. A little later, when we went through the lobby on our way to the coffee shop, I saw Paul in a far corner, reading a newspaper. I have never known whether Jane saw him.

Jane left me immediately after breakfast, still a little ill but looking happier than I had seen her in a week. Louise, we knew, could not really matter. We would soon be together again. Meantime I could understand. I walked away from Jane's taxi feeling a vast joy I'd never expected to feel again.

A few minutes later, Paul told me his surprise. Louise had agreed to go to California within the month. I was glad for him, glad for myself. In a little while both our problems would have solved themselves.

I had been home but two weeks when Paul wrote that Louise had left with Betty for California. And that Jane had followed within three days.

"The only thing left, as I see it," he wrote, "is to tell Jane's father when he comes back next week, and have him help me set them up in an apartment. I want to be fair. But, damn it, there's nothing else left! Then I'm going out and bring Betty back—I understand from Jane's mother that Louise wired three times before Jane finally decided to go. I'm open to suggestions if you can make any."

It took me two days to compose a sensible answer. I wondered why, with every letter I wrote, I found more and more eloquent reasons to dissuade Paul from telling Jane's father before he gave Jane warning and the chance to save herself. I knew I could count on Paul's real affection for Jane's father to give sense to my plea.

13

Overlapping Affairs

I TRIED TO catch some picture of myself as I had been before
Jane. I told myself that she was not an extraordinary woman
—she had no more intelligence or charm than many others. She
did not even have real beauty. But the secret of her spell over me
remained beyond my reach, and self-reproach could not make
me want her less. With Jane I had come closer to the ideal in
companionship and affection than I had ever expected to come
with another human being.

At table, I would remember that Jane used to tease me for
waiting for my coffee to cool, that she was fond of cheddar too, or
didn't like tomatoes. Over my bookshelves in my room hung her
seascape in sinister colors, the Breton seascape she had given me
because I loved it best of all her paintings. On the end table by
my reading chair was a copy of *Jules Laforgue,* her first gift to
me, when I had known her but two weeks. The pen I wrote with;
the maroon scarf that went so well, she said, with my blue suit;
the electric clock; the blue pajamas hanging in my closet. Everything everywhere, at dinner, at reading, at writing, reminded
me of her. And all the while her eyes looked at me, and her lips
smiled ever so slightly from a picture on my desk, as if to ask if
I still wore her ring on the middle finger of my left hand; as if to
ask if I'd be patient with her.

My narrow little world, created tenderly and carefully, had
collapsed completely. I did not even have a job. Six weeks had
passed since my interview in Detroit and I had heard nothing
from the president beyond a courteous note, saying that my

application was "Under consideration." I wondered how, if my dean had suggested my abnormality, I could ever get another teaching job, or how I could support myself if this one prospect did not materialize. I felt new sympathy for the woman who peddled vanilla extract from door to door in our neighborhood.

To make things worse, I had to rely on Gerald for my support. Having sent John money every month, I had saved nothing. Mother made no effort to hide her resentment that I had given up my job. I could not bring myself to tell her I had been fired: better for her to think it was pure impulse, as perhaps it had been, really. I could stand her anger.

I ran an announcement in the papers, did not neglect mentioning having studied in New York and Berlin, and within a week I had five piano pupils, all under ten.

It was the end of September when the president of the college wired me. I had given up all hope of the job when an apologetic telegram explained that the enrollment had exceeded expectations and asked if I were available.

The night before I left home I took a large wooden box up to my room and wrapped my etching, my painting, my clock, my books, my pajamas, everything that Jane had given me, even her picture and my ring, and stored them far back in my closet.

School had been under way a week. Fellow teachers were very kind in helping me to get started, but no one interested me. For too long I had been in a state of overexcitement. Now I was dulled into lethargy. I snapped out of it only when I heard from one of the elderly dormitory matrons, who meant well, that my colleagues thought Paris had made me snobbish. I didn't want to repeat the mistake of the last year, and I did care profoundly whether my students thought my teaching good teaching.

During the year I heard from Louise twice—a note in October mailed from Los Angeles told me of her tormented conscience and her hope for my happiness. She did not mention Jane. I answered briefly, with a civilized sentiment. A postcard a month later told me that Jane had made her promise not to write again.

Jane herself first wrote me on my birthday in the fall, a date she had made much of. My heart leapt to my throat when I saw the envelope in her writing, but her best wishes for happiness sounded very strange in their formality and I wished she had not written at all.

Several more letters came at irregular intervals during the year —all written with labored facility, all asking me to write; the last one said she wanted me, and I brooded for days for I knew it was only a fleeting mood. I could mail none of my answers; they were either too bitter or too affectionate. The year's scattered correspondence ended with a letter from Louise just before the end of the school year; she asked me to meet her in Chicago on my way home for the summer. Curiosity overcame discretion and I met her in the bar of my hotel.

Over cocktails Louise told me of her winter in California with Jane, months of guilty tears alternated with happiness that was spotted with Jane's nostalgia for me, and months of constant fear of Paul. I had not heard recently from him. He had not answered my letter—for months—and then he had written only a short note saying he was turning his worries over to God. His phrasing had led me to believe he was joking, but now, in answer to my questions about Paul, Louise was telling me, as casually as if she were speaking of the weather, that Paul had become an ardent convert to religion.

"I can't imagine what got into him," Louise added. "He studies at it evening after evening. If it makes him as happy as it seems to, though, I guess it's all right."

This news was no more astounding than Louise's lack of perception. Though I could not imagine the satisfaction of the escapist's lot, I could sympathize. I wondered then, as I still do, exactly how much my own rôle in his existence had had to do with it.

But their story is no longer my own. The amazing twist came after their story was told, when Louise took my hand across the table and said,

"But the most awful part of the whole thing is that I love you too. And Jane knows it."

I like to think now that I was struck dumb by the broad farce of such a near-perfect triangle in which practically everybody loved everybody else. Only my failure to love Louise kept the triangle from farcical perfection.

I tried not to be unfeeling, but my sympathy for Louise's neuroticism had long since dried up. A little later, I felt a curious satisfaction when she asked if she might spend the night with me. I did not want her and I was afraid she would be tearfully affectionate. On the other hand, the prospect of being able to hurt Jane through Louise was suddenly an ambition. Louise had said that Jane knew she was with me. Revenge would be very sweet. I had often wondered why, in my whole life, the emotion of vindictiveness had never been a part of my nature. I had often thought what a satisfaction it must be. It would not have occurred to me now had Louise not made it obvious.

She clasped my hand as we started to my room. I felt sure of myself, contemptuous of her. Inside the room Louise took off her hat and raised her lips to me. I hadn't thought she would look so sweet and appealing with her hair loose. I kissed her and held her in my arms, even a little casually. She startled me. It had not occurred to me that caressing Louise could be so delightful. I had never kissed such full, soft lips, and I felt a strange creeping pleasure in the touch of her instantly warm flesh—everything the nicer for my disinterested recklessness.

When at length Louise pulled me down beside her on the bed, my detachment completely gave way. The thought pierced me for the first time: I was no better than Jane. I didn't even have Jane's excuse of affection. Further, I was "getting even" like a shopgirl, and using a weak-willed neurotic to do it.

Louise's lips lingered on my arm; finally she said, "I want to be yours, darling." It was a trick of Jane's, a common enough trick, but she said it with Jane's intonation. I had it coming to me.

I held her away from me. I tried to be tactful, but it took me only a minute to explain. As I might have known she would, Louise reacted with a generosity I did not deserve. When she left me, shortly after, I felt nothing but simple-minded foolishness that my joke had soured without warning and so very quickly.

Indirectly, from her, my vague notions about lesbian *mores* took on unavoidable form which I had long shied at accepting. Normal or abnormal, nymphomaniac or not, Louise's complete freedom from any thought of infidelity was indicative of something askew about lesbian morals. I hated the thought. Without making the mistake of generalizing from her example of instability, I nevertheless feared that certain conclusions were inevitable. Just what was the attitude of lesbians toward sexual loyalty, fidelity? Did infidelity imply dishonesty, as it did in the heterosexual relationship? Was I ridiculously idealistic in imagining that an outlawed human relationship could last of its own strength?

There had been Elise, Elizabeth, then Jane, and now Louise, all of them following a solitary destiny that was without discipline, all of them shirking loyalty, and more than willing to temporize. But why? I asked the question as naïvely as I answered it, as if the attitude of their kind could not be mine. Perhaps, I thought, they had found that it was too costly to take love seriously. Perhaps they had learned to condition themselves to loving lightly. Or, really, was my answer naïve?

Of course it was natural enough that the homosexual would

approach intimacy more quickly than the normal person. The very lack of any kind of social recognition of the union gave it a kind of informality. Normal love, having to consider property and children, had to assume responsibilities that were of no consequence to the homosexual. Fear of conception, a deterrent to the consummation of normal love, was no problem to homosexuality.

I wondered at the overlapping of affairs. Jane's love for Louise had impinged on my love, and Jane, with respect to Louise, apparently considered herself no less faithful for having told me she wanted me. Although I could rationalize it all, understand it, still I hated it. Overlapping seemed messy, and I scorned a system of hunting, opportunizing, guarding as a frantic, cheap substitute for the kind of love I wanted: one based on mutual interests, companionship, sympathy, and loyalty.

So far as I could see, the odds against happiness in the lesbian relationship were double what I had first imagined them. No longer was it a single question of enormous social pressure from without; but even more insidious, of slipshod mores from within. The lesbian liaison had no more strength than the weaker of its two partners.

It was not a question of conventions, or lack of them. It was a question of human nature. Human nature didn't have size enough by itself; it had to be harnessed by rule. If it couldn't be made to conform to rule, as it had to in the normal world with church and law acting as referees, it wouldn't conform at all. Granted that human weaknesses showed up the rules as anything but foolproof, the fact remained: formalization was a guarantee, a consolation, that these same human weaknesses demanded.

The lesbian's development of a callous casualness might be compensation by over-compensation; it might even be a kind of heroism. But I had observed somewhere, somehow, that the promiscuous voluptuary finally comes to savage loneliness in his search for a life more satisfying than conventionality permits.

14

I Meet Leslie

VERY FORTUNATELY, pain burns out and apathy becomes intolerable to the active person. My second year without Jane began with more success as I tried to regain self-assurance in the sterile rewards of the academic world. I had written enough to experiment a little now on my defenseless students with a few "cultural articles" on French life. These would be my main contribution to the textbook that was slowly taking form with my colleague in Detroit.

I told myself that Jane of the present was dead to me, however vital remained the Jane of memory. No matter what I thought of her deception, her love had at least taken the bitterness out of my trial of adjustment to a world hostile to my kind. I had loved, I had been loved, and I had learned. I understood much better now. I had expected too much of love. I had given too freely and taken too eagerly without knowing the price of too intimate intimacy. If ever I loved again, it would be with reservation. If I couldn't trust lesbians, I could at least trust myself.

Mother came to share an apartment with me this year. John had found a temporary job at home, and he would remain there with his family. Now I would support Mother instead of sending money home. Just a week after school started, a college sorority sister back in town after a year abroad adopted me into her circle of friends. They seemed fun, and the sudden tempo of social life was exciting after a lonely year. It seemed very long since I had lived in a man's world, very long since I had shared anything with men. I hadn't known how much I had missed the male point of view, male attentions, male *esprit*.

Mother, delighted to see me socially active once more, scored test papers for me evenings so I could go out with a clear conscience. My immediate favorite among the men was Hal, a young lawyer, a good-looking sombre-eyed middle westerner whose dry wit was full of surprises. Hal was easy-going, an extrovert, a strapping, healthy soul whose friendship was good. He was engaged to a girl in Boston; I could be sure that with him I'd not be faced with the problem of how to treat a man; he was too much in love to want more than a listener.

On one occasion during this period I met a lesbian, Eleanor, a friend's sister who was visiting from New Orleans. I had gone to a dinner party with Hal, and the moment I entered the room I was conscious of her. She said nothing beyond formalities when we were introduced, nor did I. Though I was afraid my imagination was playing me false, the impression persisted: I saw through her just as she saw through me.

Later in the evening Hal asked me to imitate the showy jazz pianist we had heard several evenings before at a night club. I noticed Eleanor's face as I played, and though my sudden change of mood surprised the group, I went on with a Chopin nocturne. Nobody listened now but Eleanor. That didn't matter. Her expression had lost its amused contempt. After that, it was impossible to be calm about her, and I wondered why all my senses became overclear in her presence, why both of us were so full of intuition that everything we said to each other seemed to trail off without a climax, as if the other already knew.

I cannot explain how I knew she was a lesbian, nor how she knew I was. The seventh sense of lesbian recognition is hard to make convincing. Homosexuals must learn to condition themselves to recognizing one another in much the same way that a

blind man develops his sense of touch. Mistakes are costly con-
ditioners. Eleanor gave the impression of femininity, almost of
fragility. Though she appeared to be the picture of merry sociability, her eyes gave her away. They were full of a melancholy
that seemed wistful when she was in repose, half-malicious when
she was speaking. Her engagement ring did not deceive me any
more than did the fact that she was very popular with the group,
most of whom she had known before. It was quite possible that
being familiar with this circle of friends she would have no feeling
of self-consciousness in mingling with them.

I was with her alone for only five minutes, when, late in the
evening, she followed me upstairs. I was sitting at the vanity
table in the guest room. She looked pale and tired, and when
she smiled at me I felt a stir of sympathy very close to an intimacy as unreasonable as every other emotion I had felt about her.
Eleanor walked to the window and stood, looking out, seeing
nothing, her profile toward me.

"Could you possibly understand," she asked, finally, "if I were
to tell you I've known you for a very long time?"

Her face was still averted, and her voice trailed off as if she
were speaking a line from a play. When she looked at me her
eyes were filled with pain. She turned away again; her profile
was very lovely.

Suddenly I sensed that she was dramatizing herself. This was
unexpected. It threw me off. With stilted poise I passed her
remark lightly and went on combing my hair.

"I thought you'd know," she said. "I'm afraid I've been awkward."

Only after she had gone did it occur to me that I had been
unkind. She was halfway down the stairs when, disgusted with
my niggling efforts to be analytical, I called to her. She turned
back so quickly I had the impression that she had expected me
to call.

"I didn't mean to be so stupid," she said. "I only wanted to ask something which is very personal. It seemed important then. It doesn't now. . . . I only wanted to know if you were beaten too."

She put her hand on my shoulder, as if she were seeking support. Only a moment passed between us, a searching moment in which self-consciousness shaded into ineffable understanding. The mood was shattered by Hal, who called to me. Though it was brief, it was to become a meaningful memory. It was not until some time later that I could understand any reason for her oblique confidence.

Eleanor went back to New Orleans before I could see her again. Five weeks later Hal called to tell me that Eleanor was dead.

"Overdose of sleeping powders," he said. "Just a month before she was to be married."

She was buried the same day her letter arrived. Addressed to me at the college, it bore no heading, no ending, not even a signature. But I did not need the postmark to identify it.

It was a quotation from Conrad Aiken:

> "That is not love that takes but what it finds
> In a dark hour. If frightened here, we cling.
> It is not love, it is a transient thing.
> Say afterward: We did not love, but only
> Together turned for one inscrutable moment,
> Held in the hands of the infinite, being lonely.
> This is an intimacy we shall forget.
> We shall be strangers yet."

I never told Hal that Eleanor had dramatized even her death.

I look upon this period as an excursion back into the normal world. Now that I had become a lesbian, the change I found in my point of view toward normal society astounded me. First of all, sensitive to my chilly spot in the social sun, I looked around me to see where I might possibly fit in. But Society, as Gide had said, eternally predestined one sex for the other—indeed it urged thoughts of love with monotonous stimulation, one sex for the other, in literature, the movies, the radio, the newspaper, the example of elders, the example of social gatherings, the very scene of the streets. None made any recognition of the homosexual. There was no point in daring to hope. I had been through all of that. Growing a little older and wiser had made no difference.

With young women, my physical kin, I could never feel at ease. I was neither domestic nor maternal, and their constant talk of clothes, men, babies and a home, always gave me an exasperated sense of impotence. Most of them were so conscious of being wives or sweethearts that I could not regard them as individuals, but rather as so many halves to partnerships. No matter how lightly some few of these women took their obligations to their partnerships, there was about them all an intrinsic impression of stability. They weren't conscious of it, any more than they were of their breathing apparatus or the color of their skin or anything else they accepted as a birthright. They may even have thought of themselves as restless. But I doubt if they thought of themselves as useless, or searched for justification for having been born. They were the women who carried on, who took care of their men and gave them sons and daughters to carry on. Whether carrying on had any point was not the question. The question was individual salvation, and that could be theirs. That was their stability, whether they knew it or not, and if they were wise, that was their choice.

With men, my spiritual kin, I had a choice of behavior. Feigning femininity, I had to resist those omnipresent males who are eager to protect the single woman from the bugaboos of sex-starvation—and, I noticed, the farther behind the single woman's girlishness, the more frankly physical becomes the approach. Men did not want and would not tolerate platonic friendships except as a convenience—as with Hal, or, as a gallantry, when I wore my ring. Otherwise it was looked upon as a frustration, something to break into, and then to be proud of having broken into—either by skirmishing with elaborate artifice or, at least quicker and less boring, coarse bargaining. Whether the approach was via soft lights and soft words or hard wit and hard liquor, the libido was the same; there was no sidetracking the Great Hunt, and its perseverance was an almighty bore.

Yet, if I let careful femininity relax, there was the insufferable alternative of being slapped on the rear like a brother Elk and tagged a "good sport"—which meant that my sense of humor was tested to the breaking point—and sometimes with rank vulgarity.

My excursion into normal life turned into a mere search for distraction. Shocked by Eleanor's death, assailed by doubts that I myself could ever find an orderly design to live by, I began to drink. Heretofore, guarding my natural taste for liquor, I had been purely a social drinker. Now I followed the easiest way I knew of draining myself of the fear that I would be beaten, too. I had always hated the shrillness and looseness of drunken women, and I flattered myself that I was careful for this abhorrence. Notwithstanding, only when I was fortified by liquor did the normal world seem worth the candle. I wasn't sure even then, but my neighbors, seen through a dulling haze, seemed at the time better than no neighbors at all.

Mother, meantime, was left alone evening after evening. Unwilling to let me forego any pleasure, she arranged to take in a student from the woman's college to keep her company. I was glad for her when a girl of about twenty-one, a senior biology student, wanting the chance to escape dormitory regulations, moved into our back bedroom. Her name was Leslie.

Her voice impressed me even before I met her; the afternoon

she moved in I heard her singing softly in her room across the hall. She was singing snatches of popular songs and what words she did not know she improvised with such originality that I caught myself listening. The effect was so comical, yet her voice was so happy and so appealing, that almost before I knew it I was impatient to meet her.

She was embarrassed when she came out of her room, a human skull under one arm and a femur under the other, and realized that I'd been listening. I was in turn so startled by her macabre baggage that we laughed even before bothering to introduce ourselves.

"I'm Leslie," she said. "And I don't always carry bones around. A girl in the dormitory gave these to me, and I had to keep them as long as I was there. Do you blame me for moving? I hope I don't frighten your mother before I reach the incinerator."

She dressed with taste, had a gay, wide smile, a voluptuous figure, and her speaking voice was as soft as I'd imagined it would be, with an appealing trace of huskiness. That was all I observed of her the first few weeks she was with us. We were both busy and our schedules did not fit each other's free time. Mother liked her, was not in the least intimidated that Leslie's dean had described her, albeit affectionately, as a "problem child," and said in turn herself that Leslie was interesting.

Then one night when I came in from an evening with Hal, Leslie was sitting alone reading by the fireplace. Mother had gone to bed. I was in high spirits, and I joined Leslie. We talked for over an hour. I was interested in the story of her name, and I repeat it because of its psychological significaance.

"Dad wanted a boy," she said. "There were already two girls, Alice and Jean, and Dad had concentrated for months on a boy. You see, Dad was in a law firm that had had sons in it for four generations. I was to be Henry 3d. And when I came, Mother says Dad wouldn't look at me until she came home from the hospital. I was a bald-headed baby, though, and that tickled him when he finally saw me. He wanted to name me Henrietta as second best, but finally compromised on Leslie because that could be for either sex. Then he nearly ruined me by calling me 'Dad's boy' all the time. I thought I was a boy until I was almost six. That was the great tragedy of my life." Leslie smiled. "I'll never forget it. I was wanting to hop wagons with the boys when mother told me little girls didn't play like that. 'But I'm *not* a girl,' I cried. 'I'm a boy. I'm Dad's boy.' I wouldn't believe Mother until Dad came home and Mother made him tell me he'd just called me a boy for fun. As a matter of fact, I'll never get over wishing I were a boy. And it probably sounds idiotic, but for years afterward I thought of myself sometimes as a boy. Somehow I've always felt cheated."

Leslie was curled up in a big armchair in a beige flannel robe, her short dark auburn hair tucked behind her ears, her white skin showing an impish trace of freckles, her lips full and red. It was nice that she seemed wholly unconscious of her loveliness.

Yet I knew, as surely as if she had said, "I am a lesbian." It seemed incredible. It was incredible, foolhardy, even for all psychology's dogma about the decisiveness of character formation during the first five years of life. But as days went by I continued to think of Leslie as a lesbian, in spite of my reason, in spite of the fact that I was more and more convinced that she didn't even know it herself. The thought that she attracted me was, perversely, appalling. Her very ignorance held temptation remote.

I knew my position intimidated her and possibly my superior experience in years. Anyway, Leslie came to look up to me, to revere my opinions, even to emulate my tastes. God knows why. Though I dreaded thoughts of a crush, it was stimulating to have an eager listener, it made me feel fresh and intriguing, it awakened proclivities, and restored the spirit that life in normal society had deflated.

Had we met on equal terms, my sense of responsibility toward an inexperienced girl who did not recognize lesbianism in me any more than in herself would not have held me fastened to scruples. Moreover, I resented the thought, unreasonable in my sensitiveness, that advances toward Leslie would be taking advantage of a guest in my own house.

Gradually, inevitably, I began to feel myself respond to Leslie and, unable to face another period of having to resist every impulse, I determined to ignore her. I was beyond the point of being satisfied with little. I had had my share of hungry dreams and schoolgirl flummery. I wanted all or nothing. Experience had hardened; my strength was no longer a matter of patience. Leslie could go on looking at me, her eyes hurt and bewildered. I had to consider myself. Hal was enough, perhaps, to help me out of this.

I went on with my round of dances, dinners, hated them, hated running away from myself, drank alarmingly for a teacher who pretended to care about professional reputation, and ended—I shouldn't have been surprised—in an idiocy that will be my shame forever.

Hal and I were on a week-end house party with two other couples. I had not been drinking. Hal was lying on a dark hill just above a great tiled swimming pool, and I was still in the water, alone now that the others had gone inside. I didn't want to leave the wind of a rising storm, the thrill of lightning. Having the pool to myself was glorious. When I got out to dive, Hal called to me. I wanted to be alone—I pretended not to hear—but he came down to the pool and asked me to join him on the hill. Reluctantly I did. I flung myself down on the grass, scarcely conscious of him except to wish vaguely that he'd go away and not intrude between me and the smell of the night. Then he seemed to become a part of that odor and when, suddenly, he kissed me, the hardness of his lips astonished me as much as the fact that he had touched me at all. A protective instinct warned me that I had on only my swimming suit and a loose beach robe, and even as I thought of it Hal tore my robe back and I felt his mouth on my arm. "So sweet, so sweet," he kept saying.

Doubtless Hal thought I wanted him. I had told him I wanted to stay here when the others went in. Now I held him off and looked at him, and saw his eyes shining with desire and happiness. In spite of myself I was touched to see his smile, a little shy, to hear him say, "Diana, this has been coming on for days. It isn't right. I can't do anything about it. But I love you."

My resentment melted into shame that I had felt scornful of him. He was good, he was sweet. There was no use in blaming my incapability on men and calling it their lack of taste. I could at least make Hal happy. That was something to be glad for. Maybe that was my forte in life, making others happy—giving some poor worked-up devil relief from knots I had put in him. Maybe that would make me happy too. One can't give esctasy, surely, without feeling something pleasant. So, as a gesture of penitence for my thoughts, I put my arms about him and drew his lips to mine.

I would give myself to Hal. With an objectivity more cold than reasonable, I decided that a sense of sinning would itself be a relief. Then, even as I returned his kisses, I knew that an indescribable sense of remoteness kept me from that satisfaction. It takes temptation to make a sin.

Ashamed that I couldn't even be ashamed, something happened to me. It was nothing Hal had done or said. It was the gesture I had made, and I shall always wonder whether the clarifying power of the water had anything to do with it. Whatever it was, I was not aware of it until it had taken place. It was as if my conscience had set a mirror in front of me, a mirror that flashed back a caricature of a lesbian caught disavowing her nature, violating it by trespassing in the normal world. It struck me that she was like a stubborn patient who resists ether for fear of losing the same consciousness that causes pain. And by the looks of her eyes, she was beaten.

Thrusting Hal away from me, I got up and ran toward the house.

PART IV

Leslie

Leslie and J Become Lovers

THE NERVOUS TENSION under which I had been living in the normal world, the late hours I had been keeping, and my gnawing love for Jane eventually took their toll of me. I suffered from what amounted to a nervous breakdown and was sick in bed for five weeks. Three weeks of that time are almost a complete blank. The only times I felt anything at all were the times I could hear Leslie singing in her room. Something about her voice made a swelling come to my throat; her tones were true and so lovely that I wanted to call to her to stop.

Ever since the beginning of my illness, when Leslie and I had come to know each other well, I had seen the striking parallelism between her relation to me, and my own to Jane four years before. Over and over she showed me myself at her age: independent, hypersensitive, even with the same type of flippant, defensive humor. Most significant, Leslie was brooding for release from an old confusion I knew only too well. But I had known why when I used to brood; she did not.

With no shade of conceit I saw her affection for me, fearful as mine had been for Jane, and so apparent as to make Mother comment. I was thankful for it. I needed it, every bit of it. It was warm and thrilling to look at Leslie's loveliness and the tender sensuality of her face, to think, even before I had touched her, that we would be lovers. Though I felt a little odd about it, like a seer, I knew I was on familiar ground. There was exhilaration in my detachment, an irresistible sadistic amusement mixed with anticipatory joy.

I wanted to be very careful. Leslie was inexperienced, and I could not offend that inexperience. I still assumed her ignorance of her lesbianism; she had even spoken naïvely of feeling ill-at-ease with men. Though I would never take the responsibility of persuasion, by word or action, I told myself that the chivalric normal-world reluctance "to start a girl off" was only a relic of the old-fashioned drummer's sentimentalism. At the same time, I became conscious of a gentleness with her that was almost maternal.

I had not known when it would happen. Now I knew it must be this night.

It was raining, a soft and voluptuous spring rain, and I was glad that Leslie, too, was conscious of the sound and smell of it. We had been talking in my room, late, over a glass of sherry, talking almost in whispers, afraid of missing the sound of rain on the roof. Then Leslie got up to leave.

I looked at her, standing by my lamp to examine an etching Carl had given me. Her head was a little to one side, her hair tousled, her mouth solemn, her pajama coat half-opened in careless undress, the soft contour of her breast against flesh-colored silk. A tight, wild excitement possessed me and I was afraid to try my voice. It seemed in that moment that I had never wanted anything in my life so much as I wanted Leslie. In a strange new way I knew I loved her. And everything made sense. I was confident it made sense.

I was sitting in my big easy chair, and I did not get up. Very casually, excitement suppressed, I asked if she would like to stay with me. My casualness was overdone. After I had spoken I felt cold fear that she might understand (or was it not understand?) and refuse. Quickly, before she could answer, I told her I wanted her to be very sure of herself. Still it sounded inadequate and I became entangled in my own gaucherie. Leslie said something about having to bathe, but she did not look at me, and I knew I had confused her. When she left at once I was relieved, but I no longer wondered if she had understood. Intuition, not reason, told me she would come back.

I went to bed, tense and frightened. I hadn't thought I would be frightened. Mother had long since been asleep in her room. I couldn't hear Leslie at all after she left the bath. I began to wonder if I had not made a spectacular blunder and misjudged her. Had I placed her in the position of having to apologize for what she was not and could never be?

After interminable minutes very light footsteps hesitated before my door and went away. I heard Leslie come to my door and go away three times within an hour, and, though I ached with pity and had to curb my impulse to go take her hand as I would a child's, I could not let myself do that; it would spoil everything. If she came to me it must be entirely of her own will.

It must have been another half hour before my door opened and Leslie tiptoed to me through the darkness, and stood by my bed trembling violently. I took her hands and drew her down. Awkwardly, she sat on the very edge. The coldness of her hands shocked me.

I whispered to her and kept her hand and, contrary to my fears, I felt not in the least like a scheming seducer. I remember the unforeseen sensation of sadness that affected me as she sat there. After minutes grave with fear, she put her head on my shoulder. The gesture was like an impulsive plunge taken after long hesitation.

Her hair was soft and exciting, but I did not dare caress her. Anything could happen were I hasty; I could not afford the risk of impetuosity. Finally I lifted her face with the slightest touch, and felt her cheek cool against mine. Then she clasped my hand and turned her lips to me. I kissed her tenderly, much more tenderly than I felt. When I tried to hold her away from me, to see her eyes, she shook her head and clung to me with a little involuntary cry. I knew I would remember this always.

She had not spoken a word. With an air of sudden determination, she got up, took off her robe, and then lay back on the pillow, her arms stiff and close to her sides. The responsibility which was suddenly mine made me falter in a panic, and I heard myself telling her over and over again not to be sorry. Then for the first time she spoke. Her timid whisper was very sweet and what she said surprised me.

"Diana, are *you* sure you're glad I came?"

I kissed her, and felt my own lips tremble. My tongue was so paralyzed I could do no more than whisper, "Oh God! Oh God!" so solemnly that I sounded as if I were praying when I'd meant to sound glad. I touched her face, her arms, now almost warm. The odor of her freshly bathed body was tantalizing, and, holding her closer, I could feel her relax as fear gave way.

I felt her breast warm and full against me, and when I kissed her again the change in her amazed me. No longer fearful, her abandon was a little wild. Her lips became soft and resilient in extraordinary kisses of experienced passion. Though her passion made restraint hard, the very fact that she was so swiftly subject to my will made me the more cautious.

Egotistically, it hadn't occurred to me that she might have experimented with men too. In her experience she had learned more than I had suspected she knew. Egotistically again, it was satisfying to know her experience was limited to normal love. I had never known until this very moment the gratification of being first—as great a point of sentimental pride to the lesbian as to the normal lover.

For fear of startling her, I did not kiss her body. I felt she trusted me not to startle her. But soon, when she impulsively threw her arms about me and cried, "Please let me say it—I love you, I love you!" I was acquitted of all fear of shocking her.

[186]

LESLIE AND I BECOME LOVERS

The next few days were difficult because experience compelled me to a degree of caution which seems, in retrospect, almost carping. Leslie's childish simplicity, her exaltation, made it difficult to remain as reasonable as I wanted to be, but I kept telling myself that I would never enter into another liaison with a lover who was more blind than aware. It was better to delight in Leslie's grace with lingering appreciation, to let her temper herself gradually to the relationship for which she had had no mental preparation. The mental, I had learned, not only set the tone of the physical: there was even the question of its permitting the physical.

Even so, I never feared. Leslie loved; that was enough. She was not going to have attacks of remorse and self-accusation. She was not unaware; rather she gave the impression of having been born with complexities already worked out, merely waiting for the time to make everything right. Leslie was born to know more of the technique of love by sheer instinct than Jane could ever learn in practice. When at last I could show Leslie the full satisfaction of lesbian love I was confident that her passion would be unafraid.

"My floundering is over," she said one night. "My questions have all shot wide. Now I know. My body and my brain are sort of synchronized. Each knows what the other is up to. And for the first time in my life, my mind can approve."

Her attitude seemed too simple. She had not wept, bewildered, with her first experience, as Jane had. She had only lain lifeless, insensible, scarcely breathing, and when I kissed her lips she tried so heroically to respond that I told her not to move. At length I covered her body and felt the flesh warm. To my surprise it quivered at my touch. I reached for a glass of water on my bedside table, but she whispered that she didn't want to drink. So very long she lay without moving that I became worried. When I spoke to her she laughed ever so lightly and then, in a

[187]

half whisper, swore an exuberant stream of oaths. I was at once amused and taken aback. I felt foolish to know, with all my resistance, that I had been overcareful. Then, because her flesh had quivered, I knew she was not finished with wanting me.

Leslie's joyous appetite soon led me to see how unsatisfying my sex relations with Jane had been. Now, in Leslie's passion, as hungry for my body as it was demanding of its own satisfaction, I knew a pleasure I had never known before. The little shiver of surprise I knew that Leslie should be so eager to please me was a constant delight and, more than any other one thing, told me that I had never appreciated before what mutuality in the sex act could mean. Nor how instantly trustfulness in the lover could free the mind of doubts. Leslie's skill dissolved all the bitter fears I had known with Jane: the fear of strain in an effort to grow together, or of anxiety that consummation might not be achieved.

The surprise I felt that Leslie would have no understanding of Jane's shame marked—and I do not believe I exaggerate—the end to a large and general dilemma.

With all my heart I envied Leslie her hard-shelled realism even as I marvelled at its strength. I wondered how it would feel to be free from a consciousness of being queer enough to horrify the squeamish. She would, I knew, be fairly safe from hurt, and I was willing to profit, if possible, by her happy example. It was with profound surprise that I came to realize, within our first few months, that the pupil had turned out to be the teacher. Leslie had been born with a wisdom it had taken me years to acquire.

From the first I was frank with her. I told her I wanted never to love again as I had loved Jane; indeed I wondered if I ever could. I ought to have known better, but the chance to be honest was too novel to resist. I knew Leslie was by nature a little hard and wild, anything but a sentimentalist, and she seemed to

understand when I counted on her to forgive me for being sentimental about Jane.

"I'm lucky to have you at all," she said. "I'd be a fool to complain about anything. That is over. You're partly the way you are
because of Jane. I couldn't very well hate anything that made you
the way you are, could I?"

It was natural enough, I suppose, that I would overdo now
on the side of frankness, as I had once overdone on the side of
ignorance, but I was to be a long time in learning my mistake.
My love for Leslie was no less thrilling for its certain protective
detachment, a recognition of self removed from affection. Love
was a close loveliness and sharing, a strength and a vast tenderness.
No one could ask for more. But it would never again make me
servile to its witless power or tear down a feeling of separateness.
I never lost sight of exactly what Leslie meant to me, physically
satisfying and mentally stimulating or, unselfishly, what my
affection meant to her. As the year with her drew to an end, I
was ready to admit that this was the healthiest happiness I had
yet known.

There is in the homosexual relationship one peculiar problem
of intimacy which until now had plagued me ever since I had
known I was a lesbian. Since adolescence I had avoided as tactfully
as possible the commonplace of women's use of the bath in one
another's presence. During my life in the sorority house I had
tried to harden myself, but I was never able to accept such intrusion without embarrassment that had to be covered or draw a
natural jibe. Telling myself that I was finicky over a trifle never
helped me get over the sickly shock of feeling like a Peeping
Tom.

After I realized my homosexuality I avoided the use of the
toilet in common with other women even at cost of physical dis-
comfort. Where the sharing had been distasteful, it now offended

me as something obscene. And I deeply appreciated the esthetic sense of the rare normal woman whose respect for the physical niceties restrained her from seating herself until I had left the lavatory, whether in a dormitory, theatre or shop.

In my relationship with Jane the problem of this intimacy had been one that habit never made less irksome. I hated to admit to the annoyance I felt in her disregard of my privacy. She was unconscious of my distaste, of course, but I wondered eternally why she was also oblivious to the fact that the intrusion was always hers and never mine.

My attitude is a common one with lesbians who never learn to accept other women as freely as they themselves are accepted. Leslie shared my repugnance. At risk of sounding slightly ridiculous, I admit that her tact was a Godsent relief from years of helpless embarrassment with the thoughtlessness, even crudities, of normal women.

It was difficult for Leslie and me to hide behind careful amiability before Mother. The guilty necessity of checking the spontaneity of a lover's greeting, a lover's smile, was irritating. Leslie, not so conscious of the need of hypocrisy as I, had at first been cross and impatient that I would never let her come into my room until Mother had gone to bed. But we had no choice. I had had a miserable hour giving excuses to Mother about my sudden decision not to see Hal any more. She liked Hal, and I did not want to risk hurting her any more than I already had that year.

Night after night Leslie came stealing into my room. If I was asleep she would arouse me by crawling into my arms. And how tender I would feel to know that she had come in to me—how alive to her touch that shot like a delicious current along the surface of my body until, trembling unbearably all over, I would turn and crush her to me.

Never would I let her stay until morning, and never did she

come that I was not stricken with the fear that Mother might have heard her, or our whispers, and might possibly suspect. But this was another useless fear. I should have realized that Mother, like Jane's mother, belonged to a generation whose knowledge of homosexuality was remarkably limited. Jane's mother had simply been confused; mine, separated from me since I had gone away to college at sixteen, and for years deluded, was not likely to suspect that there was anything abnormal in my friendships.

Jane had resented the intrusion of the normal world by being ill-tempered to my friends; now Leslie, in different ways, was even more difficult. At least I had known what to expect from Jane, but I could never learn to predict what temperamental trial lay a minute ahead when Leslie and I were with a third person. Sometimes she would turn glum and look into space with a resigned martyrdom that infuriated me, or, more often, she would be seized with the impish impulse to shock my colleagues with her flippancy, particularly if they were old maids. In this mood she would flash quips at me which, under the circumstances, always seemed personal and in poor taste. The fact that they were sometimes devilishly comical made me feel the more helpless.

It was impossible at such times to realize that the stranger opposite me was my lover. It was natural, of course, that I should expect Leslie to expose the varied facets of her nature to people who appealed to proclivities I did not. Such revelations are normally intriguing. But Leslie's surprises oppressed me—a series of trifles that mounted up to a pyramid of shocks. I knew it was constant strain that accounted for her wayward impishness, and also impatience with my caution. Reasons for her temperamental foibles, however, made them no easier to endure. Leslie had much to learn about grace in lesbianism. I wondered, since women companions were unbearable, if men would be better for us.

In the spirit of trial and error, I persuaded Leslie to accept a date and join me with Allen, a young art instructor whom I liked.

I had not been accepting dates, but this foursome would be an experiment.

The four of us drove to a country club for dinner. The Spanish tango orchestra was exciting and Allen danced well; I had missed dancing. I looked at Leslie, charming, gay. I had never seen her dance before. She was beautiful, her skin an unearthly white against black velvet. She didn't say much to me, only smiled occasionally, a sweet smile that made me ache all over for wanting to hurry home with her alone. I realized now that it meant more emotional strain to play the game with men, but it was better, I reflected, to be longing for Leslie than to be hurt and alienated.

My hopes for a compromise were short-lived. I had failed to consider that Leslie, pretty and reckless, would have her own problem with men. I was getting into Allen's car to go home when I saw, in the flash of a second, Leslie's escort leaning over her in the back seat, caressing her. Allen said something to me, but I couldn't answer. When he put his hand on mine I caught myself too late, and in ridiculous temper scratched him viciously with my finger nails. Allen swore, startled, and the imbecility of my waspish impulse made me laugh a little as I tried to apologize. But my inadvertent virtue had relieved my anger.

Soon I heard Leslie making conversation. It was reassuring to hear her voice, calm and clear, all the rest of the long ride home. As I stood at the door saying good bye to Allen, who had not tried again to caress me, I wondered, shocked and revolted, what in the name of Heaven Leslie could be thinking as she kissed her escort good night before me—not once but several times.

My anger was not that of jealousy alone, but of violent reaction to Leslie's doing anything cheap. When, alone with me, she tried to pass if off with gestures of affection, I could not bear to have her touch me. For the first time since we had become lovers we quarrelled, and bitterly. Leslie finally ended a scene by grinding in on me the old legend of the goose and the gander. Only then did I realize that plain egotism had made me unfair.

"You've had men," she said. "I don't like the thought, but I know it can't really matter. I don't see what difference it can make what either of us does with a man. It's so much easier not to argue with them—easier to shut them up and send them on their way a little faster."

Leslie had learned almost everything, it seemed, easier and earlier than I had.

So our experiment with men was a dismal failure. There could be no real compromise in our social life. I couldn't help thinking how very much simpler everything would be if Leslie and I had been born to wear glasses.

2

Leslie Breaks with Her Family

THE NEXT FALL, after a gay summer in the West, Leslie and I came back to live alone in our apartment. Mother had decided to stay at home with Gerald. Leslie began to work in the graduate department of her college and, in addition to my teaching, I began to plan some writing. I felt that now I could.

Though my life had been one fiasco after another in the human relationship, Leslie meant a blessed deliverance from doubt and fear. Slowly, in the readjustment of values, my own personality took on new definition, my vitality new purpose. I could feel it happening, slowly, involuntarily, almost from month to month—a growth of self-awareness, an impression of discovering an intensely alive and perfectly calm self I had never known existed.

The happy physical relationship doubtless explained the impulse that soon turned into a plain need for self-expression—granting that sex is no less the center of mental creation than it is of the physical. In any case, I could grow outward; for the first time in my life I was emotionally solvent.

The energy source of imagination is clear enough. What crystallized my ambition to write was luck with a half-dozen professional articles and, of course, my experience with Carl and Claudia. I was used to thinking of writing in terms of craftsmanship instead of talent—which was a very good thing—and about clean sentences instead of art. Though it seems unreal to me now, I never thought at all in terms of the extra money I might earn.

LESLIE BREAKS WITH HER FAMILY

I began with an article, a diatribe against the amiable ineffi-
ciency of academicians. I could never forget a famous professor
of journalism who had made a failure of his own newspaper; nor
that my teacher in the short story had never been able to publish
anything but greeting card verse. Certain quality magazines welcome impertinence as fearless exposé, and therein lay my chance.
With a prayer in my heart and no mind for Leslie's enthusiastic
encouragement, I mailed my first manuscript.

Four weeks later I was lecturing in class when I heard an impatient knock on my door. It was Leslie, waving a square envelope
and dancing with excitement.

"I told you! I told you!" she said, even before I saw the return
address.

There was a check for seventy-five dollars and a note from the
editor. "We like your piece," I read, "and want you to know that
we will be glad to see additional articles."

Until that moment I had felt calm and pessimistic about my
chances. I hadn't dared feel otherwise. Now I made a promise
to myself.

"If you've got something besides a strong back," Claudia had
said, "your writing ought to be fairly finished job after about ten
years. Then for God's sake don't look back at anything you've
done. You'll weep. Give yourself another five and then, if you're
strong enough, you'll just laugh."

This was something to work for. This was, above all else,.
something to counteract my rankling feeling of social inadequacy.

Within two months a second, more constructive, article was.
accepted by another quality magazine. This I could publish
under my own name. Too bewildered by my luck to take any
pleasure in it, and convinced that the writer must practice years
for his effects, just as the musician, the painter, the lawyer prac-
tices, I was thankful that my practice showed promise. For the
present, I needed no more to make me satisfied.

It was during the third month of our second year together that Leslie's mother came to visit us, without warning, and for all our camouflage, recognized our lesbian relationship.

I shall always believe that Leslie's frequent and no doubt careless mention of me in letters had made her mother suspicious even before she came. It seems probable, though she denied it, that her suspicions led her to come. During her second evening with us, she asked Leslie to leave, saying she wanted to talk with me alone. Leslie looked at me as she left to go to the school library, and her eloquent eyes told me she understood far better than I what her mother wanted of me.

Leslie's mother was much younger than mine, of a dark beauty more violent than Leslie's own. She had made me feel even more ill at ease than my natural prejudice justified, for her eyes penetrated—and the moment Leslie was gone I felt myself being dissected with almost clairvoyant ease. Her first words, blunt as they were, were relief of a sort.

"You have been good to Leslie, Diana," she said. "But you are not good for her. She's too crazy about you. I wanted to tell you before I told her: I'm going to put her back in the dormitory before I leave. You may have to help me with her. She's headstrong."

Of course I denied and protested. Leslie was happy with me. Her friendship was perfectly normal. She was doing the best work she had ever done, and she hated the dormitory.

My words shed off like water. Leslie's mother looked closely at me.

"You've got a hold on Leslie and you know it," she said. "But she's got to give you up. I know her well enough to know that before she will, you will have to make her. You're the one to give up first."

She went on with an attempt at calm, then with nervous rapidity, telling me of Leslie, her concern several years before

[196]

when Leslie first showed signs of emotional peculiarity in collegiate crushes, her anxiety because Leslie had never been interested in men. Now, with brutal finality, she told me of her shame in Leslie's final vileness with me.

I use her word "vileness." I had listened in harassed silence until she said it. I had sworn to be calm; there was everything to gain by being calm. I had Leslie to think of now as well as myself, for her mother had cleverly put me in a position by asking my help. But from no one would I take needless insult.

With measured words, my voice very low to hide my trembling, I answered her. Had Leslie ever revealed any fondness for her mother I would not have tried. Now, without further denials, I struck back with the involuntary rebound of hurt feelings. Words that had been restrained for years came out in a sort of rhapsody of deep-seated convictions. I hadn't known how spontaneous they would be. I knew that talking would do no good, but the satisfaction of being able to answer an insult carried my reason away. A peculiar ability to detach myself helped me as I tried to reason with her. Then, in sudden sympathy for a mother's overloaded heart, I concluded by being almost gentle.

"I know how you must feel." I ended. "But please don't ask too much of Leslie. You can't change her. You can try to understand her."

I do not believe she even listened. Where she had been at least coherent, she now went on hysterically. Her voice cracked and she began to sob. I stood up; if I had to listen, it helped to be taller.

"I don't know what made her that way," she wept. "It's worse than being deformed." And then, shrilly, "I'd rather see her dead!"

Sense suddenly fled from me, and left me staring immobile at a room and a person who seemed to have drifted in from a dream. I saw the fire, the familiar books and the lamps wheeling about me in a nightmarish photomontage, something somebody had pasted on a great paper which never could exist in either waking or sleeping. With the accurate movements of the sleepwalker I got into my coat, picked up Bonk, and walked out the door. I did not even know I had left until I found myself on the sidewalk, walking fast toward town.

I walked until finally, finding myself near a hotel, I went into the drugstore, bought a bottle of whiskey, and registered for a room. I tried to drink myself into insensibility. It seemed the thing to do. But alcohol is mysteriously perverse when it mixes with memory; the more I drank the more clearly I could remember the strident voice which had pierced me clean to the heart. I had heard what I had heard. "I'd rather see her dead!"

I have often wondered just what instinct it was that took me back to the apartment at the end of several hours. Perhaps it was an instinct cousin to the one which drives the criminal back to the scene of his crime. Every step I took pulled against my will, and yet I almost ran.

When I opened the door—it was almost with a feeling of relief —Leslie was with her mother. They were sitting on opposite sides of the room, and Leslie was half turned toward the window. I guessed that she had been looking for me, and that the two had not spoken for some time. I tried to pass them and go on into my room. Leslie's voice stopped me.

"Diana," she said, "I'm staying with you." Her statement was flat, without expression. Her mother sat with her handkerchief to her mouth, without looking at either of us. I could only guess at what had passed between them. I shook my head and tried to go by. But Leslie looked at me with such supplication in her face that I could not desert her.

"Tell her, Diana," she almost snapped her words out, "tell her I've never been so happy. Tell her I've never worked so well. Tell her anything. Only for God's sake tell her I'm not going to leave you!"

LESLIE BREAKS WITH HER FAMILY

I had never seen Leslie in such a temper. Her eyes narrowed, catlike, and when I saw her look at her mother with cutting scorn I wanted, with inexplicable anger, to slap her jaws. It didn't matter that she fought for me too. I was choked with fury that she hadn't somehow avoided subjecting us both to this.

Of course she couldn't have helped it. And as I stood looking at the two, both of whom had asked for my help, I gathered courage to jump headlong into a situation where there could be no compromise. I had to make a choice. I knew Leslie's mother prayed that a word from me would end our liaison. I could feel Leslie in her panic begging me to let her have courage. I turned to her mother.

"What good would it do," I asked, "if Leslie did leave me? You've got to face it. It would only mean another woman in a little while."

Leslie's mother asked herself again where a daughter of hers could have come by such an abnormality. Her weak sidetracking was my inspiration. This was, after all, my issue as well as Leslie's. Her eyes, now more anxious than angry, urged me not to shirk it.

Perhaps what I said then was unwise. But I did not believe so at the time, nor have I ever had reason to change my mind. I had a plausible explanation to offer for Leslie's lesbianism and, in face of her mother's confusion, I was no longer hesitant about giving it. It had never been mentioned as such between Leslie and me, and she showed as great surprise as her mother. I regretted this, but it could not stop me.

"You and Leslie's father have done everything to make her a lesbian but tell her to be one," I said. "She's told me that story about 'Dad's boy.' That alone was enough to start her out in life with all her values inverted. My God, that was a horrible thing to do to a child! You didn't think about it at the time. I doubt if you ever have. But that doesn't change the effect it had. She's never been able to right herself. As if that weren't enough, her father's kept it up."

I knew that her father occasionally addressed his letters "Dear Junior"—a playful gesture, Leslie had explained, but one that never failed to give me gooseflesh. I could not spare her father. I had always considered him either stupid or selfish, in neither case deserving of sympathy. Finally, it was he who had insisted on sending Leslie to a woman's college, settling what potentialities may have been undetermined.

"I've been to a girl's school," I continued. "I've taught in one. The quickest possible way to finish off the girl who is not sure of herself is to take her away from men and put her in with a thousand females. Leslie was started off uncertainly. Even her name was uncertain. And then she was finished off."

Leslie was frozen by my nerve. But no more than I was myself. I went on, "I guess in all this I've given you my answer. It's cruel. God knows I know that. But it's true. There's nothing I can do."

Leslie and I looked at each other, terrified, and we saw things we had never seen before. Then slowly, somehow, I knew the situation was mine. Completely spent, there was nothing more to say. I only wanted her mother to get out and let us alone.

If I had been optimistic enough to hope that psychology could triumph over prejudice, I would have been crushed by the ultimate reaction of Leslie's mother. She played her trump card after she had gone—by sending a brief letter that Leslie had to choose between her family and me, and that her monthly allowance would be withheld until her note was answered. Leslie showed me the note. There were several overdone sentences about mother love and a prayerful conclusion that Leslie would realize the enormity of her decision.

"I pray God," her mother ended, "to make you come to your senses before it is too late."

Leslie, practical and even a little mercenary, wondered frantically if she had any choice but to leave me. A solution was possible, I knew, if only I could face it. My salary, coupled with the occasional checks from my writing, was adequate for the two of us if we were careful, even though I was helping Mother financially. Lesbians, I had found, are generally insistent on halving all expenses incurred in common—a custom I saw little reason to observe if circumstances were against it. But the responsibility of taking Leslie from her family was quite another matter to consider.

Normal lovers quake before the possibility of family condemnation. Yet normal lovers can always name the first born after the grandfather and hope for forgiveness. Lesbian lovers, vilified from the beginning, can hope for nothing. Except, perhaps, to be forgotten.

I could come to no decision, nor was it mine to make. In telling Leslie that I would be glad to help her, I did not try to influence her. Her answer was almost immediate. She would borrow the money from me and pay me back with interest when she was out of school and at work.

There was one point about this responsibility, however, to which I was extremely sensitive—the idea that conspicuous generosity is an index to the homosexual character. I had heard it several times, once even from Carl when I had asked him the meaning of the café society word "aunt."

"It's a homosexual who's free with his money," he had said. Then he had gone on, musingly, "Funny thing, fairyland is full of philanthropy. Sometimes it's of quite a decent sort."

Such an observation was, I believed, one of the few true observations on homosexuals that I had heard come out of the normal world. I myself had never known a lesbian who was not extraordinarily free-hearted, and though I saw good reason for this idiosyncrasy—by assuming that it came from her singular and loose feeling of fellowship which reached from the third sex to both the other two—it was natural now that I should be fearful of an accusation. For this reason, which Leslie readily understood, no one was to know that I supported her. She would pay her bills by cash rather than by my check.

To my dismay, Leslie would not even answer her mother's note. Never for a moment did she show the slightest regret. A dutiful and affectionate daughter myself, I fought against admitting how much this hardness disturbed me until I finally saw that it was, for my sake, a pose. No matter what conviction and affection said, the fact remained: I felt solely responsible for an imposing array of sentimental roots torn up, more than Leslie would admit to—most of them stretching far back before my time, embedded deep in memory and instinct. Wondering if my love for Leslie could be equal to this portentous blow, I knew I would need courage as I'd never needed it before, if only to keep her from remorse.

3

I Sell My First Story

B Y CUTTING herself off from her family exactly fifteen months after we had become lovers, Leslie became dependent on me for her entire support. It was exciting to figure how much money she would need for the week, to be careful she would want for nothing, to see her pleased when I could spare the money to surprise her with week-ends in Detroit. The masculine in me was thrilled by such an appeal to my pride, and by the challenge in her sacrifice.

Yet the feminine in me was uneasy that the game might not have an equal chance. In the normal world such odds would have been a dare to my gambling instinct; in the lesbian world they were blurred and indeterminate. The venture of defying both family and society on the one hand and even lesbian financial custom on the other laid me open to risks never before experienced. I would need tact with Leslie herself and impregnable nerve against the thought of her family. I could never recall her mother's visit without thinking of it as the most sickening thing that had ever happened to me.

I could not parry about this responsibility. Life had to be a skirting of hazards were we to have happiness. Nor would I implore Leslie to be renunciatory for her mother's sake. Such a temptation always seemed extravagant heroism; it could amount to exactly nothing beyond a month or so of doubtful ease to my conscience. Leslie would still be a lesbian.

I had by this time become experienced enough in teaching to be able to spend more time writing. I was teaching two classes daily in grammar and composition and one in the Romantic theatre. Except for two afternoons a week for conferences, all of my afternoons were free. These I spent on my writing.

Though I had started with articles, I turned now to the short story, guessing that stories came quicker and reached better-paying markets. I found out abruptly that my first guess was wrong. When I sent my first two stories to Myrna, Carl's literary agent, she did not let friendship stand in the way of replying, "For goodness' sake, forget what you learned about writing in college. You've plots enough here for two novels."

By following her instructions I rewrote my first story into three. One of these she told me how to rework into saleable form, and the other two she jovially advised me not to send out for twenty years when, she said, "Editors might buy your name." In a few weeks she had sold my story to a second-class woman's magazine for fifty dollars, a sum which could never pay for the way I had aged in the writing. Worse, it could make no impression on my expenses.

Leslie, I was finding, was a luxury. The thought of the years ahead of her began to frighten me. She wanted, I knew, to take a master's degree in bacteriology before going on in medicine. Tuition and laboratory fees and textbooks would devour sums far beyond what my salary could manage.

"I'll stay out of school a year or two and work," she said. "I'll find something to do. I can't let you work like this. Why, my fees alone will be $500 a year when I get into medical school. Think what that means."

I knew what it meant to each of us, but I could never let her quit school. Leslie had found herself, she was deeply interested in her work, and though my ignorance of it was shameful, she had communicated enough for me to be profoundly impressed by her breadth of mind. Her imagination was excited by a microscope as my own was by a piano; the great difference between us was that she appreciated my interests with intelligence and I appreciated hers with awe. To give her the same training her family would have given her—this was a challenge that I wanted desperately to meet.

I thought of supplementing my salary by giving music lessons, but I knew my dean would object. Then, worried and discouraged by my failure to do better in the short story, I had an idea. I wrote to Myrna.

"You are learning nicely," she replied. "I hate to see you give up to speed. But the pulps do pay money for their stuff. If you'll study them and let your hair down, you can soon do a lurid love story in a day or two. Remember the formula: 'Sin, Suffer and Repent,' call your hero Mike and your heroine Cynthia, and throw in twice every bromide you can think of. Most important, don't *write* the story; *tell* it.

"I don't handle these things myself, but send one or two along and I'll give them to an agent who does. Then, after you're caught up with finances, let's go back to something less soupy."

For days I saturated myself with pulps. I made trips through the shanty part of town where I had decided to lay my story. I tried to draw waitresses into conversation, to find out what they wanted in a story, but got nothing but self-conscious baffled stares. Finally, I asked Nora, the janitor's daughter, a pulp devotee, to be my critic.

Clearly, I learned, it would be a mistake to try too hard in the writing. The pulp should be loose, conversational. And so I asked Leslie to take a story in shorthand as I dictated from plot notes.

I went over my first story once after it was typed, and though I could not get anything but monosyllables out of Nora, a wide smile told me all I needed to know. I left it without a change.

It worked. I sold "My Night in Hell" for $150 and the editor asked for another. Leslie and I were ecstatic. She would stay in school! She would have the same chance with me that she would have had with her family.

To me, it meant much more. In Leslie I had someone to work for. Established in my profession now, and tired out with adjustments, I wanted to grow roots, to be useful, to have normal domestic security. Leslie gave me all that, and when she began to ask for my assurance that our life together would be permanent, I assented not because I believed it would be, but because I wanted to believe it.

Night after night I dictated to Leslie after she had finished her studying. Sometimes I had to go very slowly; sometimes I had not the slightest idea when I began just what would happen to despoil Cynthia for Mike, nor just how the two could possibly emerge from the black of despair into which I flung them so recklessly. Frequently Leslie poised with her pencil, rescued them with a suggestion that stimulated more thrills and suspense. Our greatest trouble was not in making our stories move, but in getting through them without fits of laughter.

My dean had liked my first articles and the fact that I had contributed my bit to a text; he need not know what I was working on now. Writing was excuse enough for seclusion, for ridding myself of friends who were only a smokescreen. Leslie and I were happy when we did not have to brush too closely with the normal world. Busy, I did not have time to miss social life.

I was thankful when trash began to pay regularly. Several editors encouraged me generously, and a few times when my work was unacceptable as it stood, when tone or plot or length needed readjusting, it gave me a feeling of confidence when they asked me to revise instead of sending a rejection slip. At least finances were going well, partly because, with Leslie's help, I could be prolific and twist a good plot into a half-dozen stories; partly because rates increased. And at least I had a sound reputation with the janitor's daughter.

I SELL MY FIRST STORY

The first half of our second year convinced me that I could not only take care of Leslie, but that her desire for permanency was becoming slowly and surely my own. Yet for all my assurances I could sense a new and curious melancholy in her response to me. Gallant and generous, she evaded my concern, blamed her mood on worries at school.

During the weeks my uneasiness grew. It was not like her to be cross when I asked her to take dictation, to kiss me a second later with over-elaborate contrition. "You are doing this for me," she had said. "I love the feeling that I can help." It was not like her to sit for long minutes in a fog of abstraction, not even conscious of my nearness, or not to notice when I played the pieces she liked to sing.

It was in the sex relation that her unnaturalness showed itself most plainly. Gradually I was made aware of a distortion of perspective between her mental and physical affection; for as the one stretched farther and farther away from me, the other came closer and closer. I was startled to notice that the merest suggestion of the physical, whether in a book or a scene of the streets, would excite her abnormally. She began to want me more and more often in a sex-ridden way that seemed morbid and was foreign to her natural buoyancy. I hated the thought that copulation had suddenly become separated from spiritual context, that the orgasm should be the *raison d'être* of our relationship. I had never thought of sex as an end in itself, and the idea of sexuality merely as a serviceable function depressed me. I began to dread a surfeit of passion, and to wonder if Leslie's desire had a saturation point, if her desire could cloy.

I understood that highly sexed women could experience keenest physical sensations without any physical contact, but my understanding of such matters was purely bookish. Now I found myself intimidated and all mixed up. I could not guess what might have brought on Leslie's surge of appetite, and groping for reasons only caused me to wonder if I myself were responsible. But because I knew too well the torments of lying unsatisfied, I hadn't the heart to ignore her when I knew she needed me, no matter the drain on my own strength and patience.

I tried to believe that she did not feel any less tender under the languor of caresses than she always had, but I learned during these few weeks that sensuality had little to do with tenderness. I could never keep from shuddering a little when ecstasy was forced with deliberate haste into matter-of-factness—for I recognized a grim struggle in Leslie between will and instinct which my indulgence, instead of helping, was only aggravating. It was this knowledge that gave me the nerve to try to relieve the strain she had set up between us. Experience had made me the natural aggressor and, as the aggressor, I must keep the advantage of setting the tempo. More important, the very fact that the lesbian sex act is adaptable to the single as well as to the mutual function gave me a chance to satisfy her desire without misusing my own. This could be our compromise and my protection.

But, indulging or abstaining, it was all the same so far as bringing me any nearer to understanding. I could not press Leslie too much to tell me what was wrong. I longed to be able to penetrate the glaze of her aloofness, to help her restore her balance, but I knew that in due time and in her own way she would tell me.

In due time and in her own way an explanation did come. One rainy evening reminiscent of the first night she had come to me, Leslie came in and sat on the edge of my bed and, without making a move toward me, told me that I was being more cruel by unconscious patronage than I could ever be intentionally.

"You don't realize it," she said. "That's the only reason I could keep on. But you've got to understand now. Nothing can be permanent the way things are. I feel like an interlude, just something you can lean on until you have Jane back. I didn't used to be afraid because I thought I could make you love me. Never as much as you loved Jane, but enough to justify my being a fool over you. I've given up everything. I had to. I guess that's why it's hard now, because I swore I'd never depend on anyone. But I've outgrown waiting and hoping. That's all. I swore I'd never tell you." For a moment I thought she was going to weep.

"I can't stand this. It grows. I want you. Oh, yes, you're good, you're sweet, but that's not enough. I want everything just as Jane had you. I want you to lose yourself to me, as I do to you, and you never have more than two or three times. You're remote, sometimes, even when you're making love to me. I can't get at the *you* I want. I've tried to forget Jane, and the harder I try the more she haunts me."

Leslie stopped for a moment, and then she went on rapidly, "One night you were dictating and you said, 'If love is to have any meaning it has to be a growing thing. Emotional roots reach deep and weave their strength into a pattern of life that prepares for the future. Sentiments take on substance, and practicalities matter more and more. A young couple wants to establish a home now, cultivate friends, have children. These things are their salute to the future, are proof of their security.'

"I remember those words because I saved them. I remember you caught yourself and stopped and said, 'My God, what am I saying? That won't do. Strike that out. Put instead: Molly wanted a home and when Joe had enough money she wanted babies. Fine boys that would be sturdy and curly-headed, the way Joe had looked when he was a baby.' "

Leslie looked at me. Ordinarily she would have laughed.

"Those were just sentences before you caught yourself. But they are perfectly true. You meant them. You see my point." Almost contemptuously she added, "We're not reaching into the future, beyond the evening meal. We can't get around a damned ghost that's between us every waking moment."

Suddenly timid, I embraced Leslie. Somehow I must make her
know how much she did mean. Damn the ghost. I was happy.
This would work out. It had to work out. The pattern of my
existence was fixed. Leslie herself had designed it.

Without bogging in psychiatry, suffice it to say that Leslie's
sexual extravagance had been linked with her feeling of frustration. The inference is clear. Feeling defeated, she had gone to
extremes in an effort to break into my separateness. I do not have
any idea whether she did it consciously. Yet it was only upon
failing that she could bring herself to admit her feelings.

The circuitous psychology of the defeatist attitude was interesting to me once I could stand off and look at it and realize what
had happened. Particularly interesting was its dénouement: Leslie's high wave of passion receded to normalcy with no more
than the release she found in talking with me.

It never came back again. I hadn't realized how hard it had
been to endure sensuality until it was over and I felt a light-
hearted freedom I had not known in months. I had almost forgotten how sweet Leslie could be.

A letter from Jane came just two weeks after I had vowed to
get rid of her ghost. Actually, her letter was not at all an unnatural event at this time. She had just seen an article of mine in
a magazine of which she had long been a reader. I had supposed
she would come upon it; I had even imagined she might write.
But it seemed that this thrust of circumstance was viciously timed.

Jane was in Detroit living in a hotel while her family was in
Florida. She spoke of being lonely, and I wondered what had
happened to Louise. "For years (or can it be only months?),"
she wrote, "I have tried to dare ask if you can feel anything for
me now. We had so much, Diana. We still do. How dreadful

pride is. But that is past now, lost in loneliness. It is better so, for I am not afraid any longer to say I'll always love you."

I read this end to her long letter and, at once, impelled by an instinct I am still regretting, betrayed its sentiments to Leslie. Perhaps it is understandable that my passion for honesty in private matters was overdeveloped to balance the constant lying about every other phase of my living.

Leslie said nothing, and went into her room. I threw the letter into the fireplace and followed her. She was lying on her bed, her face deep in the pillow, only her shoulders betraying her sobs. I had never seen Leslie cry. I hadn't even thought of her as being able to cry. I touched her, tried to speak. She jerked away. Perhaps she realized that I needed to be alone myself.

Had I been living with Leslie in a generation that knew the wisdom of ignoring tension in the human relationship, my life these next few months would have been very different. But Leslie's idiom, even more than my own, was Freudian. It was scornful of reticence, and was full of expressions about "laying the cards on the table," about finding out what made us "tick," and "watching wheels in our brains go round." The expressions fanned thoughts into action.

Now, pleading with me to lay my cards on the table, she would not let me forget Jane's ghost for a moment. Thought of Jane worked itself into an obsession that stretched a long way back into passionate jealousy.

I had answered Jane's letter and had told her of Leslie. "I love her," I said. And I had mailed the letter with a loose feeling of relief. Though Leslie knew what I had done, she was still not satisfied.

Of the several currents of tension one alone stands vivid in my memory: Leslie's hammering insistence that I see Jane the next time I went to Detroit, to decide whether I still wanted her. She insisted, in spite of my protests, that the dead would not stay buried, that my refusal to see Jane precluded any hope of our own permanency. In a sense I could sympathize with her feelings. I could understand that Leslie, realist through and through, would rather have nothing than half. Yet at times I almost hated her for having an overdose of the curse of all lesbians I have ever known—introversion.

Recurrent scenes, all faintly ridiculous, got us nowhere. Intelligence was sidetracked by overwrought nerves. Leslie's neurotic reasoning would have been pathetic had it not been so irritating. Still I knew that her obsession was more than a matter of obstinate jealousy. I believed her when she said, "If you end up by telling me you're going back to Jane, I swear I'll not say anything. I'd rather take that chance than go on like this. I keep thinking of a story I read when I was little. A prince was captured and held in a den of thieves in a mountainside. Finally one day Chief Somebody-or-other told the prince he'd have to move, and he'd let him choose which one of two caves he'd prefer to go into— the one to the right or the one to the left. The prince knew the cave to the right contained poisoned air, and he'd die right away. He didn't know what was in the one to the left, and the chief would just throw back his head and laugh when he asked him. The prince chose the cave to the right. The other had led to freedom. . . . I'm that kind of a fool."

Leslie's story made its point. Knowledge of any kind was, to her mind, better than indeterminate fear. And her inevitable reminder that I must still care more than I pretended or I shouldn't make so much of seeing Jane again, tore more and more at my nerves. So at last, one spring night after a quarrel that left us both miserable, I relented. I agreed to see Jane. In three months I had been able to do no work, no writing. Leslie had me in a blind alley, and I had to go one way or the other.

I SELL MY FIRST STORY

I was not only Leslie's lover, I must remember, but also her means of support. She made loyalty hard, but it would not change. For her I would see Jane again, steer clear of sentiment, perhaps even come to realize the brilliant trickery of an imagination that had become glorified in time, and come back happier than before. If my imagination had played no trick, *tant pis*. I would have to come back anyway. The fact that I had made no pact with Leslie did not at all lessen my sense of responsibility. Lesbian informality to the contrary, I had a sense of duty. The only thing that kept me from the common self-administered lesbian ring ceremony was my natural aversion to making myself ridiculous in the sight of both God and mirror by giving in to a travesty on normal mores. Ceremony as such was not of the slightest consequence. Conscience was.

How very much simpler this kind of problem would be in the normal world where one could offer proof to the doubting lover, proof of ceremony and social sanction, proof of friends, all those warming assurances that are the privileges of the normal!

With grim matter-of-factness I did three decisive things at once. I told Leslie that she was to go with me; I knew her nearness would make it easier. It didn't matter that, terrified, she used every excuse she knew to get out of it: Leslie had started this business and now she must see it through. Then, taking a chance on selling several more stories, I applied for passports and made our reservations for a June sailing to England. Last, I wrote Jane that I was to be in Detroit for the Easter holidays and hoped to see her.

Jane replied by return mail that she would make a reservation for us in her hotel. This unexpected move very suddenly brought the situation to a head. My impulse was to wire at once that we had reservations elsewhere. Instead I wrote and thanked her. To refuse her hospitality would be to betray my panic to Leslie. That I would not do.

4

Jane and Leslie

LESLIE AND I were to meet Jane our first evening for dinner. We had located in our hotel, bathed, dressed, ordered a drink, and it was almost time for Jane to call at our room. For two years I had been building for the time when I would see Jane again, and now, two minutes away from it, I felt like an actor who has had no chance to rehearse his lines. If only, I thought, I could get through my fit of trembling without Leslie's noticing.

"What can you be feeling now," she asked, "if I'm this scared?"

And I lied bravely. "My imagination has already exhausted my emotions. They're squeezed dry. I'm so calm it's wonderful."

Leslie smiled at my nerve. The smile froze on her face. There was a knock on the door. There was Jane, her arms wide, her eyes excited, a vision so beautiful that I stood like one entranced. Too late I recovered my thought of turning my cheek—for there stood Leslie—and with a rush of tenderness I kissed her as she meant me to kiss her.

"Please," she said, holding me at arm's length. "Just a second. Let me look at you."

I knew what she meant. Just a second more alone, before I must bring forward this girl whom I'd told her I loved. And even as Jane and I stood so briefly, expression dying from our faces, I became conscious of shock at the sight of white in her hair.

"Does it surprise you?" Jane read my thoughts and laughed. Then I felt her eyes go beyond me, beyond me to the far corner of the room, to Leslie. Clasping my hand and drawing me along, Jane went, quickly now, across the room and took her hand.

"Leslie," she said softly, and turned toward me. "It is easy to see, Diana, why you are looking so happy."

This was a remark to which any kind of reply would have seemed too much. As always, I was a little awed by Jane's poise. Though it made me feel like a blundering schoolgirl, it gave Leslie confidence I would not have expected.

"I had no idea Diana was so good at describing," she smiled. "I'd have known you, Jane, no matter where I'd met you."

"Oh, but let me make my own impression!" Jane said.

We walked into the dining room slowly, as if to put off the moment when the three of us would be expected to begin keeping this up all over again. Jane sat in the middle. Quite suddenly she said to me, "Diana, do you burn everything the way you used to when you tried to cook? Or is Leslie as touched by your helplessness as I was?"

The remark was good-natured, but Jane watched its effect on Leslie and on me.

"Wouldn't it be interesting to know," Jane went on, turning to Leslie, "which of us is the better cook?"

Such uneasy and clumsy banter would have been a bombshell in another five minutes. Frantically, guarding my temper, I began to talk about books, the theatre, the Nazis, anything to put away thoughts colored by sick uncertainty. It was up to me to avoid irremediable blunders. Somehow my unspoken anxiety carried to both of them, and, except for a certain wordless expectancy, I managed to make conversation normal and general. I was grateful to Leslie for being charming in spite of fright, and to Jane for having the good taste not to overdo in her efforts to be kind to her. Suddenly, unexpectedly, as the dinner ended, both of them seemed sweeter than I had ever known them to be, and when Jane was leaving us I had a mawkish urge to take both their hands in a private tenderness of understanding.

Jane brought us to the door of our room. I told her good night.

Then she put her hand on Leslie's shoulder and said, "Don't mind, Leslie, but I must ask you if I can have Diana for dinner tomorrow evening. Dinner in my room. We won't be too long."

This was a swift anticlimax I had not foreseen. Jane had known better than to ask me alone. Leslie agreed solemnly, unconscious that she was helping Jane to make me a victim.

Once inside our room, she stood and looked at me, her eyes stricken, and then she walked across the room and began slowly to undress, no longer daring to look.

"Leslie!" I spoke sharply.

There was a long silence while I waited, and then quickly she ran to me and came into my arms with such force that I lost my balance and stepped on her foot, and we both had to laugh. I would never have guessed that a good hearty laugh, in the wrong place, too, could clear the air so quickly. In a little while, with Leslie asleep in my arms, I could imagine once again feeling almost the way I had told her I felt.

I had no faith in Jane, and good sense would keep me from getting into a position where she could hurt me any more than she had already. Yet an old idealism remained untouched. God only knows why. Logic was never a part of my love for Jane. I now saw her past deceitfulness not as anything wilful and malicious, but as a weakness, and as such I pitied it. Her remorse had moved me and I had not the slightest desire to harp on reminders that would bring it back for my own gratification. At the same time I was afraid of weakness and repeatedly assured myself that the terrible insecurity of loving Jane was enough to keep me from ever going back to her.

The next afternoon I left the hotel for an hour to keep a business appointment, and when I came back to my room I found a note from Leslie:

"Jane called for you and when you weren't here she asked me up. Said we might as well enjoy hating each other! I'm still scared of her, dear. Come up and get me when you come back."

Instead of going, I called her. The idea that the three of us could ever meet again without an anticlimax was too much to hope for. Too, I was annoyed with Leslie for having gone. I knew she was fascinated by a threesome that had such psychological potentialities, but I prayed heaven that she wouldn't overstep in speaking of me to Jane. My hope collapsed the moment she came back, and yet there was something pathetic in her immediate question.

"Do you mind if I told Jane how much I love you? I hadn't meant to. But she brought it up. I hadn't known how much I did want to talk about you with somebody who'd understand."

I could tell the effect the minute I went up to Jane's room for dinner. She took my hand, rather formally.

"Can't we pretend," she asked immediately, "that there's nobody but just you and me, just for an hour? Leslie didn't matter until today, somehow. She was just a third person, any third person. She had no color, no body, no form. Now it's different, and I need to forget her. She's come alive. And, darling, I'm all cold inside."

My impetuous answer brought a sudden and grateful light to her face. She pointed to a small table where there was a package of my own brand of cigarettes and a decanter of apricot brandy. I could not resist a smile at this, but I hadn't the heart to tease.

I had never been able to remember Jane's being as handsome as she really was. Now I watched her moving about, lighting candles and pouring our brandy—her dark skin soft against the cerise of her lounging pajamas. Her hair was once again in the quaint knot low on her neck, the way she knew I loved it. Most of all, I was struck all over again by the majestic grace of her movements, and the sense of awe her very height imposed upon me.

Little by little—I could not stem the force—something went slowly to my head and possessed my senses, and I quaked in helplessness. I could only cling to the hope that Jane did not see.

Had she handed me my drink a minute later it would not have happened, but she saw my hand tremble as I took the glass, just as I saw it. I could not meet her eyes.

More quickly than the telling, she lifted the glass away and almost fell on the divan beside me, clasping my hands to her mouth, kissing them again and again, her eyes closed. I dared to free my hand and touch her hair, lightly, hoping she would not know. Shadows from the candlelight could not take away the grey that moved me so. Nor, when she finally looked at me, the torture in her eyes.

Every nerve in my body ached with longing. Too late, I tried to make my mind a blank. Perhaps she knew this when she crushed me into her arms. Had my body been chained, and my soul with it, I could not have been more powerless when I heard: "Child, you do care!"

It was a sound so sweet that it hurt me as grief would hurt. I had forgotten the shape of her hand, the curve of her shoulder, the yielding touch of her lips. Swiftly, in a moment wedged between past and future, I knew them again.

"Diana, Diana, Diana," she whispered. "Just to say your name and have you hear it! You do love me, Diana. We want each other. We always have."

The impossible had happened, and so entirely apart from any sense of reality that I felt almost like a spectator. This detachment was to save me, this and a relic of self-discipline. I had come by that discipline dearly, and it was stored away deep as the habit of conscience. Somehow it sprang forward through tingling nerves, even as I heard Jane whispering, and it passed judgment with astonishing clarity.

I knew that I would never come back.

I held Jane off a little, and I was conscious of screwing up my courage to speak when I heard a knock on the door. Our dinner had come.

I could not help noticing Jane's glow of pride as the waiter spread our dinner on the table, that she had remembered my favorite dishes of Paris. There were onion soup, veal in mushroom sauce, endive salad. I dreaded to have the waiter leave us alone; it was impossible to meet Jane's smile. The moment he left I spoke, hastily, to keep her from speaking first.

"I've got to say it, Jane, now." Because I could not insult her with lying gallantries, not when she said she wanted me again, I told her that in Leslie I had found my security.

"I am proud of that security," I said, with stiffness no more surprising to her than to me. "Leslie is dependent on me, and that's given me the heart to try to write. Every hope I have is set. Every ambition."

Then I heard myself pleading, "I can't give them up." That was not fair, not fair to Leslie. I got up from the table, an uneasy tightness in my throat. Standing, it would be easier to speak.

"This came too late," I said. Then, to be fair to Leslie, I tried to say right away, "I love her." I wanted to say more, much more, but a feeling of futility stopped me. Telling Jane that I was afraid of her would only rub it in; she knew. Better to leave quietly now, without risk of being maudlin. Without time, even, for full realization.

Now Jane told me that Leslie had admitted to her that she had been fighting a ghost.

"I believed her," Jane said, "because I needed to. Then a little while ago I believed her because I thought I could see for myself."

Of all emotional moments in an overtaxed evening, that came nearest to undoing me. Leslie had given the lie to everything I wanted Jane to believe I felt. Now my silly little straw of illusion was beyond my grasp.

"That used to be true," I answered. "It was easy enough for Leslie to tell you what you'd meant to me. What she couldn't tell you was what she meant."

Yielding to a chivalrous sense of renunciation, I stood there saying things I did not mean, acting courageous in spite of inward trembling. Or perhaps I acted like a simpleton. I don't know. What strength I had was not mine, but Leslie's. At last I took Jane's hand and left without daring to embrace her. With a suddenness that was startling she caught up with me and turned me to her, catching my arms above the elbows. Her eyes were angry.

"It's better for me to go now." I tried to steady my voice.

"You're not coming back?"

"No."

When I opened the door I heard a sharp intake of breath I'll never forget.

I had to wait for the elevator to take me six flights down to my floor. I'd had three reasons, I told myself hurriedly, for knowing I could not go back to Jane. What were they? Yes, Leslie. But what were the other two? Jane was faithless. But the third? My mind was blank, I couldn't think of the third. I was almost to the hallway to my room before I thought of the third. Ambition. That was it. Jane overbore me. I couldn't write with Jane.

By the time I reached our hallway, I saw Leslie coming out of our door. She was surprised to see me; Jane had just called her to come up for a few minutes, and she had assumed that I was there too.

This curious request of Jane's upset me, but I could not tell Leslie not to go. That was for her to decide. I had no more idea what Jane wanted than she had. Excited in spite of herself, Leslie kissed me quickly, handed me the key, and left.

I went on to our room and saw where Leslie had been passing time at the desk writing my name on bits of stationery, doodling like a lovesick college freshman. Printed at the top of a large sheet, I saw this:

Proclamation

I, Leslie, being of sound mind (?) and body, do hereby declare that I shall love Diana Frederics with my heart and soul as long as she will let me and want me, be it one more night or a lifetime. I pray it is the latter, for I don't know how I could keep from loving her forever and ever.

Underneath, sketched in firm lines, were two withered crones in front of a fireplace, one knitting, the other peering myopically at a huge book whose title was obscured to make room for the author's name, "Diana Frederics." A sleepy parrot stared out of his cage at the two, with a comical expression of approval. He was saying, "Diana, you've done well to stand Leslie this long." The knitter was labelled "Diana—90"; the reader, "Me—84."

I undressed, turned down our beds, and tried to relax with a book. Surely there was some way to keep my temples from throbbing. It was only a little aften ten o'clock, yet the evening had been aeons long. The room seemed huge and bare without Leslie, and I got up to look at her caricature again.

I waited a half hour, then a full hour. It occurred to me that I had not touched Jane's dinner, so I ordered coffee and a sandwich. I was not hungry, but at least that would take up time. The waiter came shortly before midnight. I didn't even try the sandwich. After an infinite stretch of time it was 12:30. By now I was furious. I can't imagine by what miracle I managed to restrain myself until 2:30.

DIANA

Then suddenly beside myself for having waited so long, I put on my robe and took the back stairs up to Jane's room, afraid even to take time to dress. I hurried up the six flights and hesitated, breathless, before knocking. Jane quickly opened the door. Her hair was down, and she was in sleeping pajamas. The room was dark. At first I thought I had awakened her. Then, beyond her, in the light of the open door, I saw Leslie scrambling off her bed. The bed was rumpled.

I threw our key past Jane with such force that it hit the radiator with a loud clank. Then I pulled her door to with shattering suddenness and fled down the six flights of stairs to my room. When I tried my door I realized what I had done. It hadn't made any sense when I did it; it made much less now. Finally I sat down in the hall, with my back against the door, oblivious to appearances, the clank of the key still ringing in my ears. If I looked like a *fille d'hôtel* out for trade, the few passers-by were not interested.

I had no sense of time, but it couldn't have been more than ten minutes until Leslie came. When she saw me she ran and knelt down, throwing her arms about me. I wrenched away, took the key from her, and went inside. She tried to speak, begged me to let her explain, cried again and again that she loved me. I wished she'd shut up and at least have the taste not to heap insult on injury. Finally, after hearing for the twentieth time that she and Jane had only been talking about me, I began to laugh. I tried to stop; if my self-control broke loose now I couldn't check it. But I couldn't stop. Tears came to my eyes. I couldn't see; my mouth got dry. I splashed my face with cold water, held a wet towel to my eyes.

Finally Leslie came from behind me and slapped me hard with the flat of her hand, until my face stung. I fell across the bed, exhausted, my jaws aching. She put a pillow under my head, covered me, and then lay beside me. I could make no effort to get away from her.

The next morning I could take better hold of the ideas tearing around in my head. With surprising efficiency I started to pack. Leslie followed my example without a word.

I was taking a last look around when I noticed her Proclamation on the desk. For the first time I looked at her and then, slowly, with a stricken feeling that a part of me had died, I picked it up and crumpled it into the waste basket. Not a sound came from Leslie, but she reached into the waste basket and thrust it, still crumpled, into her coat pocket.

Minutes later I was leaving the cashier's window when I saw Jane coming toward me. I realized she must have been waiting. She was brisk and to the point. Ignoring Leslie, she almost pulled me over to a divan in the lounge.

"Listen to me, Diana. Don't let anything happen to you and Leslie. Last night was crazy, but it was harmless. It sounds silly to say we didn't realize how late it was. But you've got to believe that. It's true."

A little desperate at my defiance, Jane went on. Every word she said stays with me as if she said it yesterday, and not a year ago.

"God knows it doesn't matter what you think of me now. But Leslie does matter. You love her. She loves you. I'd give anything in the world now if you could have heard her talking about it. It was touching because it was naïve and young. And fresh. Just the way she is. I swear to you—it's my fault that she didn't leave earlier last night."

I looked around the balustrade for Leslie. She was standing, smoking a cigarette, her tousled hair more tousled than ever, her lips tight.

"Diana, this means everything to me." Jane followed my glance. "If you can't be happy with me I want to know you're happy with Leslie. She's adorable. I could love her too if it weren't for you. Why not? Go on with her. Forget last night. There's nothing for you to hate us for. We were thoughtless. That's all. Be happy with her."

I got up to leave, hoping she would say no more. I hadn't tried to answer. Her "Why not?" had told me more of what Jane had come to than she'd have dreamed of admitting.

She walked down the steps with me. At the bottom she stopped and said, "Diana, if Leslie ever does anything to hurt you, I'll want to murder her!"

I left her standing there. Leslie waved good bye, and followed me into a taxi.

I've had many occasions since to think of Jane's parting remark. It almost impressed me at the time.

There was only one thing more I wanted to do before I left Detroit—call Louise. Jane had not mentioned her.

From Louise I learned that Jane had left her the year before, without warning, for an actress. Six months previous, only a month or so before Jane had written me, the actress had gone on a tour. Two and two fitted together. I was infinitely glad I had called Louise.

Jane had come a long way since her subconscious had left off warring with desire. Like a boarding school girl too long repressed, she was spending all her energy making up for lost time.

Jane the Huntress

DETACHMENT grew in the calm that follows shock. I leaned over backward in attempting to see Jane in all her shallowness, her trivial ambitions, her enormous conceit, her sentimentality. Yet for all my vituperation I knew the truth about her lay somewhere in the middle. The cold fact was that Jane was a lonely, hungry woman looking out for herself, let the chips fall where they may. She had a tremendous capacity for affection ready to be expended with wholehearted generosity on any woman who appealed to her. Unfortunately, her vitality was not disciplined, and she gloried in a sense of power. Scruples were beside the point.

My independence of her had not only astonished her; it had cut deeply into her pride. Jane had always got what she went after. So far as I know, that was the first time she had ever met humiliation in the human relationship. And from that point on, her course with Leslie became obvious enough. Jane was not destined to be a loser. The situation became, psychologically, a "natural" for one of her temperament. Not belittling Leslie's attractiveness, I did have the distinct feeling that Jane's play for her was motivated largely by spite. Leslie herself was first to mention this thought.

"Jane sprang to the door the second you knocked," she said, "just as if she'd been waiting for you. She didn't even give me time to move. It's clear, I guess, what she wanted to do to you. It was clever, but not clever enough."

Less melodramatic than Jane, more honest, Leslie gave me the

[225]

truth that belonged somewhere between my suspicions and Jane's designs. Nor did she try to subordinate her own rôle in the imbroglio. From the first she had been fascinated by Jane, though she insisted that her penchant for "watching wheels" was more responsible for her interest than the person of Jane herself. Leslie's response had been, I was willing to grant, not to a single stimulus but to a whole exciting situation. Jane had been built up in her mind; Leslie was victim to my own weakness.

Though shame colored her thought for days, I could be no less angry with Leslie for her behavior which galled me as bumptiousness of the most brazen kind. No matter what the reasons for her momentary defenselessness with Jane, the fact remained: Leslie had been abominable to me, and a definite part of my affection for her was gone. Deeper than hurt, wiser than anger, my feeling toward her took on a layer of callus that was but a further protection.

We had been home but a week when Jane sent Leslie a sketch she had made of her from memory, and a letter. Leslie asked me to read it, but I felt so skewered afterwards I wish she hadn't. I recall nothing of it but a sentimental flavor that cloyed and the fact, had I ever been in doubt, that it was an admission of Jane's lie to me. But this was not all I read from the letter. Most significant, it was a picture of Jane trying to escape self-accusation, trying to esthetize herself.

Leslie replied with a note, regretful and slightly formal. There was no answer.

So far as I was concerned, the thorny problem was over. I was not going to feed upon regrets. Our immediate plans to go to Europe for the summer were exciting enough to point us away from the past to the future, and in anticipation our sense of direction came back. When, several weeks later, Leslie wanted me to take the crumpled paper that had changed so swiftly from a joke to cheap irony, I was caught by a timidity in her expression that was, somehow, more articulate than tears.

It was following this experience that I wrote a story whose heroine was a character such as Jane might have been. It was a story that was born in spite of me, for it grew out of the scraps of a pulp, where it had no place; and, contrary to my previous experience, where I had forced the story along, now I was forced by the story.

My heroine, a Spanish girl, had the unfortunate talent of appearing indomitable, so splendid was the strength of her beauty. Life took advantage of that appearance; friends, family, and men expected more than ordinary strength from her. Yet she, who looked the part of refuge, who shielded her vulnerability by pathetic devices, was at heart a coward. She it was who should have done the leaning.

When her lover was brought home maimed from the Madrid front, she stood in stricken silence before this final sacrifice which destiny pushed at her. Too weak even to evade, forced by circumstances to accept him, her salvation lay in toughening her sensibilities—and because it was an emotional rather than an intellectual thing, toughening meant simply coarsening.

She was a narrow but complex study and her mental dissolution interested me, I confess, profoundly. Just as the sight of a strong woman weeping is more pathetic than the tears of a frailer sister, so my heroine's inner nature seemed the more pathetic because of an exterior which belied it. My story was violent and sordid, and certainly it left the reader holding on to nothing, but what mattered was the fact that it did, in a narrow sense, redeem the trash that I had been writing—which, reasonably, pleased me far more than Myrna's check for $450.

What merits mention of my story here is the fact that I did

not know at the time that I was drawing the essential Jane to the life. I have wondered many times if the character I had depicted had existed full-grown in my subconscious.

It was near the end of school. One afternoon I came home late, tired from work, and saw a large tan coupé in front of the apartment house. It was Jane's coupé.

I could scarcely bring myself to open my door, and when I did go in, it was with no grace whatever. Jane was sitting in my easy chair sipping an iced drink. Leslie's face showed her almost febrile confusion.

I ignored Jane's outstretched hand. The natural impulse to tell her off jerked at me, but I knew such a move would only bring on a scene, and I wanted to steer clear of Jane's vindictiveness.

Surprised that I had at last learned to look beyond her, Jane explained her reasons for stopping to see us—she was en route to Florida to join her family. Her excuse was neat but unconvincing.

I did not know whether she had been there since morning and I was afraid to ask. Soon, without effort at civility, I suggested that she go on her way.

"I'll go," she said, "but before I go I want to say something that's needed to come out for three years." Jane got up, waved Leslie out of the room and then stood facing me, her eyes full of assurance. I wished the immobility of her face did not disturb me so, nor her fingers toying with her pearls.

"I want to say this calmly," she said. "You see I can't forget that you once accused me of loving pyrotechnics."

Whatever Jane meant to say, she had already stolen the scene.

"I know exactly what you think of me now," she went on. "You couldn't help it. But that is not what I wanted to say. What I want to say is that I can't help it either. What's happened to me would never have happened if I'd not once loved you too much.

Something I had before I loved you is gone now, completely gone. I can't give it a name. I wish to God I could. Maybe it's a sense of direction, but it's the result that's important. It makes me run from myself. I started running three years ago and I'm still at it. The point is, my dear, it's your fault. No, no, I'm not going to take on about it. I'm getting quite used to the thought by now. But it is your fault. Don't deny it. *You* were the one who was always so damned sure of herself, who made me feel like one of your maladjusted students you used to talk about. *I* was the one who had to learn. Oh, my God, even about my own self!"

Jane's voice was rising despite her effort to be calm. Startled by her passion, I stood trying not to see through what I had to listen to.

"That's why I wanted to hurt you," she said. "That's why I'll always want to hurt you. This business of Leslie started because I wanted to see you squirm. But listen to me. I've found out now that I want her for reasons of my own." Jane paused to let her words dig in. Then, as if to polish them off, she said, "Why not?"

"For God's sake!" I cried, "stop saying 'Why not?' Be trivial if you have to be. Only I don't want to know how trivial you are."

"You are, of course, wrought up," Jane answered. "I've tried to be honest, in spite of the fact that you ordered me out of your house."

She picked up her hat, her bag, walked into Leslie's room for a few whispered words with her, and as she passed me on the way out—her shoulders eloquently disdainful—I heard the last thing she ever said to me.

"Every damned thing that's happened to any of us is your fault. My conscience is clear."

Jane was scarcely out of sight when I offered Leslie her freedom. Shocked, she pleaded with me, cursed Jane, pleaded again.

"All afternoon I begged her to leave before you came," she said. "I knew what you'd think. But I swear it, I had no more idea she was coming than you did. Darling, I did slip once, and there's no point in denying it. God! you know my thoughts before I have them. But I'll not take the blame for this. I want to forget it just as quickly as you do."

The absurdity of the whole situation, as well as Leslie's uncharacteristic impatience, convinced me she was telling the truth.

Four days later I was packing for Leslie while she took examinations. In her table drawer I found two little notes folded crisply, a large thin "L" on the outside of each. They were written on Jane's own note paper.

For long seconds I stared thunderstruck at this impossible sight. It wouldn't hold still before my eyes; I had to pull it back into focus. As I stood there, rooted by shock, a slow sickness chilled through my body from my head to my toes.

It was not necessary to unfold and read the notes to make sure. But I did it. What the notes said no longer matters, even if I could remember all. One question stuck in my mind. "Shall I be waiting for you, darling, when Diana sails?" I read it over again, many times, before the full sense of it finally twisted itself into my consciousness. A terrible intensity seized me and with methodical haste I began to look in the old familiar places for more notes. Scattered through Leslie's big leather notebook were two or three single sentences scrawled in the center of blank pages. All of them were signed "Your Jane." On a back sheet of the notebook was a letter Leslie had started to Jane.

"My darling," it said, "I cannot tell you anything. I don't know what has happened to me. Please give me time to think. It's all so wonderful—but you know how I feel about Diana. That hasn't changed. I don't think it ever could." The next three sentences had lines drawn through them, as if they were to be left out of the final draft: "It isn't that I feel obligated to her—she's always said that the only reason she'd be reluctant to keep me up, was that I might be. But there are so many reasons for loving her and, reason or not, I love her for every one of them. You said you wanted me to be honest with you about her." That was the end of the deletion. The letter began again: "But now there's you. Everything else seems unreal when I think of you."

There she had stopped. The letter was not dated.

Last, in a silver cigarette box, full of keys and stamps, I found a receipt for the rent paid on a post office box, Number 580. Above the stamped date, which was the day of her visit, Jane had written, "My first present to you. I hope you use it!"

I walked, half running, to Leslie's laboratory. When I reached the door I looked through the glass and saw her with several students, all in white aprons, huddled around a long table watching the instructor inject something into a big white rabbit. I waited until the instructor had walked on to the next table and then went in. The odor of chloroform struck me full in the face.

Leslie hurried to me, her eyes questioning.

"Get excused," I said. "Come with me."

She never asked what I wanted. A few minutes later she followed me out of the building and I led her toward the city limits where we had often walked on a lonely bridle path.

Finally, we sat down on the grass, and simply, even calmly, I told her I had found the notes in her drawer.

"I read them," I said. "They mean the end of you and me, of course."

She made no reply.

"Count me out of it," I said. "Something in me has curled up and died. And I will not submit myself to a whole damned neurotic series of episodes over Jane. I've had my fill of repentance. Love isn't worth it. Do what you want. It's no longer any of my business what you do. You can leave right now if you've any place to go. But I won't let you go to Jane."

That I repeated, as if I had full authority over her.

"You can keep on living in the apartment until you find work," I added. "I won't let you go hungry."

Leslie sat with her head down, biting at a blade of grass. I noticed her hands twitching. There was a long silence when, unexpectedly, she looked up at me with contempt in her face.

"Why don't you raise hell?" she asked, her voice bitter. "Why don't you come right out and call me a bitch?" Then, almost tauntingly, "Why must we have such noble dignity?"

I got up with furious deliberateness and walked away from her, going down the path which led to town. My masculine abhorrence of scenes was plain cowardice, and Leslie knew it, but this was one thing reason had never been able to help. Hurrying home now, burning from Leslie's taunt, I despised myself more with each step, but still I could not turn back.

In an hour she came in, her eyes full of shame. She walked over and tried to take my hand.

"You were right," she said. "There's more to it than a blast of temper. I've quit feeling now. I'm thinking instead, as you were trying to do. I'm trying even to think your thoughts. 'I've got to be merciful,' you were thinking. 'There are reasons.'"

Leslie stopped, bit her lip, and I knew she could not go on. I heard my own voice, in a flat calm, going on from where she had stopped.

"Yes, there are reasons. First, there is money. Second, my home is your home. We've got roots. They can be torn up in no time if they're emotional roots. But ours went deeper. It's likely to be messier."

Gradually, the air cleared; we could face each other with simple honesty. When Leslie began to speak she talked freely, but her stilted phrases were not her own, and her words often passed into a whisper. Jane, she said, had written the notes the day she came to the apartment. She had come because Leslie had not answered her second letter. I had not known of a second letter. Leslie was bewildered and even embittered by the fascination she felt for Jane, but she begged me to believe she loved me no less.

"Please, Diana," she said, "I don't deserve to have you believe it, but it's true."

Jane had urged her to spend the summer in Canada. As I sat listening to Leslie, who made no attempt to spare herself, I learned to hate Jane as I never could have hated her had I not once loved her so much.

That night Leslie moved out of my room. I was glad she was quick about it. But she came back after I was in bed and stood over me, her face drained white. I could scarcely hear what she said: "If you want me to get clear out, you'll have to send me away. I'll never leave you unless you make me."

The Post Office Box

I CANCELLED our reservations for Europe and arranged to keep my apartment during the summer months. At least I could try to get some writing done, and I meant to continue writing whatever I wanted now, if I could once get started at anything. My Spanish story had given me courage. There would be no more sacrificing for Leslie.

Leslie managed to secure a grader's post, which paid her tuition; staying on in summer school for lack of anything better to do, she worked long hours each day in the laboratory. She asked nothing of me, not even recognition of her cool and patient obstinacy. Which was well.

Because, working—or trying to—I fell into the habit of irregular hours, I seldom saw her even at meals, and when we did take dinner together we both carried books to the table in the manner of people who are afraid of being trapped without an exit.

For two months I'd had more emotions provoked than I'd known I possessed. I was exhausted by melodramatics to the point where my response to Leslie herself was apathetic. Now, whether my love for her was or was not a thing of the past, my first concern was to keep her away from Jane.

I had not told Leslie I knew of her post office box, nor of her letter to Jane. The necessity of being furtive was hateful, and I loathed my stealthy trip to the post office every day after the mails were in. I have often wondered why I yielded to this hateful compulsion day after day. I didn't have the excuse of morbid jealousy, nor could I feel any satisfaction in spying on Leslie.

Yet I had to, as if this guilty secret were my only hold on self-protection.

Knowing whether Leslie had lied would mean waiting, waiting to know what I could believe. Meantime, for my own relief, I would try to make the disquiet that lay between us as livable as possible. Forcing myself to work helped.

The first letter was in the box exactly one week after Jane had left. Or perhaps it was a second letter; I don't know. Through the glass door of the box I could see a large grey envelope addressed in Jane's hand. I could even see that it was postmarked "New York." I stood rooted for a long minute, anguish chilling through my body. How I could have believed I'd steeled myself against this reality I do not know. I only know my sense of shock was out of all proportion to my reason. Perhaps because I finally understood my complete helplessness to do anything, anything at all.

Tuesday and Wednesday the letter lay there. Thursday when I saw it again I was almost happy for a second. Friday noon the letter was gone.

Leslie, as usual, did not come home from the laboratory until late afternoon. She gave no sign. But late that night she came into my room for the first time since she had moved out and asked, a little timidly, if she might kiss me good night. Without meaning to, I caught myself looking at her incredulously. Embarrassed, she became awkward. What she finally said sounded so grave and childish that I was moved in spite of myself.

"I miss you, Diana. Please forget about Jane. I have. Please give me a chance. I can stand waiting for you to feel all right if you'll just say you believe me."

Jane seemed to be in the room, listening, watching, waiting for my reply. To ignore her made an empty mockery of any attempted solution. To speak of her was impossible. And so I said nothing, and Leslie went back to her room. She had no way of knowing how very much, at that moment, I had wanted to kiss her good night.

I tried to stand off and look at myself. Objectivity was, it seemed, easier with practice, and I had a lot to go on.

Once I had said to myself: No more cold-blooded rationalization. Then, with Jane, devotion had come before family, friends, job, even my sense. The effort to lose self in absorption of, and with, another individual had, in the end, been sickening. In the gradual recognition that a human being is isolated, is unique, is apart and lonely, I had found my balance and my knowledge of human dignity.

Fulfillment

A FEW WEEKS after summer school started, Leslie came home with the surprising news that she had a job. I did not even know that she had been looking for one.

"I'm going to sing for my supper," she said. "For days I've walked the streets looking for a job—anything. I wanted to tell you, but it was awkward. Then I went to an employment agency. I had to do something to start getting on my own. The woman asked me if I could sing. I was so discouraged I'd have applied for a trapeze act. God, how could I have done it!"

Something told me that she was reluctant to say where she was going to sing.

"It will be three hours every evening," she went on. "I can spare that since you don't dictate to me any more. I'll get seven dollars a week besides my dinner. I can't pay you back anything yet, Diana, but I can manage on that the rest of the summer." She spoke simply, without embarrassment. "I lied to the orchestra leader, just as I'd lied to the woman. I told him I'd sung with an orchestra. I was petrified. I didn't know it would be so different from the piano. The man said he'd keep me if people liked me. Next fall, too. It's at Heinrich's."

Heinrich's was a beer garden on the outskirts of the city, a respectable enough and pretty place. In spite of Leslie's timidity about it, it was not at all the fact that she was going to work, even in a beer garden, that startled me, but the fact that she would sing before people. Shy as an introvert is shy, she had always fled, terrified, from "putting herself on exhibition," as she called it. She had an appealing mezzo voice, she must have known; but she had never even consented to sing for friends who dropped in. As I looked at her now—her delicate mouth always intimidated me when it looked determined—I knew that she must have braced herself to physical courage to ask for such a job. Perhaps, after all, I had underestimated her strength.

I tried to take pleasure in her humiliation. Let her alone, I told myself. She's no longer your responsibility. Let her get adjusted as best she can. But I could take no pleasure in it.

The first night she sang she came in and, without speaking, went straight to her room. I noticed that her face was pale and drawn, and her eyes swollen with tears that would not come. In a little while I dared to go in and ask the obvious question.

"I got lost in two songs tonight." That was all she said for a long minute. "The introduction Heinrich gave me, and. all those butter and egg men clapping and staring at me—now I know how my bugs feel under my microscope."

"I can help you," I suggested. "Maybe you need more practice."

Leslie looked at me gratefully, and then a quizzical expression crossed her face. It must have struck her that I was offering to help her more quickly to the point where she could be self-supporting and free of me.

Possibly if Mother hadn't come to visit me I'd never have gone to hear Leslie sing. Mother asked me to take her; she thought vaguely that Leslie's family had met financial reverses, called her a brave child, and was incredulous when I guiltily admitted that I had never heard her at Heinrich's myself.

Mother and I took a table midway in the garden and in the center of a cluster of other tables; we were less conspicuous there. It was Mother's idea not to tell Leslie we were coming. "She begged me not to," Mother laughed. "She said it would make her nervous. I hope she won't see us."

We ordered dinner and I settled back to dread the moment when Leslie would appear. Suddenly it dawned on me that we were taking advantage of her; mother hadn't meant that, of course, but we were. It was too late now for retreat. The orchestra was already beginning one of her songs. Instinctively I sat farther down in my chair.

From behind a gaudy lattice work, Leslie appeared, smiled to the orchestra leader and, as the lights dimmed, took her place before the microphone. She wore a low-cut turquoise dinner dress; it was pretty in a cheap and theatrical way, and I assumed it was one of the "sex-appeal uniforms" that Leslie had said Heinrich furnished to his entertainers. But no matter. Her fine forehead, her tremulous smile—they answered a gown's cry of cheapness. They answered the men whose glances followed curves.

The crowd was looking toward her now, and by the light of recognition I saw on some of the faces, I could tell that Leslie already had her followers. I had not thought about this bridge of understanding which reached from audience to performer until I saw Leslie acknowledge the applause, with something of gratitude in her face. In turn the satisfaction her answer aroused in her listeners—that was what they doubtless called her "personality." It was a tenuous thing, almost a sweet thing, but it was full of vitality and it excluded me. This was Leslie and her audience, a Leslie I had never seen.

Quite unexpectedly I resented their claim to familiarity, their right to salute good-naturedly. Perversely, the moment they had intruded and excluded me, Leslie ceased being a stranger. She came so close that I imagined I could feel the touch of her hand. And so suddenly and bitterly did I resent these intruders that when I raised my head to look at her a turquoise silhouette swam before my eyes.

[239]

"Listen," Mother whispered. "When she gets home you impress on her how nice everything was. I don't know what's wrong with you. You're being stand-offish about something. But she's down now. She needs kindness."

Though I was ill-adapted to withstand music, it was not the tenderness of the song nor anything Mother said that made me tingle with sensations I had thought buried. It was Leslie's poise, her gallant devices which were so transparent to me. "I'm glad I can stand close to the piano," she had said. "It looks natural, I hope, when I put my hand on it. I get so dizzy with fright."

She was standing with her hand on the piano now, waiting for the second chorus. Then she saw us. After briefest visible astonishment, she looked from Mother to me and, with a naturalness that shocked me, managed a smile so grave and so eloquent that my mind went spinning. For an instant there were no intruders; there was not even Mother. There were Leslie, her eyes pleading, and I.

I did not dare admit what had been revealed so clearly in that second between us. It was an inner signal, almost a prayer. It was more than we had said to each other in two months.

Mother left the next day, and I went back to my writing with a furious energy that soon made me feel as I wanted to feel— remote from the sentimental mood of the beer garden. That meant nothing. Leslie showed no more sign than I had that it had meant anything. She had even told Mother on the way to the train that she was moving in the fall. "I've got to live alone," she had laughed. "I'll be cutting up dead cats and Diana turns up her nose. Oh, yes, I'll see her now and then anyway."

I shall never blame Leslie for breaking into my isolation. It must have been exasperating. Trying to make myself believe I could be any good as a robot had begun to get on my own nerves.

Though Leslie was anything but passive by nature, she had

never been aggressive with me. When I saw it coming, I admit it was a fearful pleasure I deliberately prolonged. I had sensed it since late summer—a gradual breakdown of cool patience—an unfolding of confident self that was good for her and interesting to me. I knew my apparent indifference had started it and had goaded it along. Looking back now, it seems perfectly natural to me that she ended by doing exactly what she did. Leslie had come to the point where suspense possessed her and logic had no persuasion. The only possible answer was an emotional one—and in asking the question she gave me no choice.

She came into my room one night just after I had turned out my light and gone to bed. I had been working very late, and my first thought was one of surprise that she should still be up. She left my door open, and in the faint light from the hall I saw the determination in her walk as she came straight to me. She sat down by me, and this time she did not ask if she might kiss me. I thought she wanted to talk, but in a moment I knew. I patted her hand gently, caught by a strange new sympathy I had not expected to feel. She had come quite simply, without histrionics, without conscience. It was the entire naturalness of her action that made it, somehow, heartbreaking. For the briefest moment as she leaned toward me I could see almost physical anguish in her face. A stubborn set to her jaw thrilled me far more than anything she could possibly have said.

Then it happened—an impulse beyond mind and time and self-reproach. And though I'd known, it startled me. As I felt her body trembling I felt in myself a tremor of tenderness and pity, and something forgotten. It didn't matter that she hurt me, pressing too tightly. She didn't know; I couldn't tell her. I lay smothered in her arms, biting my lips to keep from crying out a hundred things that had to be said and yet could not be said. To disentangle this lonely child from the spirit of the semi-neurotic would be, I knew, forever impossible. Slowly she moved from me, now a lover who knew tenderness, holding my face between her hands and trying to tell me. Finally she spoke, and I sensed impending tears.

"For three months I've tried everything I know. Aren't you ever going to feel all right again?"

Even as she spoke fear was no longer in the room. The need for words had dissolved as suddenly as it had come. The touch of her hand, quickly familiar, seemed for an instant the one innocent thing I knew in an experience of tricky innocencies. At first I did not know why. Then, gradually, as if the body can sense what the mind cannot, I knew that Jane had been swept into time, into the forgotten. Even thought of her seemed obscure. Leslie and I had extricated ourselves; no longer need there be anything at all to remind us of Jane.

I could feel how it had happened, but I could not have foreseen. Slowly, half-prayerful, half-exultant, it had come to me— the testimony of her patience was enough—I could turn toward Leslie and know that her loyalty was no less than my own.

"Don't you think," she whispered tremulously, "there's such a thing as vows meaning more just because they are secret?"